PRAISE FOR W. G.

ENORM

"An enthralling, apocalyptic fusion of *Gulliver's Travels* and *The Food Of The Gods*, *Enormity* comes at you with big ideas, voluminous scope and colossal pace. Marshall has the high-tech savvy and breadth of vision of a great SF writer, coupled with considerable daring. Watch his stature grow."

—James Lovegrove, *New York Times* best-selling author of *Redlaw*, and *The Age of Zeus*

"Hilarious, fast-paced and just plain mind-blowingly cool. W. G. Marshall's *Enormity* is part Michael Crichton, part Jonathan Swift, maybe even a little bit Tom Clancy, but in the end genuinely unique. Marshall's inventiveness had me guessing all the way through. *Enormity* is a page-turning thriller that will make you remember why you fell in love with Science Fiction all those years ago. This is some seriously good stuff!"

—Joe McKinney, author of *Apocalypse of the Dead* and *Flesh Eaters*

"*Enormity* is at once tight and sprawling, a vibrant rush of Phildickian apocalyptic menace. What feels at first like the collision of genres in a particle accelerator blends seamlessly into a whirling dervish of a novel that goes down like Everclear with a quark-gluon chaser. If you like spy movies, heist novels, Tom Clancy, and crazed speculations on the underlying structure of the universe, you'll eat *Enormity* up with a spoon."

—Thomas S. Roche, author of *The Panama Laugh*

ENORMITY

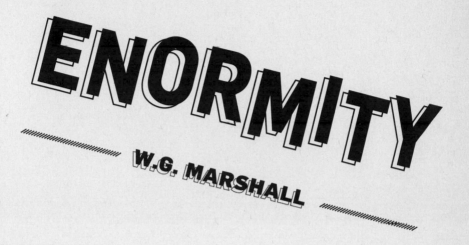

ENORMITY

W.G. MARSHALL

night shade books
san francisco

For Cindy, who started it all.

"Who shall bring me down to the ground?"

—Obadiah

PROLOGUE

THE LEAF-BLOWER

"That damn phone doohicky will rot your brain."

Joey Shapiro's mom. Not an educated woman by any stretch, but a lady of great conviction. That Old World wisdom can't be learned in school. You have to go to Jersey.

"Mom, I'm not playing a game, I'm networking."

"Networking! *Networking?* Don't you mean *not working?* I knew I should've never let you get that thing, but stupid me I let you talk me into it. It's a good thing your father's not around to see this; I know what he would say: 'Give that lazy S.O.B. his walking papers!' But you know you can take advantage of your poor mother, who can't say no to her only child, her baby. Oh yes, I remember when your little bottom fit in the palm of my hand. Why, God, why?"

"Mom, I'm twenty-six."

Joey's always been a problem child. Sallow. Skinny. Ben Pakula next door said the boy belonged in the Army—"Boot camp will wring the milk out of him!"—but Dottie Shapiro, bless her soul, hoped Joey was cut of finer cloth and kept him home. Besides, he was her only family since her husband died in that roofing accident.

"Don't get high and mighty with me, kiddo, or you'll find you're not too old to get a slap in the face from your mother. Oh-ho-ho-yes."

"Jeez, Mom, it's my day off."

"Your day off. Well isn't that fine? It's his day off." She threw open the window and yelled out, "Stop the world, it's Joey's day off!"

Joey hung back, making faces. Real chicken neck on that kid. I should've probably gone upstairs, but I was working on a cup of coffee and Dottie had stiff rules about food in her rooms. A sensible woman, and not unattractive for her age.

"Isn't it too bad that the *rest* of us don't get a day off like Mr. Joey Shapiro! *Some* of us just have to *clean up* after him!" She snatched up his phone gizmo and flung it down in the wastebasket by my chair. Good for her!

Joey squealed, "No!" He fished out the thing and frantically tried to make it work. "*Dammit*, Ma—!"

"Don't curse at me!" She loomed up over him with the flat of her hand. "Don't you *ever* curse at me. Oh no, I won't take it. Uh-uh, buster. No."

"But Mom—"

"No ifs, ands, or buts. Instead of wasting your time playing games, why don't you do something useful? Here—" she handed him the garage key, "—go out and clean the leaves off the property. Get some fresh air. Then later you can pick up a few things for me at the Stop 'n Shop."

"Come on, the Marzi brothers hang out in that neighborhood!"

"The Marzi brothers! You're a man now; it's time you stopped letting other people push you around."

"For God's sake…"

"Don't you take the Lord's name in vain! Are you gonna move, or am I gonna have to throw you out by the seat of your pants?"

"*Mom*—"

"You know I will. You know there's only so much I'll take." She squared her bosom, ready to charge.

Joey hung there for a minute, looking—if you want to know—kind of feeble. Very sad thing, a widow with such a son. But you never heard her cry about a broken heart. All guts. Finally he went out and slammed the door. Dottie winked at me, that minx, and went into the kitchen.

A few minutes later, I heard Joey start up the leaf-blowing rig, wielding it as if it were a flamethrower, blasting imaginary enemies off the driveway. Sad, sad... When I was his age I was clearing airstrips in Nha Trang. Of course, a young man had something to fight for, something to believe in then. The thought made me almost sorry for Joey. Joey, Joey, Joey. All that kid had in his miserable life was hope.

It was about two months later that a cardboard tube arrived in my mail. Special Delivery. At first I thought it might be something from my son in Guam, who I hadn't heard from since things went crazy in the Pacific. That kid wouldn't write if it were a paying job. Then I saw the return address: Hercules Enhancement Products. Damn—it was for Joey. A few weeks earlier he had asked me if he could use my name to order something by mail, and like an idiot I agreed.

"I hate to ask, sir," he had said, "but it's kind of private, and my mother opens all my mail."

"It's not porn, is it?"

"No, sir!"

"You're not asking me to accept a shipment of illegal drugs or anything?"

"No, sir, it's nothing illegal! They advertise it on the Web. It, uh, has to do with...personal enhancement."

"What do you mean, like a degree program?"

"Not exactly. It's kind of a guy thing; my mother wouldn't

understand. I'm trying to make myself more, um, *dynamic* to the…female persuasion. You know." He lowered his voice to an almost inaudible whisper. *"Bigger."*

"Oh, Jesus."

Feeling embarrassed for the kid, I said okay. Then I forgot about it. Well, here it was, whatever it was. Not wanting to know, I didn't look inside, just tore my name off the address and put the parcel on Joey's dresser next to his Star Wars crap.

Soon I started having second thoughts. Mama Shapiro and I were just starting to hit it off—we went dancing at the Elk's every Saturday. If she heard about this mail-order baloney it could sour my big play. Why had I started such Father Figure nonsense in the first place? I turned around and headed back to the basement.

Joey was coming up. He had the mailer in his hands. "Mr. Lieber?"

"Hi, Joey."

"Uh, did you put this on my dresser, sir?"

"I guess I did."

The kid's bat ears were bright red. "Does my mother know?"

"No. But this is a one-time deal, y'unnerstand? I may be a crusty old man with a heart of gold, but that doesn't mean I'm gonna be your personal P.O. box."

He nodded, relaxing a little. "You won't mention it to her or anything?"

"Are you kiddin'?"

Joey's face collapsed into an embarrassed grin and he said, "Thank you, sir."

"Hey, I just hope it does the trick."

"Me too, Mr. Lieber, me too." Then he was gone down the stairs.

≥≠≤

"What am I going to do with that damned kid?" Dottie moaned over her vodka tonic at the VFW.

"It's just a phase he's going through."

"A phase! Fat chance."

"I'm telling you. Give him time. It's hard on a boy, not having a father."

"Hard on him? Hard on *him*? What about *me*?"

"I know, shhhh."

"Don't shush me! That boy is a spoiled brat. He's had everything handed to him on a silver platter! That's all. I've been too weak with him. That's always been my problem—I'm just too nice. People walk all over me. I could've sent him to a boarding school but I didn't. I could've put him in foster care. I could've gone out and had a high old time instead of squandering my beauty raising that ungrateful, lazy brat. But I'm too damned soft-hearted. Well no more. No more, pfft! From now on I—"

"Whoa there." I leaned forward into the candlelight. "Lady, you didn't 'squander' anything."

She looked baffled, grinding gears as I took her hand. "What?"

"Ma'am," I whispered, "you make Joan Collins look like pickled herring."

When the tears started flowing I knew I had her. It's all timing. Needless to say, we didn't get home until after midnight, and Dottie and I had big news to tell Joey in the morning. Yessireebob, it was going to be a big day for all of us.

≥≠≤

It must've been three in the morning when the earthquake hit.

I was knocked out of my bed, the whole house warping and cracking around me. Books tumbled off shelves, windows shattered, and chunks of ceiling plaster came crumbling down. I heard Dottie screaming upstairs and ran for her room. Except for a faint glow of moonlight through the windows, the house was pitch-dark.

"What the hell was *that*?" she cried hysterically as I rushed in. She was sitting up in bed holding a pillow over her head, surrounded by puzzle-pieces of ceiling stucco.

"I don't know," I said, crouching next to her, "but I think it's over now. Are you okay?"

"No, I'm not okay! Call 911!"

I tried the phone but it was dead. "Looks like all the power's out."

"Where's Joey? Joey!"

"Don't worry," I said. "I'm sure he's fine down in the basement. He's probably still asleep." That kid could sleep through a stampede of rogue elephants.

Mrs. Shapiro bolted to her feet, heading for the door.

I caught her arm. "Let me," I cautioned. I had a terrible premonition of something—I wasn't sure what.

"He's my son."

"No—"

"He's *my son*!" She wrenched free.

Feeling her way to the hall closet, she dug up a big flashlight among boxes of camping gear—the late Earl Shapiro had been something of an outdoorsman. I was surprised there wasn't more commotion outside: sirens, car alarms, jabbering neighbors.

I couldn't see a thing out the windows; the world was dark and dead quiet. Inside, the hallway had a hazy, dreamlike quality, and our voices were slightly out of sync. Weird. Staggering a little, I leaned against the wall to catch my breath. The air seemed too thin; I felt lightheaded, high as a kite.

"Phew, I think I'm still drunk," I said.

Dottie must have felt the same, because she moaned, "What is *happening*, Bill?"

"I don't know, honey."

For once she didn't know everything. For once…she needed someone. I hugged her tightly and she cried softly into my shoulder like a young girl.

The downstairs looked like a tornado had hit it.

"Oh, don't scratch the floor," Mrs. Shapiro said as I cleared a path through the debris.

Holding the lantern before us, we made our way down the basement steps to Joey's room. The stairway had been twisted and mangled in bizarre ways, as if it had softened like taffy and then hardened again. The door at the bottom was open.

"*Oh* my," said Mrs. Shapiro, her voice cracking.

Joey was not there. His room was wrecked—even more than usual. As with the stairway, it looked *warped*, the walls bent into strange waves, the ceiling beams perversely askew and out of proportion. A strange layer of luminous vapor hovered above the floor like swamp gas, making islands of the furniture. I hoped and prayed I was still drunk.

"Joey!" his mother called.

"He must have gone outside. That's probably the smartest thing to do for us, too. This place could collapse any minute."

We went back upstairs, giving the kitchen a quick once-over.

"Joey?"

"Hello? Joey honey?"

Tracks in broken sheet-rock led to the open back door. Looking at the dark void, I had a sudden feeling of dread.

There are times when the mind goes blank, just puts up the Gone Fishin' sign and checks out. I would have thought I was long past it, me an old campaigner and jaded leatherneck who lost his innocence in Da Nang and later four toes and ten men during the Tet offensive. But in the face of...*this*...I was cold-cocked, flat-footed, green as grass.

What we should have seen out there in the moonlight was a view of Dottie's postage-stamp backyard: her grape arbor, flowerbed, birdbath and cast-iron patio furniture, hemmed in by a wood fence and the high gabled houses of the neighbors. There was none of that. There was nothing.

Instead, the back porch seemed to step off into outer space, a huge unobstructed night sky, close enough to touch. Dottie gasped and grabbed my arm. I looked down: Casa Shapiro was standing all by itself on a small jagged plateau in the middle of an otherwise empty landscape—a featureless desert that fell away to the edge of the world.

Low in the distance was the downhill curve of the horizon, dark against the pale blue rim of the sky. It was as if we were perched on a weird alien moon. A low mist covered the ground, and here and there were beds of sparks like kicked-open embers, glowing under weird coral formations of smoke. I thought I was going crazy: the heavens seemed to turn as I watched them.

"What the hell happened to Hoboken?" I asked.

Dottie squealed, "Oh thank God! There's Joey!"

Joey Shapiro was in his undershorts, sitting on the porch roof like some kind of Indian guru, his legs crossed and his expression one of ecstatic revelation, tears running down his face. Oh, I could tell right away that he had figured something out. A cloud of tiny flies was buzzing around his head like electrons around an atom.

"What is this, Joey, what's happening?" his mother begged. "Come down, honey. What's the meaning of this?"

I was incoherent, raving out of my head, "Where's New Jersey, you punk? *What have you done with my Camry?*"

Joey didn't look at us, but only gestured at something with a limp toss of his arm. We turned the way he was pointing, toward the east. It was brighter there; the sun was coming up, visibly rising, a brilliant salmon streak spreading along the base of the sky. The colors were mirrored on the surface of a calm primordial lake that stretched to the opposite horizon. There was something funny about the water, about the little crenelated island and the shore, the shrublike puffs of smoke.

"You always wanted an ocean view," Joey said.

That's when Mrs. Shapiro started screaming.

CHAPTER ONE:

THE QUEENS

Dad has a surprise for the Queen family tonight.

It's been a normal evening. Harley Jr. is dividing his attention between homework and Facebook. Mrs. Queen is sorting recyclables in the kitchen and feeding baby Willy. When Dad comes in with an Anthony's Pizza it's almost disconcerting: Pizza on a school night!

"Eat up, everybody," Harley Queen says. "We don't want to miss the movie."

Obviously they are having a crazy, impulsive treat, and neither Harley Jr. nor his mother is about to look a gift horse in the mouth. Mrs. Queen—Judy—merely asks, "How was your day?"

To which her husband shrugs affably, says, "Little change of pace."

Their pizza quickly demolished, the Queens pile excitedly into the car. It's cool out, October, the gorgeously clear sunset imbuing the suburban scene with hues of *Saturday Evening Post* Americana: Anytown, U.S.A. Nobody says much during the drive, as if afraid to jinx it. Dad could still change his mind.

Navigating around bicyclists, joggers, dog-walkers, and playing children, they finally leave the residential neighborhood, following Fairchild to the mini-mall, where they turn left at the Burger King and head up Douglas to the Keystone Theater. There is a small crowd gathered for the movie.

"Line's not bad," Mr. Queen says as they park.

"No, but then it's a *weeknight*," his wife teases.

They buy tickets, load up with popcorn, soda, and Sno-Caps, and find seats in their preferred region of the theater: seventh row, central. Judy had been worried the baby wouldn't cooperate, but he is already asleep in her arms.

"Mom, this is so fun," Harley Jr. whispers as the lights dim.

Automatically the audience stands in anticipation of the national anthem. A second later the music kicks in, the movie screen lighting up with a montage of stock images: flag, farm, fighter jets. At last everyone sits down and the previews begin, then the movie itself.

It's a silly comedy—something about a ditsy blond girl running for president—not usually the kind of thing that Mr. Queen would ever see, and Judy keeps glancing over to make sure her husband is not miserable. They have spent so much time apart throughout their marriage that she is just grateful to have him around. To be a family.

About twenty minutes in, something happens.

First, several cell phones go off in the theater, including Mr. Queen's. Then a pair of large light-boxes bracketing the movie screen are illuminated. Each one reads, ALERT FORCE RECALL.

Amid the murmuring, someone says, "Oh my God," and a number of people in the audience—Mr. Queen among them— rise to leave.

"Dad!" Harley Jr. protests.

"Lee!" Mrs. Queen grabs her husband's arm. "What are you doing?"

"Sorry, honey. You know I have to go." He lovingly squeezes her hand as he removes it, giving her and the baby a kiss. He ruffles his older son's hair. "You da man. Be good for your mother."

Judy is not finished: "Is it an exercise?"

"No. Come on, you guys are missing the show, sit down. We'll talk later." He blows them a kiss and hurries up the aisle. Then he's gone.

Things hang frozen for a few minutes, the movie unspooling with idiotic persistence. Weeping can be heard, and dire whispers. Soon a portion of the remaining audience begins trickling away, unable to suspend disbelief.

Judy steps outside into the breeze off the Pacific. For now the sky over Kadena Air Base is peaceful, luminous clouds scudding through a pool of stars, a distant flicker of lightning. It is so beautiful in Okinawa this time of year...but there's a catch. Always a catch, no matter where they move. Mrs. Queen hugs her baby close and listens to the engines of the first scrambled jets, their turbines chiseling a cruel inscription across the dusk: three letters dreaded by every military wife since the dawn of time.

"What is it, Mom?" her older boy asks.

Surreptitiously wiping tears, Judy Queen says, "War, I guess."

CHAPTER TWO:

MANNY AND RUTH

Before it all fell apart, Manny Lopes liked to say that his marriage was due to Providence—Providence, Rhode Island. That was where he met Ruth Yi at an Ingmar Bergman double feature. The Avon Cinema was showing *Wild Strawberries* with *Autumn Sonata*, and Manny had spotted Ruth during the intermission, casually leaning against the low wall at the back of the theater. She was a goddess, majestic of thigh, with long black hair that fell like a horse's tail down the curving shelf of her khaki-clad butt.

As a small man, Manny had a fetish about big women; as a buff of '70s Kung Fu flicks he had a soft spot for sexy-scary Asians; so Ruth was Manny's perfect type: the kind of girl who looked like she could beat the hell out of you. Another guy seemed to be sizing her up, and Manny decided that if he didn't make the first move he would kick himself for the rest of his life. So he took a deep breath and sidled over, saying, "This is a great old theater, isn't it?"

"I love it. I come here all the time."

When she looked at him, her pale moon face eclipsing the red light of the exit sign, Manny realized he was out of his league. She was an Oriental warrior princess, he a Creole shrimp. Far from discouraging him, the knowledge relieved his anxiety: If he didn't stand a chance, he stood nothing to lose.

"Me too," he said. "I always thought it would be great to work in a place like this."

"Yeah. This is what heaven should be like: red velvet, dim lights, soft music, a good movie always about to start…"

"Hot buttered popcorn. What did you think of the movie?"

"Oh, I love Bergman."

"Me too." This was not quite true—Manny had no strong feelings about Bergman. He mainly liked going to art films because it suited the intellectual persona he was cultivating, the mythical, idealized Self that he wanted to become: a Renaissance Man, urbane, witty, but no slouch in the physical department. Not someone who could be defined by family connections, wealth, race, or physical stature (of which Manny had none), but rather by the power of pure merit. Manny didn't know exactly when this inner transformation would happen, but felt sure it must be a cumulative thing—just a matter of racking up enough life experiences. "I especially loved that dream sequence," he said.

"Oh yeah, and Max Von Sydow is always so good."

"He is."

"And I can't wait to see Liv Ullmann in the next one—she's amazing."

"She is, isn't she?" There was a gap in the conversation. This would have been the point where Manny usually broke off and retreated, not wanting to seem a pest. For some reason he decided to keep at it. "So, are you a student?"

"No, I'm a teacher, actually. K through eight."

"Oh yeah?"

"But right now I work at a daycare center. It's just until I can get state certified. What do you do?"

"Well, I came here to take courses at RISD,"—(he pronounced it "Rizdee")—"but then I decided I didn't want to go back to college right away. What I really wanted was to *travel*. So I've been saving up money to do that, working whatever odd jobs I can find. Right now I work at a parking garage downtown, and on weekends I do handyman stuff for my landlord, but it's just until I can find a job overseas. Hopefully something with the U.S. government."

"*That's* cool. You mean like the Peace Corps?"

"No, the War Corps—the military. But I'd be working for them as a civilian. There's a constant push to upgrade the computer infrastructure on the older bases, so they need lots of independent contractors."

"What exactly would you be doing?"

"Anything. Everything."

"Jack of all trades."

"Master of none—that's me. No, but I did graduate from technical school, so I figure Uncle Sam can find something for me to do. It's a two-year commitment, but the pay and benefits are great."

"Unless you get blown up."

"Yeah, well. So, are you from around here?"

"My family lives in Mass, but I'm originally from New York."

"Really? I'm not from here either, I'm from California."

They talked for a few more minutes, introducing themselves, until the lights clicked on and off.

"Whoops, showtime," Ruth said.

"I guess so." Manny spoke before he could think about it: "Do you care to sit together?" Every fiber in his body seemed to ball up.

"Sure."

"Great." Trying to appear suave, he gestured down the aisle and said, "After you."

≥≠≤

A year later, Manny and Ruth were married. It was a simple ceremony, a guerilla ceremony, hastily conducted in a hidden glade of the Swan Point Cemetery, right on the gooey bank of the Blackstone River, with a couple of friends as witnesses and one of Manny's co-workers (a compulsive dog-racing aficionado and former corrections officer, who had obtained his Certificate of Ministry through the mail) performing the service.

"That was nice," Manny said afterwards, unexpectedly moved. Pinned to his lapel was a big orange button—their only wedding present. It read: KISS ME, I'M MARRIED.

"It was okay," Ruth said, scraping mud off her shoes with a stick. "I'm glad it's over."

Manny was a bit stung, in spite of himself. Both of them had come from troubled homes and had airily dismissed the institution of marriage from the very beginning, but Manny was also wary of too much ironic detachment—he believed in passion, in living in the moment. It had caused some friction between he and Ruth, who was three years older and by nature more hardheaded.

"Come on, it was beautiful," he coaxed. "You didn't think that was romantic?"

"What are you talking about? It wasn't even real—we only did it for the piece of paper, so that I can be on your health plan."

"Yeah, but it was more than that. It was the perfect kind of wedding: just us, in nature, without all the pressure and bullshit most people go through to get married."

"That's because it wasn't even a wedding. Nobody I care about was there; I can't tell my family—that's not my ideal of marriage."

"I suppose you wish we'd done it in a church, in front of a thousand people."

"*No*. You know I don't believe in that. I'm sorry, honey, this whole thing just made me feel a little bit like a hypocrite. We did it, it's done; you're going to Korea. Can we just drop it?" She gave him a kiss, her eyes shunning his, shunning tears. "You *know* I love you."

Manny's hurt melted. Ruth was just stressing about him going away for so long, and he knew just how she felt. It was insane, if you thought about it. They had barely gotten to know each other, and now...

"I love you, too," he said.

CHAPTER THREE:

BLACK HOLE

SEOUL, South Korea, October 23 (UPI)— A freak volcanic eruption occurred overnight near the Korean port city of Busan, causing widespread destruction that reached as far as mainland Japan, where tsunamis pounded southern Honshu.

Survivors report "rolling mountains" destroying an area tens of kilometers wide. Volcanic gases are blamed for triggering a violent storm system that has caused all air traffic and shipping in the region to be rerouted. All four reactors of the Kori Nuclear Plant have reportedly been shut down. Communications have been disrupted as far north as Daegu, and highways out of the south are jammed with fleeing refugees.

The Kyunghyang Shinmun newspaper quotes unnamed officials at Seoul's Defense Ministry saying that emergency evacuation and rescue efforts are underway despite extremely hazardous conditions at the site. American military facilities based in and around Busan are thought to have been severely impacted, and joint U.S./Korean forces are being mobilized to deal with the crisis.

"It's a black hole in there," said Lt. Colonel Paul Atwells, spokesman for the U.S. Southern Command. "As of this morning we have reconnaissance teams doing the groundwork so that we can safely mount large-scale relief efforts."

No damage estimates have been made available, but officials warn to expect the worst. A nationwide state of emergency is in effect, and the entire southern province of Gyeongsangnam-do has been formally restricted to essential personnel. All others are advised to stay away.

≥≠≤

The first thing Major Queen noticed was the weather. About eighty miles off the Korean coast, a towering thunderhead loomed up out of the clear blue sky, looking like an alabaster toadstool with gills of black rain—a classic mushroom cloud.

"Is that it?" he asked, standing over Captain Deitz's shoulder in the cockpit.

"Yep. That's the thermocline."

"Huh. Does that look volcanic to you, Mike?"

"I guess so. Why?"

"It's too white—it just looks like condensation, like a regular supercell. I'm not seeing any smoke or ash. If this thing erupted overnight it ought to be dirty as hell."

The CV-22 passed beneath the dense cloud shelf, losing daylight. Walls of wind buffeted the aircraft. Unruffled as he surfed the turbulence, Deitz said, "Part of it's offshore, so you'd expect a lot of steam. I saw that when I was in Iceland."

Queen was searching the windshield for telltale ash smears. "It should still be full of crap."

"Wait, let me check my crap detector." Mike Deitz was no expert on volcanoes, but both men had meteorological training from the 10th Combat Weather Squadron, and Deitz thought the major was quibbling. How could you argue with what was right in front of you? "Hey, I'm getting a reading!"

"Okay, so how do you explain this?"

"Well, it has to be something volcanic," Deitz said. "You can't grow a mountain without some kind of major geologic upheaval. And there's definitely something growing in there. Thermal and side-scan radar images confirm it."

"Yeah, but it doesn't make any sense. Mountains sometimes explode without warning, but they never just spring up overnight—not without the granddaddy of all earthquakes, or sustained lava flows. I was at Clark when Pinatubo blew, and that was a hell of a mess. Huge. The moderate seismic activity that's been recorded so far doesn't account for what's going on down there—"

"Moderate! A major city has been wiped off the map."

"That's just it: one city. Considering the geological scale of this thing, the earthquakes have been incredibly localized. Seismography shows them emanating downward from the surface, not the other way around. And there hasn't been any evidence whatsoever of lava activity. The hottest temperature in there is barely a hundred degrees—you couldn't even cook a hot dog on that. And its source is one intermittent plume of gas venting from a fumarole at the easternmost elevation, about eight hundred feet high. The rest of the formation is slightly cooler. If it was formed from lava it would take months to cool to these temperatures. Hell, it *couldn't* form this quick, there's no way."

"So what are you suggesting?"

"I...don't know."

"Hey, that's a first. What about recon? We have anybody down on the ground?"

"You mean on site? Not since we lost contact with Stein's people. As far as I know, SOCKOR and the 17th SOS is on hold until we get there. There's a joint forward command post set up at Gimhae. That's our staging area."

"So nobody's really had a first-hand look at what's happening in there?"

"Not and lived to tell about it. We're it, brother."

They flew in silence for a few minutes, then Deitz said, "Because, you know, I heard some pretty weird stuff…"

"What kind of stuff?"

"Just while we were refueling in Yokota—there was loose talk about intelligence reports filtering out of Yongsan. I thought it had to be bullshit."

"Spit it out, Mike."

"It's just so *stupid*—"

"Stop being so damn coy."

"Creepy-crawlies, chief. Everybody who's come out of Busan has reported seeing people get eaten alive by weird…things."

Queen hated imprecision; it was a waste of his time. "'*Weird things?*' What kind of weird things?"

"That's just it: No one knows what they are. But a lot of the refugees are crawling with them."

"What do these 'creepy-crawlies' look like?"

"Here." Deitz reluctantly fished in his flight jacket and pulled out a folded piece of paper. "A friend of mine at the 160th Airborne forwarded this to me—it's supposed to be life-size." It was a color picture of something that looked like a primitive sea-creature: a semi-transparent blob fringed with many hair-like legs. "There are different kinds, but they say this is one of the most common. You can keep that."

"What is it these things are supposed to do to you?"

"I guess they cling to you like a—a jellyfish or something, and eat your skin. They're parasites."

Queen handed the picture back, annoyed at the sudden tightness in his chest. He wasn't afraid—the thing in the photo looked dead, flattened and unimpressive and probably somebody's idea of a joke, but it added greatly to the mounting burden of unknowns being heaped on him. "Mike, until we know more, I don't want you passing this around. Or even talking about it."

"Yes, sir. Sorry."

"No, that's all right. If it turns out to be anything, I'm sure we'll be briefed."

CHAPTER FOUR:

MT. SURIBACHI

"**I** love you, honey baby."

"I love *you*."

"I miss you so much, honeybunch. I keep thinking about our evenings together, sitting on the porch listening to jazz, taking walks in the cemetery. I can't wait to spend the rest of my life with you. You are so wonderful."

"No, it's you."

"It's *you*."

"It's you."

"It's you."

Manny Lopes clutched the phone receiver to his ear and thought wildly, *I'm going to die. I'm just going to die.* He wanted to scream. He wanted to reach through the line, stretch his arm all the way across the Pacific Ocean and the Continental United States, all the way back to Providence, grab her by the shoulders and shout, *I'm dying! Can't you see I'm falling apart? Don't you care at all about my suffering? I'm in Hell!* But all he said was, "God, you're beautiful."

"You're the one."

"It's you."

"It's you."

"It's you."

"It's you."

Ruth and Manny were a cute couple, that was what his friends at work said. They looked at Manny's wedding picture and said, "Awww! What a *cute couple!*" At first he accepted such compliments at face value, viewing the photos through the lens of his own pride, but as distance set in he began to realize that others were amused by the disparities between him and his wife. "Cute" referred not to their perfect harmony of spirit, but to their charmingly ridiculous physical contrasts: Ruth's statuesque (or the word she herself preferred, "Rubenesque") figure towering above him as if he were a lawn jockey. When Tech Sergeant Sue Budlick remarked, "Opposites attract," she was making a joke. Manny's pride soured; the cuteness curdled.

Manny never let on to Ruth how he was feeling, but as the months went by he sensed that something mechanical was creeping into their phone conversations. The lovey-dovey stuff was getting out of control, becoming filler to plug up the silences.

There was a long, unusual pause from Ruth's end of the line. Manny could hear her breathing. "Ruth?" he said.

"Manny?" Ruth's voice vibrated like a taut string. "God damn it. We need to talk."

"I know," he said.

≥≠≤

After speaking to Ruth, Manny still had to get ready for work. He went through the motions of his daily tae kwon do exercises, feeling numb. It was going to be another long day, as every day was here, an interminable battle with boredom and loneliness, ending in a fruitless trip to the APO. The only personal letters he ever got were from Ruth…and it looked like those would be drying up. So much for his big dream of going home at the end of his contract. What was there to go home to?

Manny, I can't do this any more. I'm sorry.

There was no one left who understood him now. Not the military people, not the civilian personnel or spouses, not the local Koreans. In the sixteen months since Manny had arrived in Daegu, there were any number of people who had tried to get to know him, and he them, but it was always strained and uncomfortable, fizzling to nothing. He knew people thought he was weird with his retro hats, baggy suits, wingtip shoes, and pencil-thin mustache, something out of a Harlem nightclub in the '40s, but it was a look he was comfortable with, and that was one of the few comforts left to him now. He put on the clothes as if girding himself in armor.

Manny just wasn't a joiner, however much he tried. Prayer groups, bowling leagues, meet-and-greets—they just weren't his thing. Until he came overseas, Manny had never realized how dependent he was on the cultural wealth of a big, cosmopolitan city: the foreign films, the ethnic restaurants, the underground music and nightlife, the sparkling art scene and tolerant, diverse population in which to blissfully lose himself. It provided the basis for his whole personality…or, he feared, perhaps camouflaged its absence.

Such reserve was all but unknown in the expatriate community in which Manny found himself, a Wal-Mart diaspora that mocked any possibility of transcendence. Here the only culture was a weird holdover from the fifties, a frozen slice of provincial Americana forever being reheated by the wisdom of Paul Harvey and Rush Limbaugh, all other interests forbidden except the time-honored ones of television, gambling, drinking, religion, shopping, sports scores, gossip, or adultery.

So Manny spent his days bitterly alone, buried in the guts of balky mainframes, spending his off-hours at the gym, doing the crossword in *Stars & Stripes,* watching crap on AFKN, or—when he could still muster up the energy—wandering off-base so that he didn't become one of the slugs who were afraid to set foot outside their Little America housing compounds. That was how he met Karen Park.

≥≠≤

"You ready to go, Karen?" Manny asked, sitting on the edge of her desk with brittle insouciance.

"Give me two seconds to finish correcting."

"How was your day?"

"It was good. What about yours?"

"Oh, you know…" Brushing aside his martyrdom, he said, "Don't forget we have to meet Mr. Wang at four."

"Yup."

"I can't wait for this weekend," he said.

Karen Park didn't look up from her grade-book. She was a teacher at the DoDDS school on Camp George, and Manny had been there many times to fix the computers. "I agree," she said. "It'll be good to get away from this place for a little while. I need a break."

"It'll be like a little honeymoon."

Karen glanced curiously at him. "Oh yeah," she smirked. "I bet." Manny had never flirted with her before.

They had met on a USO tour to Chinhae during the cherry blossom festival, and were comfortable enough in each other's presence to take several more group tours to the countryside. Their reason for doing this was that however lonely either one of them may have felt in Korea, they were rarely left alone, being objects of deep fascination to most Koreans.

As a foreigner, an American, and particularly a brown-pigmented American, anywhere Manny went he was treated like a celebrity… or a freak…by local nationals who apparently had never seen a black man in person, many of whom were eager to practice their halting English by comparing Manny to Barack Obama or some other high-profile black person. Considering the thousands of African-American military personnel who lived in Korea, Manny was surprised the novelty hadn't worn off…but it hadn't.

Thus he found it useful to have a traveling companion in Korea, someone to share the heat. Karen was unfailingly upbeat about it. *Just smile and wave*, she would say, to which Manny would wearily reply, *I know, I know: Pretend you're Michael Jackson.*

Some locals were offended at the sight of a Korean-American woman in the company of a slight brown *miguk* and would scowl or make rude comments, while others pointed and laughed as unselfconsciously as Sunday zoo-goers. Karen was amused, but Manny often felt offended—he felt more like Michael Jackson's chimp.

Fortunately, the majority of Koreans they met went to great lengths to demonstrate friendly acceptance, to welcome them, which could be the most exhausting of all. Children were endlessly impressed with Manny's body hair, and would brazenly stroke his arms while chanting, "Mistah Monkey, Mistah Monkey."

But none of this had deterred him from exploring the place. As challenging as it was, Manny still refused to become like so many of the Americans he knew: sedentary, contemptuous of the host country, hardly venturing out into what they dismissively referred to as "the economy" except to shop or get drunk. Following the lead of his fearless companion, Karen, Manny seized every opportunity to plumb this alien culture, even when he hated every minute of it.

They explored on foot, stepping over gobs of spit ("Land of the Morning Phlegm," Karen would joke), dealing with mazes of unmarked streets, dodging maniacal traffic, risking death from indoor carbon-monoxide fumes and outdoor street vendors, holding their noses as they passed sewage-pumping "honey-wagons" and mosquito-fogger trucks, getting tear-gassed and nearly trampled during street rallies, and submitting to hostile interrogations by strangers about American foreign policy.

But they also made wonderful discoveries: The sinus-clearing joy of *kimchi*, the spicy national dish. The water-heated *ondol* floors under their stocking feet. The enormous brown pear-apples, and in springtime the lush roof-gardens that made bearable the grim concrete infrastructure of urban Daegu. Then there was always the unexpectedly excellent coffee, Lotte chocolate, garlicky *bulgogi* beef, the impeccable trains, the beauty of clay-tiled temples and villages, the broad cultivated valleys and stepped hillsides. The old folks playing Go on the sidewalk. The ever-present *mugunghwa*— rose of Sharon—which reminded Manny of Southern California.

He had come here because it was a chance to experience a foreign culture, damn it, not just a government job with free housing and benefits. Manny would survive if it killed him.

So there was nothing romantic about it; it was a partnership of convenience, and apart from such trips the two hardly spoke to one another. Karen knew that Manny and his wife Ruth were so lovey-dovey it was disgusting. And Karen was spoken for as well, engaged to a Japanese military liaison she had met on a MAC flight to Fukuoka.

It annoyed her a little bit that her fiancé, Yukio, was not as totally devoted to her as Manny obviously was to Ruth. Yukio had been so charming in the beginning, but ever since they'd become engaged he had started acting like a jerk. He hardly called anymore, and sounded put off when she phoned him in Japan. When she accused him of giving her the cold shoulder, he said, *Karen, you just don't understand Japanese culture. It's not normal for a Japanese man to say "I love you" a hundred times a day, like Americans do. With us it's more serious.*

"No, I know," Manny said to her now, disguising his awkwardness with a laugh. "Just kidding."

Karen turned back to her grade book. The way she tuned him out so easily made Manny feel that he had disappeared altogether.

≥≠≤

Their plan for this weekend was to take a USO bus tour to a famous restaurant called the Moon Viewing House—a fancy *bulgogi* place with elaborate sculpture gardens—and then to avoid the long return trip by jumping off the bus in Busan, where they would spend the night at the Paradise Beach Hotel before returning to Daegu by train.

That was tomorrow. First they had to go with Mr. Wang and earn the money to pay for it all. Just as they were leaving school, Mr. Wang was driving up to the camp gate in his white Hundai luxury sedan with gold trim. At the sight of them, he tooted his horn.

"*Annyo' hashimnikka*," they chirped, getting in the car.

"*Anno' haseyo! Chossumnida*," said Mr. Wang. To Manny he offered his fist, saying, "What-up-dog?" Mr. Wang had dealings with many African-American service members, and prided himself on speaking their language.

Manny awkwardly met the proffered fist with his own. He had never been the least bit "ghetto", and in fact scarcely thought of himself as black, since his mother had been white. He rejected all racial classification. "Yo," he said. "*Komupsumnida*."

"*Chon'moneyo*, G. Soddy to keep you waiting."

"We just got here ourselves."

"Good, good. Ready to go?"

"Yes."

"Off-da-hook." He pulled away from the gate, maneuvering the big car down narrow alleyways lined with shops. They merged onto a busy road and left the city, catching sight of green hills in the distance. "How are you liking Korea?" Mr. Wang asked, as they drove through the suburban Suseong-gu district.

"We love it."

"What do you think of Korean peoples?"

"They've been very kind to us."

Karen added, "Wonderful."

"Korean peoples and American peoples very good friends."

"That's true."

"Korea very small country; America very big. Some Koreans think America too big, but I love you very much."

They nodded and smiled appreciatively. Mr. Wang had good reason to love Americans—he owned a lot of rental properties and was also heavily involved in the black-market sale of AAFES goods and pirate DVDs. They knew a few Americans who made a pretty penny off this trade as well.

Mr. Wang grinned at Karen in the rearview mirror, "You are very tall for a Korean woman."

Karen laughed, "That's what they tell me. I'm only half Korean."

"Yes. At first I think you too tall, too much fat, but now I think you very beautiful."

"Thank you," she said. "*Komupsumnida.*"

"You and your husband together too much," he chided.

Manny and Karen didn't say anything. They both wore rings, and had gotten into the habit of allowing the locals to assume they were married; otherwise it would be considered unseemly for them to be together. The whole platonic thing didn't fly here.

"Not good for man and woman to be always together so much. One of these days I take your husband fishing maybe." To Manny he said, "Do you have fished before in the States?"

"Sure."

"Very good fishing in Korea—Pohang. I show you best places."

"Great."

"Wife not allowed, just you." He laughed.

Manny laughed along, feeling slightly peeved—he knew Mr. Wang's friendly overture was actually a backhanded way of saying he was pussy-whipped, a well-meaning attempt to restore his manhood.

They arrived at the university, a large modern building with a *mugunghwa* hedge shaped like a Buddhist swastika. Mr. Wang led them upstairs to the language lab and introduced the couple to a team of young recording engineers who didn't speak English. The crew sat Manny and Karen in a soundproof booth with thick scripts, headphones, and a microphone, then retreated to an editing console and signaled them to start.

The script was a series of simple dialogues—elementary stuff for Koreans learning English. Manny and Karen had been expecting that. What they hadn't expected was that the script would be quite so *long*. This was supposed to be a fast fifty bucks, an hour's work at most. Hoping to make short work of the thing, they threw themselves into it, reading as quickly as they could while still trying to imitate the perky cadence of NPR hosts. Once they found a voice and a rhythm, they began to enjoy themselves. For the first time that day, Manny was able to forget about his talk with Ruth.

About 45 minutes into it, just as their throats were getting dry, Mr. Wang stopped them.

"Too fast," he said, his voice ringing in the headphones. "Slower, please."

"Slower, got it," Manny said. "Where do you want us to start from?"

"At the beginning, please."

"The beginning of the page?"

"No. Start page one, okay? Go slow."

Manny and Karen looked at each other. "We have to start again from the beginning?" They had read over eighty pages.

"Yes, please to start at the beginning. Numba one, okay."

This time they read with painstaking care, but it was only a half-hour before Mr. Wang cut in again: "*Sillyehamnida*. Slower, please."

"*Slower?*"

"Yes."

"We go any slower, we'll be going backwards."

Mr. Wang exhibited no amusement. "Slow *down*," he insisted patiently.

This time they were ultra-cautious, doggedly pronouncing each syllable as if speaking to the hard of hearing. Manny's voice was almost shot, but Karen's teacher pipes were holding steady, and they got through eighty pages, a hundred pages, a hundred and fifty pages, two hundred pages, and were closing in on the end when Manny came across a misprint that caught him off-guard. The sentence was supposed to read, "The Marines planted the flag on Mt. Suribachi," but instead it read, "The Marines planted the flag on *Mr.* Suribachi."

It was not the first misprint Manny had come across—the script was full of typos and minor grammatical errors that they caught and corrected along the way. But now he and Karen had been reading steadily for over three hours, and Manny was giddy with exhaustion and thirst. When he read, "The Marines planted the flag on Mr. Suribachi," he was suddenly seized with a delirious image of tiny soldiers poking a toothpick-size flagpole into the scalp of a wincing giant…a giant who resembled Mr. Wang.

Manny choked, tried to stifle it, snorted and felt tears spring to his eyes. The tears were of pure grief—the last thing he wanted to do was laugh. But then he glanced at Karen and realized she was involved too, set off as much by the typo as his grimacing reaction to it. (She would later tell him, "You looked like steam was about to shoot out of your ears.")

That was it: The two of them exploded, breaking down completely. They turned to rubber, sagged in their chairs, practically slid to the floor, their guffaws only exacerbated by the stony patience of the Koreans. For a few minutes Manny gave in to this blessed release, venting not only the stress of this evening, but all the frustrations of the past two years. He sobbed with laughter, and then just sobbed, thinking of Ruth's brittle voice in his ear: *Honey, I just can't do this anymore. I'm sorry.*

Finally, after a few relapses, Manny and Karen got hold of themselves and apologized to Mr. Wang, trying to explain just what they had found so funny. The grave-faced Korean man listened with clinical indifference, then leaned down to his mike and said, "Okay, start again, please."

CHAPTER FIVE:

THE LAST SUPPER

Hugging his punctured ribs, grinning like an idiot, Dr. Fred Isaacson stumbled across moonless sands toward the East Sea. Except for where his hand cupped the hot blood oozing from his side, he was cold to the bone.

"Wimps," he wheezed through bloody gritted teeth. "Oh yeah—the wimps shall inherit the Earth. You can bet your bottom dollar."

The beach was not completely deserted: a number of incandescent tents glowed like paper lanterns across the long strand, their sides flapping in the wind. From a distance they reminded Isaacson of the *luminarias* he had seen during Navidad in Los Alamos. He made his way to the nearest one, catching a whiff of cooking oil and charcoal.

It was a little outdoor buffet like the ones he had passed on the street in Itaewon: Seoul food, *al fresco*. Lots of deep-fried goodies on sticks, which customers washed down with beer or *soju*—Korean white lightning. Isaacson found such places picturesque, but he would usually never set foot in one, not with his triglycerides. Also, he had forsworn alcohol as part of his recent covenant with Yahweh. It was too bad; he could have used a stiff drink.

He threw open the plastic canopy and babbled, *"Help—American—need help, please!"* but the quaint Asian faces he was expecting were nowhere to be seen—the tent was empty. A string of bare light bulbs bobbed above an abandoned banquet table covered with pans of batter-fried peppers and squid and yams, vegetable fritters, fresh and cooked shellfish, an enormous red spider-crab. Braziers and steaming pots sat untended. Gusts of wind made the walls shudder and the light sway, as if the fragile refuge could come uprooted any second. Swooning from the pungent kitchen warmth, Isaacson collapsed on the bench.

"Please God, please God," he prayed, face down on the table. "I hope I have done Thy bidding." He heard someone come through the flap behind him, bringing in a gust of cold air.

A shrill, grating voice said, "Excuse me. I see you are practicing your custom of 'saying grace'. Do not let me interrupt."

"It's too late," Isaacson groaned, not looking at her. "You're too late; I got rid of it, praise Jesus."

"Jesus is a fairytale, a nursery rhyme to put children to sleep. We don't believe in fairytales, Professor, unless they are about our Great Leader. Otherwise they are a corrupt Western invention. But if you like nursery rhymes I will tell you one. I learned this at Pyongyang Information Ministry; you may know it: Little Jack Horner? I believe it goes, Little Jack Horner sat in a corner, eating a Christmas pie. He stuck in his *thumb*—"

A horny, powerful hand suddenly pinned Isaacson's head to the table while a long-nailed thumb jammed deep into his wound. Isaacson screamed, writhing.

"—and pulled out a *plum*, and cried, 'What a good boy am I.'" Grunting with the effort of holding him still, the voice rasped, "Be a good boy, Professor, and tell me what you have done with our…plums?"

Dr. Isaacson's consciousness came unplugged—he was swept up in a vivid dream that it was still morning, before all of this had begun.

≥≠≤

That morning, Fred Isaacson had anxiously huddled in his suite at the hotel, waiting for his ride to the airport. He had just wanted to get out of Korea, get far away and wait for the Rapture. In spite of some misgivings, he had accomplished what he set out to do, as mandated by Yahweh. And God was well pleased: "NOAH HIMSELF COULDN'T HAVE DONE IT BETTER," He had told Isaacson in the shower. "YOU CAN TELL HIM I SAID SO."

Isaacson was sitting on the end of the bed watching stilted Armed Forces TV commercials ("Say, Betty, did you hear about the Colonel's new plan to test those nuclear artillery shells on the golf course?" "Shhh! Be careful, Bob. You never know if the terrorists might be listening." "Gee, you're right! It's everybody's responsibility to practice good OPSEC.") when there was a loud knock at the door. It made him jump.

Through the fish-eye lens of the peephole, Isaacson saw what looked like a hydrocephalic fetus bulging out of a shiny brown suit. It was actually a gaunt, grave-faced Korean man—his official, and unofficial, liaison.

He opened the door, saying, "Good morning, Mr. Wang. You're just in time—I'll die if I have to sit through *Guiding Light* again."

"Good morning, Dr. Isaacson." Mr. Wang bowed stiffly. "*Annyo'hashimnikka*. You are ready to go?"

"Quite ready—bags all packed."

"Very good. I hope you have enjoyed your stay in Korea."

"I always do."

It was the fifth time Fred Isaacson had been to Korea—and the last. His church sponsored a mission there, and he had visited twice in just the past year, taking part in organizing food aid shipments to the North. This dovetailed conveniently with his recent duties as a nuclear scientist appointed to oversee the transfer of reactor technology as part of a non-proliferation agreement with Pyongyang—not to mention as a holy agent of the Apocalypse.

Ever since his salvation Korea held a special fascination for Isaacson, its perpetual struggle—North against South—so much a macrocosm of the individual human soul. Visiting the Demilitarized Zone as a tourist, the professor had felt the living presence of the Eternal Serpent a hair's breadth away. Yet he had been surprised at what a vale of green the DMZ was: not a denuded minefield as he would have expected, but a veritable nature preserve, thriving forbidden in the shadow of death. Animals long extinct in other parts of the country still existed there, rare as the happy accident of war that sheltered them.

He had been told the story of a tree standing in this garden, a tree like the one in Genesis, which had appeared so innocent and yet had harbored evil fruit. Isaacson had recurrent dreams about that tree, terrible dreams in which he played the role of Captain Bonifas, idly standing guard as local nationals went to prune branches which were blocking the view of a lookout post. Lulled by the peace and stillness, Bonifas heard a sound and glanced up...glanced up to see something that defied explanation. An optical illusion? A trick of light and shadow? Anything but what it appeared to be—that's why serpents hide in the leaves. Bonifas and another guard were slow to move, disbelieving: how could there be *men* up there? And then as the North Koreans dropped down there was no time. No time to unlimber a weapon, no time to do anything but run. Run from that inconceivable vision of axes raised against you in the clear light of day, amid birdsong and new-mown grass. And then to feel the bite of that first steel blade. To fall. Isaacson always awoke drenched in sweat, heart pounding.

Proximity to such evil always gave Isaacson a sense of real

urgency—of opportunity. He felt *needed* in Korea...but he could never stay long. He was not a professional missionary, or a diplomat. He was a scientist—a senior researcher at the Brookhaven National Laboratory, divining the nature of matter. Just as Panmunjom gave him insights into the nature of Satan, quantum physics revealed to him the face of God. In the play of mesons and bosons, quarks and leptons, muons and gluons he counted angels dancing on the head of a pin. And as his burgeoning religious fervor distanced him more and more from his unsaved colleagues (and even his own family), it was little wonder that Fred Isaacson became convinced that he had a key role to play in the inevitable showdown...a conviction that was dry tinder for that fateful night, alone on the couch, when a loud, disembodied voice had first boomed, "FRED." When God spoke his name.

≥≠≤

They had been driving for a while when Isaacson became concerned—they should have been at the airport by now. Instead they were skirting the industrial sprawl of the container port, headed for Pohang. Catching a glimpse of the ocean, he said warily, "Nice day for the beach."

Mr. Wang's voice revealed nothing: "Too cold for swimming."

"Were we going swimming?"

"No."

They passed a bleak little yard in which a single dusty persimmon tree stood, its fruit startlingly orange.

"Do you like to swim, Mr. Wang?" He couldn't imagine this stolid-faced man in a bathing suit.

"No."

"If you don't mind my asking, what do you do for fun?"

"Fun."

"Fun? Recreation?"

"Fun is a decadent American vice."

Isaacson was amused in spite of himself at the characteristic Korean bluntness; they weren't shy. "Oh come on," he said. "Koreans know how to have fun." As he said this they were passed by a motor coach full of boogying travelers. It swayed to the beat of the music like a rolling disco.

"You've seen Americanized Koreans brainwashed by bourgeois concepts of pleasure. These are not healthy traditional pursuits; they have no ideology, no higher purpose except to reduce people to the level of animals so that they may be more effectively exploited." Mr. Wang said this not in an angry way, but as a rote statement of fact.

Nodding thoughtfully, Isaacson felt his stomach flutter: *The jig is up.* He surprised himself with his own cool—perhaps he had been expecting this all along.

They left the city proper, passing through an outlying area of rice fields surrounded by shimmering strips of reflective tape. Solar scarecrows. Drying rice was spread along the breakdown lane, and Isaacson wondered if it was flavored with lead or other toxic emissions. But he had always admired Korean utilitarianism. He closed his eyes to wait, putting his faith in Yahweh.

Arriving at a semi-industrial seaside town, Mr. Wang parked before a row of shuttered businesses. Weather-beaten banners and signs lent a sad carny air to the place, as of better days. Everything appeared to be closed for the season. No, not everything—at the far end stood an outdoor cafe with several small tables under a canvas awning. One of the tables was covered with an array of freshly severed pig heads, each one resting on a stand made from a bleached jawbone. The heads all faced the same way, sleepily grinning. A huge fish tank full of eels cast a Coke-bottle-green shadow on the concrete patio. Following Mr. Wang's lead, Isaacson pulled up a chair and sat down. He checked his watch: It was now definitely too late to make his connection.

"So, am I under arrest?"

Mr. Wang ignored the question, calling orders to a stooped old woman in the doorway. She brought them pickled yellow radish and some sort of raw seafood with a dish of hot sauce. Then she dipped a net in the tank and scooped out a large eel. The eel was a live wire, muscular and slippery, with a dark gray top and a pearly belly. It looked unreal. With practiced deftness, the woman transferred the eel to a pink plastic shopping bag, twisted the top into a rope, and beat the creature against the ground until it stopped writhing. Then she took it inside.

"Phew," Isaacson said, grinning nervously.

"Very fresh," said Mr. Wang, who took up a pair of metal chopsticks and ate one of the seafood polyps.

Isaacson tried one and found it bitter. "What is this?" he asked, chewing.

"Sea squirt. Good for potency."

"Ah." He put his chopsticks down. "Mr. Wang, let's not drag this out."

The Korean nodded blandly. Clearing his throat and spitting, he said, "We at the North Korea Friendship Society question the motive behind your interesting gift, Doctor. Our friends have expressed…concern."

"I've already told you how dangerous it is. That's the whole point."

"Dangerous, yes. But to whom?"

"What do you mean?"

"We suspect that this is some manner of trap. The only reasonable explanation is you are acting in accordance with your government to test our security apparatus."

"That's baloney. I represent one person, and that's my Lord and Savior. I'm His advance man on this Earth, and it is my sacred mandate to pave the way for His return. In representing Him I represent the cleansing wrath of Yahweh, who has chosen your people to be the instruments of Armageddon. I thought we'd been through this already."

"Of course, of course…then perhaps you can tell me once more what this peculiar object is supposed to be. My superiors are not convinced of its value."

"It was an accident."

Mr. Wang's lip curled with undisguised contempt.

"WIMPS," Isaacson said. "We were studying WIMPS—Weakly Interacting Massive Particles, also known as Dark Matter. Higgs bosons. The hidden fabric of the Universe."

"Which you say has never been directly observed."

"Except by us. Only by us. We not only observed it, we made it."

"How?"

"As I said—by tsunami. We detonated a very small amount of antimatter in the Japan Trench, which had the unfortunate side effect of triggering a major earthquake. Whoops. What we were really trying to create was a magic carpet. It's a wonderful idea, isn't it? A magic carpet! Take you anywhere you want to go, no emissions, no fuel, no moving parts to wear out. That was the notion that started all this; that was where the funding came from. An honest-to-goodness magic carpet…who wouldn't want one?"

Mr. Wang grunted, less than delighted.

Isaacson continued, "Of course, it's not easy to get people excited about something so airy-fairy—you have to break it down to basic principles, such as isolating the elusive graviton. It sounds like something out of science fiction, but it's no more outlandish than anything else in quantum physics. It's like catching butterflies: You take your net and go a-huntin'. If you catch something, you pin it down and take a good look at it. Figure it out. If you're lucky, they'll name it after you and award you the Nobel Prize. But antigravity—there's a word that'll get you labeled a kook real fast. Talk about pie in the sky! We heard it so much we made it our project logo: a flying pie. To come up with antigravity you have to find gravity, which is no mean feat. Funny when you consider that it's the flypaper that holds the Universe together, that it's literally everywhere, connecting everything to everything else. But try getting it under a microscope.

"We did the next best thing, though: We learned how to poke a pinhole in it, to create a graviton-free zone in the center of a terbium-based superconducting ceramic flask. The way we did this was by exposing a small amount of antimatter to conditions of extreme pressure—conditions which exist at the bottom of the sea. The antimatter was encased in a special alloy that liquefied during the reaction, forming perfectly spherical vacuum bubbles. We then captured some of the larger bubbles for study. By attaching electrodes to their poles, we turned them into mini cyclotrons, using the Relativistic Heavy Ion Collider to generate a Fermion superfluid which we injected into them, creating a high-velocity vortex of degenerate Fermion gas. As the plasma expanded and spun away from the center, baryons and antibaryons annihilated each other within a shell of perpetually orbiting Cooper pairs that amplified the magnetic repulsion effect at the core, creating a negative spot like the eye of a hurricane—a perfect void. Not like the dirty void of deep space, mind you, which is a soup of waves and particles acted upon by gravity and time, but pure nullity such as hasn't existed since before the Big Bang. *Nothing*. We had literally bottled pure Nothing! And that's what I've given you: a whole lotta Nothing!"

"Most generous, I'm sure."

"Oh, Nothing is funny. You might think Nothing is nothing, but we found it's actually the mother of Something; it's the incubator. Create Nothing and you create conditions suitable for a baby universe to be born—a Little Big Bang. What's interesting is that it happens relatively slowly, perhaps due to the damping effect of our existing universe—more a Big Ooze than a Big Bang, and what's interesting is *what* it oozes."

"What?"

"Pure, Grade-A Dark Matter."

"And this is lethal?"

"Well, not *per se*. Remember what Dark Matter is: It has mass and volume, but no other detectable properties—that means it's invisible, but reveals itself in the way it influences visible matter. The danger of hatching a new Universe is that it's like a cuckoo's egg—a cuckoo's egg universe crowding into ours. We can stop the singularity at the quantum level by flooding it with a quark-gluon plasma, but left alone it must eventually get too big to control."

"What would that mean?"

"Our observations at the subatomic level suggest that WIMPS infiltrate ordinary matter, increasing its volume exponentially and forming a kind of chromodynamic scaffold between disassociated particles, multiplying or otherwise altering their properties. Think of it as a cancer on reality...or a hellish Jiffy Pop. Since tremendous mass is introduced, it could theoretically create a gravity well that would destroy...well, everything. Create a Black Hole right here on Earth that would consume the planet, and eventually the whole Universe. Much ado about Nothing, indeed."

"Hmm. How would such a reaction be triggered?"

"Now that's what caused the project to be shut down—hypothetically, it's very simple: disrupt the stasis field. Breach the containment. Believe it or not, destroying the Universe may be as easy as cracking a walnut. We made hundreds of those terbium vessels for Nullity studies before we realized the risk and had to neutralize them...or most of them. It was an incredible boondoggle, really, considering the danger was purely theoretical—there could easily be limiting factors we don't understand. But I'm sure your people will find a way to put them to good use."

"I see. Yes, I think I understand, Mr. Isaacson." Mr. Wang pushed back his chair and stood up. "And I'm afraid we must decline your most generous offer."

Isaacson watched, astonished, as the old lady wheeled out a huge clay jar on a hand truck. It was a crude earthenware jug identical to every other *kimchi* pot in Korea, but Isaacson knew at once that it was the very one in which he had last week placed his strange and terrible stolen cargo, concealing it among a thousand others in a vast shipment of food-aid to the North.

Blinking stupidly, he said, "What? What are you talking about?"

"We are returning your gift."

"You're giving it *back*?"

"Yes. Very embarrassing—there will be an internal investigation to determine why this mistake was not recognized at once. Clearly we were deceived by your credentials."

"But I didn't deceive you! This is crazy!"

"Crazy, yes. You are crazy—cuckoo, like you say. *Ppokkugi*. We give you back your eggs."

Suddenly Isaacson understood. They thought he was some kind of crackpot! A garden-variety loony. Well, wasn't that the fate of every prophet? He should be flattered! "You silly, stupid—" he said in wonderment. "*You're* the crazy ones, and I can prove it."

Isaacson jumped up and went to the jar. They didn't bother to stop him. The heavy lid was secured with rough twine; he cut his hands trying to wrench it off, then finally accepted a knife. All the work he had put into sealing this up! Opening the lid, he was struck with the pungent cabbage smell of fermenting *kimchi*. He pried out the bag that contained the spicy vegetable mixture and plunged his hands into the straw beneath.

"Here it is, here it is," he crooned, eyes watering. "Come to papa."

Deep within the red clay jar, buried in straw, were three pale gray balls. Isaacson cautiously scooped them out, holding them up to the sunlight. "Handle with care," he chortled. They resembled antique enameled ornaments—beautiful paperweights. Close up they had the silvery organic translucence of small moons, webbed with an intricate arrangement of hairline cracks. Scorched-looking metal terminals gleamed like meteor strikes at their poles.

"Pretty, aren't they?" Isaacson said. "Who could imagine?" He looked triumphantly from the balls in his hand to Mr. Wang and the woman. "Crazy, huh? Get me a superfluid of fermionic hadrons and a nutcracker and we'll see how crazy I am."

Mr. Wang did not seem to be paying attention. His disbelieving stare was focused somewhere past Isaacson, as if he hadn't heard a word. There was a muffled *plop!* and suddenly a neat little hole appeared in the center of his forehead. The Korean staggered backward, steadied himself and then abruptly collapsed, spouting a delayed jet of blood.

Isaacson shouted in terror and dropped to the floor.

"When you've got Nothing," squawked a harsh baby-doll voice, piercing as a rusty spring, "you've got Nothing to lose."

It was a woman. The old stooped woman. Only she had shed her hunchback and her *hanbok* and her dirty rat's nest of hair and half her years; now she was standing tall in an albino alligator jacket and miniskirt, with black-and-white striped leggings and stiff, fuchsia-tipped platinum braids that encased her waxy skull like a crown of thorns. She was a hard-bodied go-go doll with the head of Medusa, her murderous dead stare freezing Isaacson like a bird in the thrall of a snake. He knew what he was looking at, or what was looking at *him*: a human weapon tempered and made razor-sharp by God-knew-what depths of poverty and abuse and state-sponsored depravity, sent South to murder and spy and shelter murderers and spies under the guise of a simple old peasant woman bent double from an innocent lifetime of planting rice—it was all written in those black-smudged eyes, that blank-brutal face, and the collapsed veins in her arms.

Whatever her superiors felt, she believed him. And now she was going solo. After a lifetime of harsh obedience she finally saw her chance to practice in its purest form the uncompromising North Korean philosophy of *Juche*: self-reliance.

"Give me your balls, Mr. Isaacson," she said.

Just as certainly as Isaacson knew the flavors of leptons and quarks, he knew this woman was going to kill him…no matter what he did. He was about to die. This should not have scared him—he had spent quite some time now on familiar terms with the Almighty and looked forward to expedited admission to Elysium—yet it did. All at once he most desperately did not want to die.

Isaacson didn't think, he just threw her one of the spheres. "Here!" he cried, lobbing the ball high and wide, so that she had to run for it. And as she ran one way, he ran the other. She could not watch him and the ball both; she certainly could not aim and shoot—Isaacson ran in a frenzy of wild hope. Having once been a respectable starting forward on the CalTech team, he thought there was every chance he had sunk the ball in that eel tank, where she'd have to fish for it. *"Home free,"* he gasped. *"Please, dear Jesus…"*

He was so flush with adrenaline that he didn't know at first that it was a Teflon-coated 9mm North Korean-made bullet that punched him in the ribs; he didn't hear the gun at all. He thought perhaps he had been hit with something else, anything, and kept running. Then he thought it was a cramp. Then he found the blood and knew: *She* was coming.

Trying to staunch the bleeding as he ran, searching for a place to hide, Isaacson ducked into a low-tech industrial complex: a maze of small workshops making knock-offs of Gucci and Chanel leather products, as well as quantities of "eel-skin" goods (he fleetingly, empathetically thought of the eel in the bag). They were obviously not operating at peak—there was only a handful of people around; mostly women doing vinyl piecework. It occurred to him that anyone engaged in these shady enterprises would probably be reluctant to get involved. Chances were that if he made a big commotion they would give him away to his pursuer, intentionally or not.

He passed a loading dock for one of the larger manufacturers. Several delivery trucks stood waiting at the platform, loaded with express-mail packages bound for America. There was no one in sight. Protecting both his wound and the two remaining terbium flasks, Isaacson heaved himself up into a partially loaded truck, making a cave out of boxes before sinking into exhausted limbo. The stench of epoxy masked the smell of his blood and sweat. As he was passing out, he read and reread the labels all around him, comforted somehow by the fact that they were printed in English. It made him feel less alone.

They read:

> MADE EXCLUSIVELY FOR HERCULES ENHANCEMENT PRODUCTS, USA, BY SANG-DONG MFG LTD, ROK. HANDLE WITH CARE.

≥≠≤

The streak of blood down his side turned ice-cold when the tent flap opened, waking him to misery. At first Isaacson thought he was still in the truck, but then he remembered that he had fled the truck hours ago, when he heard people being shot in the warehouse. Questioned and shot, one after another. After that, everything was a blur of running and running in the dark until at last he collapsed in this *soju* stand.

He couldn't see with his face mashed against the table, but he remembered who was doing the mashing: *Her*. So who was entering the tent now? Not daring to hope, Isaacson felt his attacker tense as the intruder demanded, "Hello? Hey, what are you doing to him? Oh my God!" An American!

"What is it?" cried someone else in English—an American woman.

"I don't know, stay back! Run to the hotel and have them call the police! Just do it, Karen!"

Seizing the distraction, Isaacson's fumbling hands found the neck of a big brown bottle of OB beer. He had been on a courtesy tour of the OB brewery only a few days before, along with the rest of the nuclear delegation (most of whom had embarrassed him by availing themselves a little too freely of the free samples), and suddenly he felt that this was significant—a portent. Since finding Yahweh, Isaacson's world was rife with omens and other manifestations of the Almighty…of which this slim chance was clearly one. He swung the bottle as hard as he could against his assailant's head. The glass didn't break as in the movies, but it seemed to do the trick: for an instant her claws let up and he spun clear, wildly swinging.

"Yeaaaagh!" he screamed.

The bottle connected with something hard—a glasslike object in his attacker's clothing—and both of them gasped, frozen in terror as if perched on a landmine. When nothing happened, Isaacson broke first, scrambling across the table while the other calmly raised her small black pistol, aimed, and shot him twice in the back. Mortally wounded, he still didn't stop, but squirmed hideously away and out of the tent like a maimed animal.

The assassin was prevented from shooting again by Manny Lopes, who finally found the presence of mind to do something: He grabbed for her gun and inadvertently took a tiger by the tail—in a blur of motion he found himself slammed breathlessly across the table, skull clanging like a bell as he stared cross-eyed down the smoldering barrel. His bladder let go.

"Damn Yankees," squealed the fierce woman, sounding like an unholy Betty Boop. In throwing Manny down, she had torn off his coat sleeve, and now she shook it in his face. "All the time sticking your nose in where it don't belong!"

Then something happened. Manny would never be able to satisfactorily describe it later—it had the qualities of a hallucination, as when he spiked fevers as a child and could barely drag himself to the bathroom, slogging as through waist-deep wet cement: clammy pajamas, baking breath, feet of lead anchoring his gigantic, queasily floating head.

First there was a *clunk* as something heavy fell out of the scary woman's jacket and onto the table. It bounced once and there was a crisp *pop!* like an exploding flashbulb. Manny flinched, assuming he was shot. Time stopped for a millisecond, shuddering on its sprockets, then instead of a bullet he felt himself struck by what seemed to be a wave of invisible slush; a dense, wet avalanche that swept over and through him as though his body were a sieve, soaking him to the back of his soul and drowning him in its harsh metallic roar.

At the same time he had the strange, violent sensation of speed; that he was rising in the air—floating right up and out of the tent into the night sky and gratefully leaving the gun and the killer behind. Perhaps life itself. His senses blurred: the very Earth seemed to contract beneath him like a blanket being drawn down a hole, and strobing forks of electricity flashed all around, briefly illuminating rolling combers of smoke that slowly spread outward like the rings of a tremendous bulls-eye. The punishing strain and noise reached an awful crescendo and then abruptly ceased, leaving low ripples of thunder and a settling mist. At the center of it all, Manny lay still.

CHAPTER SIX:

ON THE GROUND

A convoy of ten Humvees, ten RATTs, and a lumbering Hazmat Analysis Mobile Lab set out from the forward staging area east of Gimhae. There was a warm, filthy wind blowing, a zero-visibility flying junkyard with random gusts a hundred miles an hour—the insertion aircrews had never been so happy to lift off in their lives. This was the gateway to no-man's-land; everything east-southeast of here was blasted ruin, scoured by the typhoon. The only daylight was a sickly green line above the western horizon.

Driving into the black mouth of the storm, the vehicles skirted buckled roadways and collapsed bridges, only rarely stopping or backtracking. They made good progress. Blazing a trail, the dune-buggy-like RATTs courted the worst punishment, their space-helmeted drivers flirting with disaster as they weaved around obstacles and each other like a pack of hunting dogs searching for a scent. As often airborne as not, the snarling quad vehicles appeared to be in constant danger of flipping over. But it was one of the Humvees that was lost in a deep gully when the eroded bank gave way, the men escaping without harm to squeeze sheepishly in with another crew.

There wasn't a building or tree standing anywhere; it was as if the Earth had shaken off mankind and all his works like a dog shaking off soapsuds. Fishbone rebar and flapping rags of plastic were all that remained to show that this had been a heavily populated, industrialized region. It was not lost on the men in the vehicles that a repeat of such violence would put a very abrupt end to their mission.

Despite the lunar desolation they encountered straggling groups of survivors, walking corpses huddled together against the wind and the pelting, greasy rain. They looked bad: many were injured, some grievously, and Major Queen reported their positions while KATUSA interpreters reassured them that help was on the way…eventually. The squad could offer nothing else—they had a specific objective and were duty-bound to keep moving, even as wails of supplication rose around them and mothers pressed dead infants to the windows. Queen was ashamed at how grateful he was to be wearing his biohazard suit—those people were crawling with bugs.

It was really awful—he had never seen anything like it: They were covered with open sores that seethed with living jellied beads like masses of frog eggs, squirming and spreading infestation with busy, burrowing tendrils. Queen could see them splitting in two, multiplying as he watched, taking over the victims' whole bodies like a sticky caul of tapioca. Hideous, flesh-eating tapioca.

And this was not all: there were other things growing on them— colonies of rubbery white stalks like bean sprouts, and grotesque warty buds the size of new potatoes.

It was a relief to get going, to get beyond the threshold of civilian survival, where the team only need be concerned with its own existence. The convoy proceeded fifteen miles and was finally forced to stop before a towering bank of rubble. It was too steep and loose even for the RATTs—though they attacked it gamely, plowing upward, toppling back, and charging up again before the major called them off.

"This is it," Queen announced over the radio. "The first of the pressure ridges around the epicenter. We're less than two miles from ground zero." He held his GPS device at various angles. "We're losing the signal—it's this weather."

"No, the compass is fucked-up too," said Deitz. "It's some kind of magnetic interference. Check this out." He showed them his compass, its needle pointing straight ahead as if tied by a string.

"Wow." Queen called the men in the hazmat truck. "You guys picking up any radiation?"

Dennison's garbled voice replied, "A minor amount. Nothing to worry about."

"What's a minor amount?"

"It's elevated, no question, but that's not unusual with any big earth upheaval. It's no big deal. I'm more worried about the carbon-dioxide level out there—it's around thirty percent…and increasing."

"Thanks for telling me. Anything else we should know about?"

"Well, the temperature has risen forty degrees, in case you didn't notice. It's running around a hundred out there now, with a hundred percent humidity. Uh, there's a strong magnetism that's causing some glitches with the electronics. And get this: We've done a quick analysis of the rain, and it's approaching the salinity of seawater. There's also a great deal of organic matter in it— lipids, proteins, bugs—it's a friggin' soup. I can't even imagine what the smell must be like. Solomon's running more lab tests right now."

"Well, strap on your spare air, because we're going for a walk."

"All of us?"

"No, I don't want to expose everybody to risk. Just you, me, Ron, Allen, Patrick, Lieutenant Soon and whoever he wants to bring. Everybody else hold the fort."

The major opened the door of the lead Humvee, a specially-equipped GRC-206 Mobile Communications Vehicle, and stepped out into the gale. It almost blew him over, but he held on to the door and planted his feet. He shouted, "Look out, it's really blowing." His billowing suit wanted to carry him away. "Jesus!"

"You okay, boss?"

"I'm fine! Let's just get everybody on a tether."

It was a challenge to move—surprise squalls blasted in from every direction, and the intense, glutinous rain made it hard to see through the faceplate. Queen felt like an overmatched astronaut on an alien planet. "God, this *slime!*" The extreme adversity almost made him laugh—and this was a component of his personality that had gotten him through the SEALs and the Special Forces and now AFSOC…and had driven a wedge between him and his family. This was the craving that defined Harley Queen's life:

It was so bad he was beginning to enjoy it.

Looking like retro space-invaders in their fluorescent yellow suits, the eight soldiers made their way in a line up the unstable slope, slammed from behind by powerful updrafts and only too glad for once to be weighed down by weapons and equipment. It was slow-going but steady. They soon lost sight of their vehicles, and even at the crest of the ridge it was impossible to do a decent visual—their spotlight beams congealed at point-blank range in a blinding frizzle. Between sheets of slop they had glimpses of still higher elevations beyond.

Trying to get weather readings off the Kestrel 4000, crouching in a circle with the others, Queen shook his head and said, "Barometric pressure is off the scale—this is it right here, the inner rim of the storm: On that side is the heat column and on this is the turbulence as it collides with denser cold air from outside, funneling it up into the atmosphere and turning it back on itself like a breaking tidal wave. If we can get over the top and into the heat sink on the lee of this range it ought to be a lot better."

You hope, thought Captain Deitz. To him, things were looking less promising by the second. The unearthly moan of the wind was getting under his skin—at any moment they could get hit by lightning or carried away by a tornado. The hill could collapse. Not to mention the possibility of another volcanic event. He wasn't afraid of death so much as loss of control—he didn't like being lashed to the others under these conditions. As a pilot he was used to having ultimate autonomy. "How much farther, do you figure?" he asked.

Queen's voice over the headset glinted with humorous reproach: "What, afraid of a little *volksmarch*? We used to love this kind of thing back in Kaiserstrasse." As they closed up the equipment cases he began whistling the theme from *The Sound of Music*. Deitz noticed the three Korean officers looking at each other in amusement, and it embarrassed him. Finishing up, the major said, "Let's get a move on."

Blown this way and that, keeping down, they scuttled like beetles up one gravelly rise after another, each one broader and more gently graded, until at last they found themselves on a rocky plateau some six hundred feet above sea level, totally exposed to the weather. To make things worse, the rocks began small but soon became a difficult-to-negotiate field of boulders.

"Well this is kind of spectacular," shouted Lieutenant Carl Dennison, sounding troubled.

"What?" asked Queen.

"Look at these things—they're like pure quartz. And that looks like mica—whole giant crystals. This is amazing!"

"Huh," said Deitz miserably. "Pretty."

"Pretty my ass. It's like a mineralogical Disneyland. I've never seen anything like it."

Deitz said, "What, are you a geologist now?"

"You don't have to be a geologist to think this is weird. Every one of these things belongs in the Smithsonian! And what the hell's this?" He kicked at a large white pod wedged between the rocks, an odd rounded shape. Hollow and tapering at both ends, apparently bone or ceramic, it was elaborately molded with a pattern of dimples, bumps, and striations that suggested either organic function or whimsical Christmas ornament. Shaking his head, Dennison said, "Would you call that art nouveau or art deco? Look, there's more!"

"It's weird, it's weird, I got it," said Queen. "File it and move on."

As the boulder field began to slope downward, the steaming rain and wind became intermittent, a few last swift kicks for good measure, then abruptly thinned to nothing. The eye of the storm. There was a rather stunning silence, broken only by rumbles of thunder.

It was as if the men had passed through some kind of membrane: They stood drying while rain hung all around, a vast undulating drapery that enfolded them in gray, eastward-curving wings. In the thick overcast they could see now that the rolling berm they had climbed described a similar circle; it was part of a miles-long earthworks abutting a weather-seamed brown cliff hundreds of feet high. It reminded Queen of the bizarre rock formations he had climbed in northern New Mexico during his Special Tactics training: palisades of eroded sandstone resembling baked dough, dotted with pinyon pines and shrouded at the top by clouds. Having been hidden behind the storm, the ominous barrier now completely filled their field of view, stretching north-south like a fantastic bulging peninsula. Strangest of all, it bristled with whip-like spines all up its face, evenly distributed as desert shrubs.

"What the hell is that?" said Deitz.

"Must be the volcanic mount," Queen said doubtfully. "What else can it be?"

Dennison cut in: "No way. There's vegetation on it. Looks as old as Ayer's Rock."

"Topo doesn't show it—it's gotta be new."

"Maybe we got turned around," said Staff Sergeant Patrick Snead. "Are we sure of our position?"

"I've checked and double-checked. Look at the telemetry

yourself if you want."

"No need to check, please," said Lt. Soon of the Korean Army's 1st Special Forces Brigade. He was a stocky, rather baby-faced man, yet he seemed utterly unfazed by either the punishing trek or the ominous, overhanging mountain. Beaming reassuringly behind his smeared faceplate, he said, "We are in the right place. I am familiar with the region, and I assure you there is no natural landform of this kind. This is certainly the source of the ground activity. Don't you feel it?"

And as soon as he said it, they all noticed the odd, rhythmic tremors that shook the earth. It was not thunder, but consistent rumbles coming in sets of two, with about a forty-second interval. Regular as clockwork.

Watching Dennison hurriedly unpack the seismograph, Deitz said, "That can't be good."

"No need for concern," said Soon. He held up his wristwatch. "I have been timing the frequency of the seismic activity—you see? It is consistent with readings taken by our Ch'ungmu Geological Research Station since the original event. It is our contention that these predictable tremors are of unknown origin, most *un*likely to be volcanic. There is no indication of any imminent danger."

Queen said, "But there wasn't any sign the first time either, was there? Any warning? It just came out of the blue."

Soon shrugged affably as if to say, *What do you want from me?* "All the data suggests an external source for the disturbance," he said. "Perhaps something…artificial."

"What would that be?" Queen scoffed.

"I was hoping you could tell me."

"What are you talking about?"

One of the other Korean commandos said something to Soon in a low, urgent voice, and the two began arguing.

Deitz cut in, "He means man-made, Lee. American-made, to be specific. At least that's the buzz I heard. Isn't that right, Mr. Soon? Your government thinks we caused this. That's why you're here—to investigate and make sure we can't cover anything up."

"Give me a break," Queen said, half laughing at what he thought had to be a bad joke. Seeing the grim expressions of the Koreans, his mouth fell open in astonishment, "*What?* I mean, *what?* Cover what up? *That* thing?"

Deitz shrugged apologetically, suddenly aware that he had goofed by not sharing this information sooner, however absurd it seemed. "That's what I thought, too," he offered lamely.

Queen was nearly speechless. "You have got to be—are you fucking *kidding* me? That's the most ridiculous thing I've ever heard!" He stared in disbelief at the looming cliff. "How in the hell could we have caused *that?*"

Soon said quietly, "Again, Major, I was hoping you could enlighten me."

"Of all the—" Queen caught himself, and his voice suddenly took on the measured, flat tone that indicated he was truly furious: "Look, don't waste my time. I'm here for one thing and one thing only, and that's to do a risk-assessment with a view to establishing an LZ and base camp. Other than that, I don't have a God-damned clue what's going on around here—o*bviously.*" He shot a dirty look at Deitz. "Where the hell did this asinine notion come from, anyway? It sounds like a Worker's Party press release or something."

Suddenly Lt. Soon looked uncomfortable, and Deitz said, "Bingo, chief."

"Oh, come *on*. Now I've really heard everything," Queen said, disgusted. To Soon, he demanded, "Since when do you guys pay attention to DPRK propaganda?"

Lt. Soon was offended. "We do not," he said. "As you will agree, major, this is a very unusual situation. Many thousands of lives have been lost, a whole region devastated, and we do not yet know how or why. Until this matter is fully investigated, it is my government's position that we cannot afford the luxury of either blind prejudice or blind trust. Is it your assertion that your government would do less?"

"Oh, for Christ's sake." Queen's anger faltered—what the Korean said was true enough. "Fine," he said. "Just tell me this: How in the world could we have done this? It's ridiculous!"

"Major, this is not a public inquiry, and I have no officially sanctioned basis for accusation. What I do have is an event that defies conventional explanation—therefore I seek an unconventional one. That's all."

"Well, we're all in the same boat, then." Dismissively turning away, Queen said to his men, "Start scouting around for a ground station, ASAP. Let's put an end to this nonsense."

The team found a relatively flat area at the bottom of the slope, a few hundred yards from the base of the cliff. Queen and Deitz decided it was the closest thing they were likely to find in the way of an airfield. The boulders there were littered with peculiar debris—cracked slabs of yellowish, fibrous material that had scaled off the overhanging wall like old plaster. Dennison mentioned that it looked a little like magnesium silicate—asbestos.

"So?" asked Queen. "Is that a problem?"

"No. Just making an observation."

"Gotcha. Stick to essentials until this is done, okay? In your expert opinion, do you think we can land a chopper in here, or will the vibration bring that cliff down on our heads?"

"From the amount of rubble, I'd have to say it doesn't look good. But it's this or nothing, isn't it? So before I render my *expert* opinion, what I suggest is that we take a closer look."

Leaving half the men behind to begin setting up the equipment, Queen, Deitz, Dennison, and Soon ventured into the recessed space beneath the bulging cliff. It was very dark under there, cavernous. The deeper they ventured, the more slippery the footing became, like a polluted shore at low tide: Everything was encrusted with saltlike deposits and caked with fatty, yellowish goo. In places they had to slog through deep sumps of it, pools of rancid curds scummed with sickly colored alien flora, of which

Dennison took samples.

Hyperaware of the terrain, always intensely focused on the next tricky step—one fall, one rip, could cost them valuable time, valuable equipment, or their very lives—the men were gratified to finally arrive at the base of the overhang, where no further advance was possible. Swinging their lights around the low, sweltering crevice, they took a breather.

They knew the place was strange; perhaps they thought a good close look would alleviate that strangeness. It did not. If anything, close proximity to the thing only made it more disturbing.

Hanging over them was a freakish moonscape, a barren inverted planet like a parched lakebed: quilted folds of what appeared to be baked and broken clay, peeling up from the substrate in filo-like layers, dimpled here and there with shallow pits that suppurated cloudy, sap-like liquid. The scaly, arthropoidal tree stalks, thirty or more feet long and perhaps ten feet apart, were all curved as if swept by a high wind. Those at the bottom were bent and driven into the rocks beneath, as if the mountain had rolled over them. It was not a heartening thought.

"It's moving," said Captain Deitz, dry-mouthed.

They all noticed it: A subtle swaying of the "trees," a continuous drumming vibration apart from the regular tremors. A distant roar like surf. The sense of volcanic instability, of vast menace, was almost suffocating.

Dennison made his way up a slimy pile of scree and cautiously touched the peeling brown wall. Collecting scrapings and a vial of fluid, he said, "Geothermal. It's hot, but not dangerously so. Pretty weird stuff, though." Then his face became quizzical and he pressed up against the cliff as if listening. "Feels like there's a subway train going by on the other side," he said.

"Seriously?" Deitz asked.

"Well, no, I'm sure it's just magma cooling."

"Must be pretty damn cool already, for you to hump it like that."

"That's true," Dennison agreed absently. He looked up the

bellied mountain in wonder. "I still can't figure out what the hell kind of rock this is. It's the damnedest thing I've ever seen."

"I thought you said it was asbestos," Queen said.

"I said it *looked* like asbestos—that was the only thing I could think to compare it to. But it's more like wood or something. Plastic. See how resinous? I don't know, I could swear it's organic." He unsheathed a razor-sharp tactical knife and tried sawing off a piece. "It's tough stuff; it holds together pretty good. I don't think there's much risk of an avalanche, not way out by the camp—I say let's try calling in the whirlybird."

They went back and set about making an airfield. It was hot work—the air from their rebreathers was not cooled, only filtered and circulated. Using a Nikon Total Station surveying set, the team tamped down the scree to create a reasonably level landing pad, laying out a pattern of pocket-size landing lights. They also set up a remote miniature weather station and opened a microwave uplink to the waiting vehicles, as well as to the mobile command center back in Gimhae. An MH-60G Pave Hawk helicopter full of supplies was immediately dispatched to them, as were air drops, road crews and heavy equipment, and a small army of full-bodysuited humanitarian-relief workers—just a trickle, but behind it all the affronted, pent-up industrial might of civilization, eagerly poised to rush in and restore order. It was only a matter of time now.

"Hey, Major," Dennison said as they awaited the chopper, "I want you to take a look at this."

"What is it?"

"It's some of the test results Solomon's sending from the mobile lab. Weird."

"You're abusing that word. Show me something here that's *not* weird. Hell, if it *wasn't* weird it'd be weird."

"Sorry. Uh, well, he's analyzed a number of our 'bugs' and found that they're some kind of rudimentary, single-celled life form. They seem to, uh, secrete a toxic enzyme that breaks down proteins, which they then absorb through their surface membrane. They eat us like a kid sucking a Popsicle."

"What the hell are they? Where did they come from?" Only half-joking, he said, "Outer space?"

"We're still waiting for USAMRIID to get back to us on that."

"So, what you're telling me is you've never seen anything like them before."

"No…actually I have."

"Thank God. Where?"

"Under a microscope."

"Say again?"

"I know this sounds…weird, but these things are dead ringers for common, everyday prokaryotes. We've identified cocci, bacilli and spirilla, ribosomes and all—it's really kind of mind-blowing."

"Look, I'm not a doctor like you. What does that mean?"

"Bacteria. They're ordinary bacteria."

"Ordinary!"

"No, not *ordinary*—obviously, bacteria don't grow this big. That's why they call them *micro*-organisms. They must be some kind of mutation or something, but structurally they're typical of germs that live all around us. *On* us: *Staphylococcus*, *Escherichia*— all the reasons we wash our hands before eating."

"Beautiful. Does that mean we can get rid of them with soap and water?"

Dennison didn't laugh. "I doubt it; you're not going to kill these babies with a little antibacterial soap. The capsule protecting the cell membrane is too tough. High heat might do the trick, or dryness—you notice we're not seeing many of them around here. They need a liquid medium in order to be mobile, and without a food source their lifespan is very short. Once that rain out there stops they should all die off. They're already dying off—a lot of them seem to be infected with monster bacteriophages. Viruses."

"*Viruses*." Queen felt a sickening chill. "Oh no."

"I don't think it's a problem. Viruses attack individual cells and hijack the cell mechanism to replicate, but these ones are much too big to infect us—I'd be surprised if they even recognize us as a host. Their DNA is gigantic compared to ours—it'd be like trying to repair a watch using a jackhammer. I'm pretty sure they're only a threat to these mutant bacteria."

"Really? Carl, you just made my day."

"In the meantime, though, the whole region is quarantined."

"I should hope so."

"It's not just because of the bacteria. There also seem to be some freak strains of fungi present—parasitic ones."

"Is that what we saw growing on those people? Christ."

Dennison nodded. "They're just like the hyphae of something I used to treat every day at the dispensary. They feed on keratin in the skin, then branch out and form sporangia—spore-bearing nodes. It's very common."

"What the hell are you talking about? I've never heard of anything like that before."

"Sure you have." He picked through the ground litter and came up with several lumpy objects resembling strange seedpods or nuts. "The spores are everywhere, just waiting for a host. Except for the size, these ones happen to look a lot like *Trichophyton interdigitalis*."

"What's that?"

"Athlete's foot."

Queen blinked.

"You son-of-a-bitch. You're fucking with me."

"I wish."

"Well, what the hell does all this mean? Some kind of bio-warfare?"

"Your guess is as good as mine. But I'll tell you one thing." He cocked his head in the direction of the cliff. "That thing's no volcano; it's not the result of tectonic subduction or crust shearing or a thrust fault. I doubt it's geological at all."

"What do you think it is?"

"No idea. But check out these TIMS images I pulled off AWACS." He handed over a sheaf of false-color printouts. "They've been verified as accurate to within a couple of meters."

Major Queen looked at the photos. They were all high-contrast thermal images of what appeared to be a sprawled human body, dark red against a yellow background, taken from different angles and distances. "What's this?" he asked. "There's a survivor in there?"

"Look at the scale, Lee."

Queen focused on the tiny grid markings at the margin of the picture—one inch was equal to a kilometer. He shook his head. "What's this supposed to mean?"

"I don't know, but it's for real. JPL confirms it, too."

"Confirms what? The Jolly Green Giant?"

"No one's saying that. In fact, we've been advised to make no mention of it. Officially it's just a geographic anomaly. But the security situation is going haywire—Central Command wants an explanation."

"I bet they do. Holy hell." It was too absurd to think about. "Look, they've got to realize this is a fluke, some kind of accidental formation, like Jesus in a potato chip, or that face on Mars."

"Yes, sir."

"The man would have to be a thousand feet tall!"

Dennison was grave. "More like six thousand, Major."

Deitz's voice suddenly came over the radio: "Underdog, this is Touché Turtle, come in."

"Ten-two, Turtle," said Queen. "This is Underdog."

"Major, we've found some downed aircraft over here—at least three Army Blackhawks, from what I can see. They must be that recon flight that went missing—Colonel Stein's birds out of Camp Walker."

Queen looked at the GPS coordinates Deitz was sending. He and two of the Koreans were out doing a perimeter survey—they were only a few hundred yards north, hidden by haze and low embankments of rubble. "Any sign of survivors?" Queen asked, already knowing the answer.

"No survivors, no bodies. Nothing. The choppers are fairly intact, though—looks like they could have walked away if they wanted." Deitz didn't have to say what the major already knew: that without protective suits, Stein's people couldn't have gotten far.

"All right. Try sending up a flare, just in case."

"Roger that. Stand by." There was a distant, muffled report, and then a whistling red star that arced slowly downward through the gloom.

Queen waited until the signal flare sputtered out of sight, then said, "No?"

"Nope. Sorry, boss. I'd say the area's deserted." There was a hubbub in the background. "Wait, Henderson's found something…" There was the jerky sound of Deitz hurrying over uneven footing, then he said breathlessly, "Looks like human remains, chief."

"*Looks* like? Are they or aren't they?"

"They are."

"What do you mean, 'remains'?"

"Bones, for the most part. It's a lot of bones scattered around in the rocks."

"And you're sure they're human?"

Deitz sounded manic, wired. "Uh, affirmative on that, Major. I'm looking at a skull in a flight helmet—says Captain Rodriguez. And there's other gear around. It's definitely Stein's crew."

"Any idea what happened to them?"

"Same thing that happened to those civvies: they weren't wearing any DEET."

Dennison cut in, "Not if their bones are scattered—the bacteria wouldn't do that. How spread out are they? What's their condition?"

Deitz sounded distracted: "What's that, major? I didn't copy."

"Carl wants to know if those skeletons look abused. Torn up."

"Well, they're all over the place, if that's…hold on a minute…"

Whatever Carl Dennison was suggesting, Queen didn't like it. Making a snap decision, he said, "Mike? Just wrap it up and get back here. We can't afford to lose your silly ass."

"Wait a minute, chief." There was a rustle as Deitz shifted, then he said, "Something's moving."

"What is it?"

"I can't—I thought it was a boulder. Holy shit. They're everywhere."

"Mike, get out of there, now. *Now*. That's an order."

Suddenly Queen flinched at the burst of loud static in his earpiece—the garbled sounds of gunfire and someone screaming. At the same time, there was a maddening commotion close by, so that he couldn't properly hear. "Say again?" he shouted. Straining to listen, it took him a second to realize he had problems of his own.

At his side, Dennison shouted, "Major, it's Snead! Snead is down!" All the men at the base camp were scrambling for their weapons.

Major Queen looked up the slope to see his staff sergeant fighting with some kind of lamprey-like monster, its dark translucent body pulsing like a wet inner tube, the gruesome flaps of its mandibles clamped on his right leg. It was trying to pull the man down under the rocks. Queen was not so surprised as pissed-off to have been surprised, cursing himself even as he knew there was no way anyone could have foreseen such a threat.

"Shit!" he hissed. His hands automatically found and snatched up his SAW—his M249 Squad Automatic Weapon, of which every painstakingly cleaned and oiled part was as tenderly familiar to him as the intimate features of his wife's body—more so. The gun made sense to him, unlike the mundane disorder of everyday life, and when he could fire it with impunity, as now, he felt he was fulfilling some personal destiny that had been arranged for him by capricious Greek gods: his own grim, golden stake in the universe. It was something he needed and loved.

Bullets pelted the unreal monster, scoring its tough blubber, yet the thing seemed oblivious, imperturbably drawing Snead deeper underground with each flex of its body. All at once the man's leg separated from his hip with a cartilaginous pop and a rending of flesh and rubberized fabric. He fell back screaming from the garish fountain of his own blood.

The others converged on the escaping creature, getting in a few last rounds as it retracted out of sight with the severed leg. Queen let drop his empty rifle and picked up Snead's M4A1 SOPMOD 5.56 carbine just as the monster disappeared.

"See to him!" he barked in frustration, well aware that Patrick Snead was a lost cause. As Dennison tore open the medical kit, and Soon took one of his men to scout out Deitz's lost patrol, Queen grabbed the satphone.

"Alpha Tango, this is Romeo One-Niner," he said urgently, scanning the ground for any further signs of danger. "We have at least one man down and require emergency evac, over."

Through a shower of static, the operator replied, "Copy that, Romeo—your ride is hot on its way—ETA two minutes at most. Hang tight."

"Roger that." Switching to his squad radio, he called, "Touché Turtle! Mike! What's your status, over." For a long moment there was no reply.

Then a gloriously welcome, ragged voice broke through: "Volksmarch my ass." It was Deitz. He sounded like he was running. A staccato burst of automatic fire could be heard from over the hill, closer than before. "Returning to base under heavy… animal attack. Two men lost. Weapons ineffective. Request you lay down a heavy suppressing fire as I approach—try to slow them down."

"Soon is halfway up to you right now, and there's a chopper on the way. Just keep moving. What's after you?"

Deitz didn't seem to hear. "They're right on my ass. Sorry about bringing them down on you like this…"

Now Queen could see the small dark figure of Deitz cresting the hill, only thirty or forty yards above Soon. He was waving frantically, and Queen was alarmed to see that he was bareheaded—an astronaut without his helmet. In fact he had shed all his weapons and gear, stripping down to one slim straw— the last survival strategy and the first, hardwired in from the days of Australopithecine: Run. Run fast.

And as he came, Queen saw humped shapes rising behind him. Not more of the giant worms, as he had expected to see, but huge lumbering beasts, like a herd of bison or rhino. These animals were nothing so mundane, however: Covered with thick plates of polished amber, with pulsing organs visible within, each one had many crablike legs and no proper head at all— just a grotesque, sowbug-like body that terminated in massive jointed antennae and a wicked set of jaws. The ground shuddered with their approach, and volleys of Soon's covering fire could be heard. Dennison and the others looked up, torn even from their desperate task of staunching Snead's bleeding by this outlandish new menace.

Then came another sound, a familiar deep drumming threaded with the silvery whine of turbines—a sound as welcome as the bugle of cavalry: the helicopter. It crested the hill at high speed, trailing a ribbon of mist from the storm. Queen hardly had time to toss out a smoke canister before the careening aircraft was upon them, swooping in so low along the rocky slope that the men on the ground reflexively ducked, blasted by its downdraft. The bug-like monsters scattered before it, springing in all directions. It came so close that Queen could hear the pilot—Ned McPherson of the 353rd, a funny guy, but not usually given to barnstorming—shouting into the radio as his Pave Hawk buzzed them and erratically continued on, nearly colliding with the cliff face as it arced sharply up and away. He didn't seem to have any intention of landing.

"Where's he going? Hey!" Queen yelled. "The fuck does he

think he's doing?"

"Evasive action," replied Deitz, stumbling up and collapsing. Pointing westward, he gasped, "Look!"

Now a second flying object came barreling through the clouds—one much larger and less familiar...though vaguely similar in its wasp-like configuration. Instead of matte dark gray, however, the newcomer's bulbous fuselage was bright yellow and black, massively armored in overlapping jointed plates, bristling with antennae, and churning the air with fantastic iridescent wings that created a violent shockwave with each stroke. Its undercarriage was a mass of six articulated grappling claws. It was a flying nightmare—the ultimate war machine. Yet it was *alive*.

Spellbound, the men watched in dread as the pursuing thing overtook the zigzagging helicopter. With an elegant, impossible maneuver, it turned over in midair and snagged the craft from below with lobster-like limbs, whirling the Pave Hawk upside-down and ramming its spike-tipped abdomen into the chopper's fuel tanks. There was a dismal whine of straining engines, then the rotor blades flew apart and the helicopter swung dead in the grasp of its insectoid captor.

Now the immense creature plummeted with its burden, dangling those long, articulated legs and landing so heavily that the helicopter was partly crushed beneath it. The monster itself appeared utterly unfazed by the impact, busily intent on its gruesome business. As Queen and the others gaped in horror, the thing reared up and briskly peeled open the cockpit with steam shovel-size mandibles—literally jaws of death. Glass and avionic debris rained down as it prized Captain McPherson from his harness and bit him in half. Blood and soft tissue gushed from seams in its antlike maw as the creature chewed, splattering the rocks below. The co-pilot, Lt. Oscar Kirsch, pride of the AFSOC Men's Choir, was plucked up and devoured as he tried to crawl free.

Major Queen and his men did not suffer this horror in dumb

shock, but immediately cut loose with their weapons. The monstrosity was downslope, less than a hundred yards away, and quite as big as a balloon in the Macy's Day Parade—they could scarcely miss.

"Go for its eyes!" Dennison shouted, and the hail of fire converged on those two glittering baubles, each one a many-faceted crystalline hemisphere at least four feet across. As with the earlier worm-thing, their small arms barely seemed to have any effect, though they emptied every gun in their arsenal, from their M9 pistols to the devastating 12-gauge 870. It was unbelievable—anything they threw at it just pranged off like windblown grit.

Tired of fucking around, Queen unstrapped his trusty M203 40mm stand-alone grenade launcher and fired a round into the ruin of the helicopter. This was a little more satisfying: The ruptured fuel tanks blew up, enveloping the straddling monster in an enormous fireball. Sunset colors played across the bleak cliffs as the insect writhed in flame.

"That got his attention," said Deitz wearily.

Incredibly, the thing was not destroyed. As the men stared, faces gleaming in the firelight, the monster's great wings suddenly flexed, causing an explosive concussion that instantly dispersed the fire, blasting rocks and burning helicopter wreckage in all directions. Snead, unable to take cover, was all but beheaded by a whirling metal plate. As the other men dove for meager shelter, the creature lifted off, each wing beat a violent shockwave that scoured the hillside. It rose a few hundred feet and hovered there, its sleek, Porsche-shaped head swiveling, searching, until it saw the five tiny buffeted figures hunkered amid the rocks. Then it went for them.

Shielding their faces from the explosive gusts as they awaited death, Queen and the others did not see what happened next: The creature's terrible wings, supersonic kites of smoked-glass a hundred feet long and half as wide, stronger than steel, with branching ribs like leaded cathedral windows, suddenly erupted from above in darting sparks and shrapnel, as if somebody had set off a mother lode of firecrackers—fireworks enough for a hundred Chinese New Years. The wings split and cracked, fracturing further as they batted the air, rudely crazed in a thousand places. All at once, the monster wheeled sideways and fell, slamming into the boulder field with as much force as a crashing jumbo jet. But though it gouged a deep trench in the earth, it did not disintegrate...or even die outright. It continued to heave and flap in its pit, struggling to fly, as more manic firecrackers danced up its back to its head, shredding its antennae, pitting its silvery eyes.

"Gunship!" Deitz cried, and suddenly the plane could be seen, an AC-130H Spectre from the 160th SOAR, banking in from the east with its port side 105mm howitzer and 40mm cannon and five-barrel 25mm Gatling gun all spitting flame and steel. The plane made several passes, hammering the monster with rivers of hot metal until it slumped, quivering, immobilized if not dead. The guns also strafed the routed beetle-creatures, ensuring they would not soon return, and as a final boon the plane dropped a large cargo-pallet of supplies, tipping its wings as it roared away through the clouds.

"Well that was exciting," said Deitz. "What are we gonna do with the rest of the day?"

Queen wasn't in the mood for jokes. "Prep Pat's body for evac," he said. "And get yourself scrubbed and covered up." He had been in contact with Echo Company and the 353rd SOG, and they were sending a regular airlift this time, a real fleet, storm or no storm. The stalled ground vehicles had been recalled to base and now would be flown in under heavy air cover. The military did not intend to relinquish its foothold, though to what purpose Queen couldn't guess. He didn't let himself dwell on what Soon had said—it was probably bullshit...yet what *could* explain the insane events of this day? All he knew was, he didn't want his people here any longer than necessary. Queen had to admit it: There was such a thing as too much excitement.

CHAPTER SEVEN:

LIMBO

Manny awoke on the beach, face up in the gloom. The gray light of dawn startled him—for some reason he had expected to open his eyes to pitch darkness. Instead he found himself surrounded by the thickest fog he had ever seen, a dense veil that enclosed his body like a shroud. At first he thought there was something wrong with his vision, with his ability to focus—there was no frame of reference in that pale, depthless field—but then he realized he could see his own breath, substantial as cigar smoke, puffing out and mingling with the surrounding vapor as if spinning another thickness of cocoon. As if he himself was the fog machine.

Lucky nobody stepped on me in the night, he thought. Disoriented, all he knew was that he was grateful to have the sheltering fog—he wasn't ready to explain to anyone what he was doing there... not until he himself could figure it out. What happened?

Dinner. He remembered dinner at the Moon-Viewing House: Sitting with Karen under the stars, sampling all the interesting Korean appetizers—the tiny candied shrimp and dried cuttlefish, the toasted silkworms—and then frying marinated beef on their own little table brazier and eating it sizzling hot, wrapped in savory cumin leaves. Washing it all down with big bottles of OB beer. It had been wonderful.

After that, they piled back into the USO bus with all the military people, but for Manny and Karen it was a blissfully short ride—they had the pleasure of disembarking just outside Busan, having made reservations for the night at the luxurious Paradise Beach Hotel. How wickedly delightful to bid goodnight to their fellow riders, who could only watch enviously from their cramped seats (sized for tiny Asian asses) as the two of them dodged the long homeward grind to Daegu and disappeared into that brightly gilded lobby.

This is the best idea you ever had, Karen had said, beaming with tipsy cheer. Then she kissed him.

Okay, he thought wildly. *Okay*.

Alone in their elegant seaside room, Manny had slowly undressed her, reveling in Karen's bountiful curves, her creamy white neck and long black hair, her body like a chubby marble nymph—pale pink at the knees and around her compact little nipples, which were set slightly upward on her teardrop breasts; her kissable constellation of tiny brown moles; her neatly trimmed pubic thatch and the plump, powdered cleft below. If only she didn't remind him so much of his wife…his *ex*-wife, Manny reminded himself. What was it about him and big Asian women?

He sat her back on the bed and kissed her as she unbuttoned his shirt and took down his pants. Karen was careful with his briefs, easing the elastic over the bulging arrow of his penis, then affectionately clasping his genitals in her smooth hands, gently kneading them. Manny groaned through the kiss and pressed against her, languorously fucking her hands. Cupping his balls, she eased one of her fingers underneath and stroked the puckering rim of his anus.

"You're going to make me come," he said breathlessly, pulling back just in time. It had been almost two years since he had had sex. "Here, lay back." He eased her down on the bed and slowly ran his hands down her sides to her waist, then caressed his way back up her belly and around her breasts, grazing the crinkling flesh of her areolae, her perking nipples. Manny reveled in the contrast between his cinnamon hands and her white skin.

He leaned over her, kissing her sensitive neck, then kissed down to her flushing breasts, nibbling and licking there as he rested one knee on the bed between her legs, pressing his upper thigh against the baking heat of her crotch. The tip of his penis bobbled against her hip, drawing clear squiggles. He kissed her belly and finally went on his knees at bedside to attend her florid, hidden altar, tugging with his lips at the tender folds and teasing her out with his flicking tongue, opening her up, tasting her, until she couldn't stand it anymore and cried, "Omigod, fuck me. Fuck me now!"

Pulling him none too gently by the hair, Karen drew Manny up on top of her and spread her legs wide. "C'mon, take me! Do it!" she demanded, as he hurriedly guided himself through the tropic aperture and settled in deep, as into a hot bath. She moaned blissfully, grinding her pelvis hard against his and crushing him between her scissoring thighs: "That's so gooood."

The ecstasies that followed were only a little dampened by the occupant of the adjoining room, who at the highest moment of passion began knocking on the wall to protest their banging headboard. But Manny came hugely, and Karen a little later, by hand. Still, she reassured Manny that she was wonderfully satisfied, and that simultaneous orgasm during intercourse was extremely rare, if not a total myth perpetuated by Hollywood.

They blissfully sprawled in bed all through the following day, checking the TV, enjoying the opulence of the huge mattress. After their second night of passion, Manny was passing out, but Karen jostled him and said, "Hey, sleepyhead! Why don't we go for a walk?"

"A walk? Don't you think it's a little late?"

"No! For a walk on the beach? It's romantic! Besides, I'm hungry."

Karen's appetite never failed to amaze Manny. To her, Korean food was delicious but insubstantial—"I feel like I just ate a bunch of salad," she would say, or, "An hour later you're hungry again." He was still full from dinner.

"What about room service?" he tried.

"Oh, come on, silly pants. This is our last night. Show me a good time."

"I thought I already did."

"Come *on*," she mock-sobbed. "I'm not ready to go to sleep—I'm bursting with energy."

"That's the difference between men and women," he said, but he got up and started putting his clothes back on.

Everything after that was less clear. Manny remembered that they had gone down to the beach, where there was a concrete promenade at the edge of the sand. It was brisk out, and there were few other strollers. As usual, Manny was glad for Karen's whims: He liked the anonymity of walking in Korea at night. It was the only time he came close to inhabiting the persona he had long yearned for, had in fact come to the Orient seeking: that of worldly sophisticate, at home in exotic foreign lands. His inner James Bond.

Feeling debonair, he bought Karen a newspaper cone of orange sweet-potato fries from a cart, to nibble as they walked. At some point they took off their shoes and ventured across the cold sand to one of several food concessions that stood like Bedouin tents on the wide shore. Karen loved street food, was always dragging Manny to such places, and was particularly keen to try these on the beach. They *were* picturesque.

But something was wrong. Manny had the impression that something was bothering Karen. When he tried to touch her she was evasive, grasping at any distraction, feigning enthusiasm about the sand, the sky, the sea air, and whatever else was at hand, to put off looking at him. Really talking to him. It was not like her—she who was rarely circumspect about anything. A feeling of disquiet spread like Novocaine through Manny, turning his roguish grin into a numb leer. All at once he knew what was going on: Karen was having second thoughts. She thought she had slept with a married man, and was riddled with guilt. She was working up the nerve to tell him she thought they had made a mistake by sleeping together. That she couldn't see him anymore.

Manny felt crushed, heavy and sagging as if an air valve had been opened in his spine. Suddenly he couldn't think straight, couldn't face even the possibility that he was about to be rejected for the second time that weekend. He closed his eyes to it as to a stiff wind. *No*, he thought. *I'm just being stupid.* He knew he was prone to paranoia, to unwarranted fits of despair. It would be just like him to go and ruin a perfect night. Well, he wasn't going to let it, not this time.

"Karen," he said, stopping and turning in the dark. "Something happened this morning that I think you should know about."

And then there was a scream.

Manny remembered the scream, a man's scream, coming from the farthest tent. It was followed by a trailing guttural moan of pure agony. Manny had never heard such a sound, and even in the midst of exploding heartache it caused his skin and every hair on his head to bristle as if yanked by tiny invisible tweezers. He lost his breath. Before he could speak, Karen said, "What the hell was *that*?"

"I don't know." Seizing the reprieve, he said, "It came from over there. I better check it out."

"I think we should just wait here for a minute and see what happens."

"No." Righteously, he said, "No, I better go see," and made for the tent. He called back, "It's probably nothing. You stay here!"

≥≠≤

What had happened after that? Still lying on his back, Manny strained to penetrate his deep inner fog, thicker yet than the outer. He had a dreamlike impression of something terrible—a man being murdered, an American, blood all down his side and some kind of Korean punk-princess standing over him with a gun. Her *face*. Thinking again of that harsh, dead-eyed doll caused his scrotum to contract—Manny remembered he ought to be dead.

Why wasn't he dead?

"Oh my God," he said. "Have I been *shot*?"

And he jumped to his feet.

CHAPTER EIGHT:

THE SHADOW OF DEATH

Materiel and personnel came pouring in, and in less than twenty-four hours the base camp began looking like a real military outpost, with geodesic positive-pressure decontamination chambers lined up like alien huts, and mini-bulldozers and backhoes clearing an airstrip. Any time now a road to the outside would be opened as well. In the meantime, Tyvex®-suited civilian engineers were flown in by the dozen, taking over what was informally known as Base Bugshit. Queen knew his part of the job was effectively over—he and his "operators" had served their purpose. Soon the flight could go back to Kadena.

Or maybe not.

"You like to climb, don't you, Lee? Recreationally?"

It was Colonel Robert Warburton, Commander of Special Operations, Korea. Queen and his reunited squad had been taking a much-needed break when the colonel showed up in their tent unannounced. The seventeen men were sitting around a folding table in only boots, shorts and t-shirts, eating MREs and drinking bottled water, swapping hard-ass tales of their fallen comrade, "Savage" Snead. Half-crazed as they were, it was still a joy to be out of those sweaty biohazard suits; the guys wallowed in purified, air-conditioned bliss. They didn't bother to salute.

Needlessly bidding them to stay seated, the colonel took Queen aside and broached the question.

"Yes, sir," Queen replied, still chewing an energy bar. "How was your flight in?"

"Free climbing? Base jumping? All that extreme stuff?"

"Sure. I haven't done it *recently*…" Most of Queen's climbing of late had been in the mountains of Afghanistan.

"Do I have it right that you once climbed a volcano?"

"I did, as a matter of fact, a couple of years ago. Ol Doinyo Lengai in Tanzania, when we were there for Operation Uplift."

"And how was that? Was that tough?"

"No, not really. It was interesting, but not really what I would call a technical climb."

"Jesus Christ. What would you call a tough climb?"

"Well, I'm not sure. Every climb is different…" Aware that the colonel was waiting for an actual answer, he ventured, "Maybe Frenchman Coulee."

"What's that?"

"A vertical icefall in Washington State."

"Sounds like a bitch."

Queen shrugged. "I really just climb for fun, sir."

Colonel Warburton ignored the comment. He said, "Think you could have done it with a full complement of tactical hardware?"

The major grinned at the outlandish notion. "I guess that would be…interesting."

The commander's gray raptor eyes bored into him. "Oh, you're gonna love this," he said.

Midway through his explanation, as Queen was beginning to digest the irksome fact that he and his men were being served with another mission, there was a low rumbling, and the ground began to shudder.

"Earthquake!" Queen announced. "Everybody outside! You first, Bob!"

Steadying himself on Queen's shoulder, the colonel said, "I'd say we're better off staying under cover until it passes."

"Not unless you want to suffocate in this thing. Move!"

As the men hurriedly evacuated, the rumbling got much worse, and with it a harsh clatter of rocks on rocks, loud pelting sounds as rubble shook loose up the slopes and came hurtling down. Thin shouts could be heard outside, vying with surprise bursts of shrieking wind. The pressurized tent envelope deformed, straining against its moorings as weather and stones pounded the tough green fabric. All at once the western-facing wall gave way, peeling open as if unzipped; the ceiling billowed and immediately collapsed, leaving Queen to cut through the heavy folds with his knife. He freed himself just as the big tent tore loose altogether and was swept away, a tumbling bag of furniture.

Queen emerged to a sight so disorienting it caused him to lose his balance, to topple forward on his hands, imagining that somehow the very earth was in free-fall beneath him. Flattened against the ground with the others, thinking, *This is it*, he witnessed an upheaval beyond all imagining, the final mad stroke.

It was the cliff. That bulbous, black-bristled wall that dominated the landscape as far as the eye could see, and which dwarfed the rapidly disintegrating military compound, was *rising*. Lifting right off the ground.

Dust billowed out from under it as it tipped mountainously upward off its sunken bed of rocks. Shockwaves sundered the earth like waves in the sea, lightning flashed, and violent winds rushed in—a hundred tornadoes unleashed all at once, strobing incandescent blue and pink as they wreathed the impossible object. It levitated higher and higher, not erupting or capsizing or collapsing as reason suggested it inevitably must, but simply continuing to climb, miraculously unsupported, until it was lost from view in the tempest.

Almost at once the ground ceased to shake, and a shaft of late afternoon sunlight broke the clouds. Queen caught his breath. Where the cliff had stood was now the edge of a vast, shallow crater. Men squirmed, groaning, in the mild light of day. The sky was rapidly clearing; there was a growing window of blue, and through that opening Queen saw what at first he took to be a vertical cloud formation: a fantastic, slowly swaying human shape rendered in vapor and shadow and gleaming dusky gold, thousands of feet high. An imaginary colossus, head and shoulders above the clouds.

Queen shuddered, and through gritted teeth sobbed, "Oh shit. Oh my fucking God."

CHAPTER NINE:

MR. SURIBACHI

Manny patted himself down thoroughly, searching for bullet wounds or injuries of any kind. He had heard stories of people who had been shot and wandered around for many hours before realizing they were seriously hurt. Or perhaps he had suffered a concussion, some kind of brain injury. That would explain his dizziness and amnesia—he still didn't have a clue where he was or how he had gotten here. And where the hell was Karen?

It was obviously not the same ocean beach he remembered from last night—that had been sandy, briny, blustery, a perfectly ordinary beach. Here the whole atmosphere was different: absolutely silent and still, not just ordinary morning calm, but the dead space of a vacuum. There was water, an inky lake of it like a steaming hot spring, its placid riffling surface more like a big puddle than the sea, the very horizon foreshortened as if ending at a cliff. Despite the mantle of vapor, the air here was anything but humid; rather, it was thin and arid as a mountaintop, and like a mountaintop the view seemed all cobalt-tinted sky.

The dry land was no more familiar, or promising. Where Manny had lain it was sandy, almost as if the sand had been scooped up and dumped there with him, but beyond that ten or fifteen-foot radius the ground became a scorched-looking gray loam. Like ultra-fine ash, its powdery crust puffed into spreading rings of smoke at the slightest vibration. Here and there in the near distance were moss-green rock formations rising like jagged headstones out of the haze. Other than that, nothing as far as the eye could see.

When he had first stood up, Manny had stepped clear of the weird, reef-like mass of fog that seemed to have accumulated above him. It reminded him of a rain cloud above an unhappy cartoon character. Elsewhere the mist was thinner, just a low murky soup about chest-high, with the sun shining bright above it. Watching his breath come out in billowing dry-ice plumes, Manny was struck again by the sense that he himself was generating the fogbank.

It's the cold, he thought. Yet he himself wasn't cold—in point of fact Manny felt overwarm, feverish. His ears were all plugged up and he had a sinus headache. But more than that he was getting a little unnerved—a lot unnerved—the longer he tried to make sense of things.

Where was the hotel, the city, Korea? There was no sign of them, in fact no sign of anything denoting the presence of people. Manny appeared to be standing in the middle of nowhere, on some kind of barren tundra, half-submerged in mist. It made him think of something out of Sherlock Holmes: moors and peat bogs and other such mystery tropes. Had he been kidnapped and carted out here and left for dead? Could he have been drugged, or fuddled with alcohol like Cary Grant in *North by Northwest*? Manny didn't think so. For one thing, he found he still had his wallet; all his money and his passport were still inside—he hadn't been robbed. But then neither had Cary Grant.

Maybe I am dead, he thought, not totally facetiously. Looking out across the unreal landscape, he wondered how he would explain himself to God, given the chance, or if he had already been judged and condemned. *Maybe this is what Hell is like, or Purgatory...or the Twilight Zone.* He absently murmured the show's creepy theme music and it made him feel a little better. *Whatever it is, it's not heaven—I feel like crap.*

He *had* lost his shoes, but at least the dirt seemed soft enough. Still, he paced within the limits of the familiar sand, reluctant to leave it in case someone was coming back for him. Discovering that his digital watch had stopped, he threw it down in disgust and finally risked embarrassment by shouting as loud as he could, "Hello? Anybody out there?" His voice sounded strange to him; muted and distant. He tried clearing his ears, to no use.

Then Manny noticed something *extremely* odd. Even by the rarified standards of this morning. "What the hell?" he muttered fearfully.

The day...the day was already waning. The sun was sliding down the inverted blue bowl of the sky, changing from white to yellow to orange like a cooling droplet of molten metal. Unless he was completely crazy, Manny could have sworn it was high overhead when he first stood up, an hour ago at most. No, he could actually *see* it moving! Furthermore, he could see his own shadow stretching out into the water, molasses-slow but plainly visible. What could possibly explain that?

Now he really began to panic, racking his brains. *Come on now, what's more likely?* he thought. *That you've been kidnapped by aliens and brought to another planet, or that you're having a psychotic breakdown?*

But he didn't *want* to be crazy! He wouldn't let himself! As someone who felt he had created his own destiny, a self-made man, Manny had always thought of himself as a fundamentally rational person, that reality was what each individual decided it should be, and that mental problems (and most other problems) were largely self-determined—a matter of flawed character, of relinquishing control. That was why Korea had been so hard for him, because for all his focused energy he couldn't make it work.

Despair settled in. As a little boy Manny had often been told how his father had done the impossible: Obsessed with the USA in all its crass splendor, Ezekiel Lopes had willed himself to leave his own poverty-stricken country and become an American citizen. Just made up a completely unrealistic plan and carried it out, without money, help, or anything but the force of his own will. All his life, Manny had tried to emulate that success, to will his own far less ambitious fantasies into being, generally with far less extravagant results. But always with the underlying faith that if he *really needed it...*

Yet all his willpower couldn't shake this surreal dream, couldn't prop up that sun. As it touched the horizon, he decided he had to start walking—*Just go, dammit!*—or he was going to be stuck here all night.

Feeling utterly lost, Manny headed inland, chasing the sunset in some ridiculous hope of delaying nightfall as long as possible. It was as good a direction as any. As he walked, he tried covering up first one ear and then the other, making various noises to test his muddled hearing. His ears were completely stopped up. Everything sounded as if it was underwater; beyond a few feet he couldn't hear a thing. *Great*, he thought. *I'm deaf. Nuts and deaf—beautiful.*

Watching his step, Manny began, in spite of his woes, to take an interest in the ground beneath his feet. Though he tread as lightly as possible, each footstep raised flattened blooms of dust or smoke; surreal eruptions like silt in a mud puddle. Peering down through the gray mist, he felt as if he was combing a shallow primordial sea.

So bizarre, man...

In the darkening twilight he realized too that it was not his crazed imagination conjuring up ethereal flashes and sparks underfoot—somehow he was causing the effect, leaving a glimmering wake.

As a swimmer he was familiar with bioluminescent plankton—
the "red tide"—but he had never heard of such a thing happening
on dry land. He chalked it up as one more red herring in an ever
more grandiose waking dream.

Yet the deepest part of him knew, knew in his bones, that this
was real, and that there was a perfectly logical explanation for all
of it—there just had to be. He was awake…and sane. It was this
knowledge that drove him and held him together.

Little by little the dead gray soil was taken over by mottled
patches of moss or lichen, square as carpet remnants. Expecting
a cool, velvety texture, Manny was disappointed to find that
the fuzzy greenery was not as substantial as it appeared, puffing
away like dry mold at the slightest whisper. There was something
unsettling about the crazy-quilt geometric patterns of it—he
began to spot grids of fine lines and fragile little clusters of ordered
matter that also vaporized into smoke before he could get a good
look. Tiny mazes strikingly like electronic circuit boards, with all
the shiny little chips and resistors, somehow sprouting from the
earth…but even more like something Manny couldn't quite put
his finger on. The light was too poor to see properly.

Swatting at the whine of a gnat in his ear, he thought, *What it
really looks like is aerial photography.*

And as this thought reverberated, he stood up straight and
looked out across the smog-layered, dusky landscape as if
seeing it for the first time. Suddenly he could make out patches
of illumination under the haze: yellow webs of fairy light and
hyperactive ant-trails of white and red, everything cranked up
to time-lapse speeds. He was overcome with the sensation of
height—he could be looking down on this manic panorama from
an airplane. Traffic, cities, a whole civilization in miniature. The
world at 1/1000 scale. It made no sense, but it was unmistakable.

"This is a joke," he half-sobbed in horrified fascination. "I don't
believe this." Certainly it had to be a prank, a trick of some kind,
an illusion. The ultimate diorama. But why, why?

Wait a minute...

Feeling sick to his stomach, Manny looked back at the dark swath he had carved through it, a spreading brown pall with roots of smoldering orange. Pinprick lights of microscopic rescue vehicles darted into the ankle-high conflagration. It couldn't be, and yet he suddenly felt his heart seize up with the utmost, hysterical conviction:

I'm Mr. Suribachi!

CHAPTER TEN:

ROAMING CHARGES

The night skies were getting crowded—everybody wanted in on the chase. Military air-traffic controllers had to ground the F117s because their low radar signatures made them a collision hazard, but squadrons of F-22s, FA-18s, F-16s, and F-15s from the 90th Fighter Squadron had more than taken up the slack. B-1s and B-52s patrolled at their bombing altitude of 40,000 feet, gravid with Joint Direct Attack Munitions. There were also a great many varieties of modified C-130 aircraft, some of which were gunships, some were adapted for communications, and some were refueling tankers for the fleet of Special Forces helicopters from the 31st Special Operations Squadron out of Osan Air Base. A single CV-22 Osprey, its fat tilt-rotors suggestive of Popeye's whirling fists, led the armada as if spoiling for a fight. The hectic pursuit was overseen and managed from high above by an E-3 Sentry commanded by Colonel Robert Warburton, of the 353rd Special Operations Group.

The object of all the attention was a single man. A mundane man in certain ways, and yet one so beyond all comprehension that no one who heard about him could quite bring themselves to believe he existed, however reliable the source. Much time was wasted confirming and reconfirming reports. Even seeing first-hand was not much help: most witnesses, however tough and jaded, existed forever afterwards in a state of hallucinatory free-fall, playing along at fulfilling their duties and obligations even as they waited for something to arrest their descent, to please relieve them of this traumatic vision. To wake them up.

"Romeo One-Niner, this is Alpha Tango. Be advised that you are being patched through to Whisky Hotel Two-Zero-Six over a secure channel. Please confirm, over."

"Roger, Alpha. Confirming encryption Two-Zero-Six, over."

"Stand by..." There was a crackling, then a hash of electronic tones, and then a new voice said, "Romeo One-Nine, this is Whiskey Hotel Two-Zero-Six, Colonel Warburton speaking. Lee, this is a privileged three-way communication between me, you, and the kitchen sink. This conversation is being monitored and recorded. Acknowledge."

"Roger that, Colonel."

A different, warmer voice asked, "What is your present status, Major?" It was General Stan ("Buddy") Chesnutt, Commander in Chief of U.S. Forces, Pacific—the "CINC."

"We are presently at seven thousand feet, General, circling the target at a range of some twenty-eight nautical miles as it heads south-southwest at about nine-zero knots. Our airspeed is a nominal hundred and twenty knots. Target is passing through the vicinity of Chinhae, heading for Masan."

"All right, that'll do for the play-by-play. What I meant was, are you all right?"

"I'm okay, sir. Yes, sir."

"I understand you and your boys came within spitting distance of that thing. What I want you to do, quick as you can, is brief me on it. Whatever you know, or think you know."

"Absolutely, General. Well, my medical specialist has done a preliminary analysis based on our station survey and aerial observations—it's pretty speculative, but this is what we have so far. It superficially resembles a man, of course, indeterminate ethnicity, but swarthy, possibly Arab—and he's wearing what... what *appear* to be wool dress slacks, and a gray turtleneck sweater under a camel's hair coat, from which the left sleeve has been ripped off. He's barefoot, and—"

Trying to fend off the encroaching lunacy that stalked every order, every conversation, every instant of this hideous day, the general said, "Yes, we have all that—he's a spissy dreff—I mean, a spiffy dresser. What else?"

Queen took the plunge: "Well, he's approximately sixty-six hundred feet high. On the ground we had a close-up look at what we now believe was his left wrist, and it alone measured at least three hundred feet across. His feet are each about nine hundred feet long—or just about the length of the Titanic. Weight is another matter: from the specific gravity of his tissue samples, we estimate that he weighs something in the neighborhood of a hundred million tons, give or take a couple tens of millions."

There was a pause on the other end of the line.

"Did you get that, sir?" asked Colonel Warburton's voice.

"Yes," the general said, clearing his throat. "Did you say million *tons?*"

"Yes, sir."

"I have another teleconference with the Joint Chiefs in ten minutes—this data is not going to come back and bite me on the ass, is it?"

The colonel said, "I don't think so, sir. It gibes with all the field reports I'm getting, as well as my own observations. His discarded wristwatch alone leveled at least twenty acres of trees and made an impact crater a hundred feet deep—it must weigh a thousand tons all by itself. A Seiko, looks like."

"All right," the general said queasily. "What else?"

Major Queen said, "We think he's going to be impervious to just about anything we can throw at him, based on the effect our small arms had on the microbial life we encountered at the site of our initial contact."

"Yes, I have a copy of that report right here—maybe you can make sense of it for me: 'Harpacticoids'? 'Aschelminthes'? What the hell is that?"

"It's Greek to me, too, sir—that report was prepared by my lieutenant, Carl Dennison; he's the microbiologist. He says our camp was attacked by a giant parasitic nematode, or roundworm, that would normally live in the soil. I could give a rat's ass what it was, except that it killed one of my men—Patrick Snead. Then there were further lethal attacks by creatures called harpacticoids—a terrestrial variety of copepod, if that helps—and by a predatory wasp of some kind, which alone took down a Pave Hawk. The bacteria you know about. All these things are ordinary, benign microorganisms that have somehow been mutated into giants. Crazy as that sounds…"

"Don't worry about how it sounds," said the general. "The trick is not to think about it too much—try to keep it on an abstract, technical level."

After all he and his men had been through, Queen was offended by this facile armchair advice. Then he realized that the general must have been dealing with mass hysteria all day long, and had probably started saying the same thing to everyone—the words sounded like a mantra to stave off panic, not least his own.

Queen replied, "Yes, sir. Now, it's Dennison's theory that they should die on the spot, crushed by their own weight, except that there's something about their molecular structure that makes them incredibly robust—it's as if they don't quite follow the ordinary rules of physics. That wasp certainly shouldn't have been able to fly, for instance, not at that scale; it's not designed for it. And this giant man is another example: there is no material we know of that could withstand the kind of compression that his body is being subjected to. It's astronomical. We estimate that each footstep has the force equivalent of hundreds of kilotons of TNT. That suggests to us that conventional explosives would be of very limited utility against it."

"I see. But your report states that you did in fact successfully employ conventional firepower against these…organisms."

"We did, but that was pushing it to the limit of our airborne artillery capability, and that was just against a bug. This man is so many orders of magnitude greater."

"So it's your opinion that nothing short of nukes will stop it?"

"Sir, in my opinion even nukes are no guarantee."

"All right. What would you suggest, then?"

"Anything but pissing it off. I mean, I'm not sure we're in any position to pick a fight, are you? And even assuming we could win against it, what would be the pathological impact of a corpse that size? I've had a close-up look at its germs, sir, and I don't think we want to breed any more of them if we can avoid it. Kill the thing and we could infest the whole planet. Besides, it looks human enough—what about talking to it? I'll bet it's as confused as we are."

The colonel cut in, sounding testy: "That's fine if we had time. Pardon me, General, but I'm afraid I have to disagree with the major's opinion. We don't know enough about this thing to make these kind of assumptions, and every minute that passes is another mile of devastation. We have to stop it before it reaches a major population center, and I think we can."

General Chesnutt sighed, "Bob, I'm going to go with the major's suggestion: Let's try saying hello first and see what happens."

An EC-130 Commando Solo from the 17th Special Operations Squadron slowly descended on the giant's head as on a mountain peak, banking in tighter and tighter spirals. The plane was equipped for Psy-Ops and could broadcast television and radio signals, as well as having a 200-decibel loudspeaker that could be heard from twenty miles away.

"All right, we're coming in range," said the pilot, Captain Janus Wisnicki. The plane began to buck as they entered the region of disturbed air—the giant was making waves in the atmosphere, creating its own storm. Its heat and respiration left a turbulent trail of clouds, and discharges of static electricity festooned the aircraft's propellers and control surfaces in skeins of blue St. Elmo's fire.

The thing's head was coming up like the Matterhorn. Mesmerized by the view out the windshield, Wisnicki gave the order to the sound engineer in the audio suite: "Begin broadcasting."

The engineer, a linguistics specialist named Archimedes Hippopolis—Archie—who had only ever practiced with this equipment, ran a sound check: "Testing, one two three. Testing, one two three." The external mike was picking him up; the levels were all good—he gave a thumbs-up to the cockpit.

Gravely reading the prepared message, he said, "Attention, please halt. Repeat, please halt. By continuing to walk, you are causing great damage, death, and suffering to the populations below. Stay where you are so we can help you. Do not be afraid. Please stay where you are, or we will be forced to respond with force. We do not want to injure you, but you must halt now. I repeat, we want to help you. Please halt."

The message was being blasted loud enough to cause permanent hearing loss to anyone within a thousand yards, but giant did not seem to hear it. Corporal Hippopolis repeated the message in Korean, Spanish, and French, adding, "If you can hear this message, please acknowledge by nodding your head."

There was no response...and then, ponderous as a calving glacier, the vast head began to tilt, rocking away from the plane. Its forest of hair swayed majestically.

"He's nodding! He hears me!" cried Archie, thrilled and terrified.

"Oh shit," said the co-pilot, Lt. Barry Cross, looking down.

From below, harrowing as any immense flux of nature, came the giant's right hand. It rose straight up in their path, each splayed finger a massive Eiger etched with aboriginal-looking whorls. Bulging joints such as burls on gargantuan eucalyptus trunks soared past one by one until followed by the bronze vastness of that enormous rutted palm: a parched flood-plain cutting off light and escape.

Trying to dodge it, the aircraft first pulled into a steep climb and then rolled sideways, attempting to dive through and out of the narrowing shadowed canyon between the giant's ear and that onrushing five-fingered juggernaut. It was a close thing. The plane barely cleared the notch between forefinger and thumb, emerging safe and whole into coppery sunlight as the giant missed it, swatting himself.

"We're clear, we're clear," gasped Captain Wisnicki, daring to breathe.

But that missed blow was a slap to end all slaps: Mountains collided—the proverbial unstoppable force meeting an immovable object—and their impact was cataclysmic, filling the sky with shrapnel-like skin flakes and spawning a shockwave as powerful as a 15,000-pound "Daisy Cutter" bomb. It rippled outward at supersonic speed to engulf the fleeing airplane, snapping it by the tail like a wet rag and instantly popping every rivet.

A cascade of smoking wreckage streamed down out of the waning sunlight to dusk-shaded cherry orchards six thousand feet below.

General Chesnutt's voice was brisk: "Well, gentlemen, the 160th Special Operations Regiment is mobilizing along the projected western route, along with armored support from the Third Republic of Korea Army and the Seventh Republic of Korea Corps. Field artillery from the 2nd Battalion, 34th, is being deployed between Masan and the Nakdong River, and the 40th Mechanized Infantry Division is taking position in the mountain passes between Chinju and Samch'onp'o. We've got full aerial coverage by all the services, and the USS Ramsdale is fifty miles offshore with cruise missiles at the ready. All in all we're in good shape, considering the short notice. Any problem with any of that, major?"

Queen said, "No, sir. I agree that we are positioned to deliver a very solid military strike. I would only suggest that we try not to hit it in the eyes—we don't want it stumbling around blind and crazy."

"Why not?"

"It'll make it harder to defend against, to anticipate. The thing has been moving in a straight line all this time, and I don't think it's been much concerned with us—that's our one advantage. The damage it's causing is totally incidental. But once it's ticked-off we will no longer have the luxury of predicting where it goes. Assembling ground forces against it will become impossible. That's my biggest concern with this whole situation, in fact— the unknown element. It seems to me that without knowing the origin of this thing we can't really assess the risks of going on the offensive at all."

"The offensive? That's an interesting interpretation, Lee. Unfortunately, we do know the risks of *not* attacking it," said Colonel Warburton. "All you have to do is look at the devastation in its wake to know what we can expect if we do nothing. Do you propose to let it reach the population of Gwangju? Or the Yeonggwang Nuclear Plant?"

"What I'm trying to say, sir, is that there have been rumors about this thing being created by us. Now if there's any chance of this being true, it would obviously aid us tremendously in dealing with it."

"*What?*" barked Warburton. "What the hell are you talking about? What rumors? I apologize for this, General—permit me to confer privately with the major for a moment, would you?"

"No, ah…" There was a hesitation on the general's line, then he said, "One thing you gentlemen should know is that a few minutes ago, the North Korean Foreign Minister formally accused us of having triggered a 'quantum weapon' on South Korean soil."

This news hung in space for several seconds, then, sounding indignant, Colonel Warburton asked, "*Did* we?"

"Officially, Washington is denying it. Unofficially, they have ordered all senior commanders to forego any strategies involving nuclear weapons. The order is very explicit: Nukes are off the table."

"Jesus," said the colonel in disgust. "*Un*officially."

"Sorry, Bob," said the general.

"What do they mean by a 'quantum weapon?' Do they mean the giant, or is he just supposed to be a side-effect?" Queen asked.

"Major Queen, I can assure you that right at this moment there are ten thousand distinguished scholars scrambling to answer that very same question. I'm afraid I'm not one of them. My sole responsibility is to determine whether or not to recommend conventional military action under these...*unusual* circumstances—and that is the question I put before both of you: Based on everything you know, should we or shouldn't we?"

Swallowing his anger, Colonel Warburton said, "We have to, sir. What choice do we have? One way or another, it has to be stopped."

"Major Queen? Do you concur?"

Queen had never been involved in a decision of this magnitude. Yet he didn't hesitate long—they had to try something, however futile. From his web jump seat, he looked down the red-lit airplane cabin at his twelve remaining operators, most of whom were sprawled out asleep. The Osprey looked like a casualty ward. Only Deitz, all bandaged up at the controls, was awake and aware, and communicated by the set of his jaw what he thought should be done. The insignia on his helmet showed a winged dagger. Queen patted it and gave him the hand signal for *stand by*.

"I concur, sir," he said.

≥≠≤

General Chesnutt stood on the flank of Mount Chii'san and scanned the eastern horizon. He had turned down his frantically squawking radio. It was a cold, clear night, and he could see the distant flashes of battle. Delayed bomb concussions, remarkably like the echoing din of a bowling alley, reverberated through the atmosphere. In the valley below there were long lines of refugee traffic creeping west. Behind him, jamming the scenic overlook, were the trucks and tents of his field headquarters, frantically busy as a stock exchange.

"Sir?" It was Lt. Colonel Jillian Kaye, looking grim. "The giant has broken through the main batteries at Chinju. We've lost contact with Colonel Vanderveer, and General Bixby reports ground forces being destroyed or routed all along the main line of defense. Cruise missiles appear ineffective. It's still coming."

"I know. Has contact been re-established with Colonel Warburton?"

"No sir, but General Finch has assumed direct command over the coordinated aerial attack, and has temporarily suspended the bombardment to withdraw his forces and regroup. He reports heavy losses due to some kind of debris cloud."

"What? Tell him to keep pounding that thing until I say otherwise—those ground forces need air cover!"

"Yes, sir. The problem is, there seems to be a communications vacuum in there. All anyone knows is that a lot of aircraft have suddenly gone missing, and there's been a priority hazard alert issued around the target—something to do with airborne debris."

"What debris? He can't issue that alert! Tell Finch he's ordered to resume the attack, Goddammit."

As he spoke, the general glanced east. Above the nacreous blue horizon, he could see what appeared to be a dark plume rising into space. It slowly arced upward and then down, fanning out as it progressed, dividing into a myriad threadlike streamers.

They plunged into the dim smog layer, leaving a spreading brown smear in the eastern sky. A moment later there was a drumming sound like thunder.

"What the hell was that?"

"I don't know, sir. We've just lost contact with 2nd Battalion."

Down the hillside, on dry-stubbled fields, General Chesnutt could see mobs of protesters screaming anti-U.S. slogans and throwing rocks at the MPs who were blocking the road. It was an organized protest; they had been bused in—which meant there had been an intelligence leak somewhere along the line. As if the situation wasn't complicated enough. And to complete the fiasco, the news media had been alerted: Korean and Japanese television crews were down there making hay of the whole thing. It was all organized—there were concession stands, for God's sake! Chesnutt would like to strangle the bastard who sold him out.

"I want that bombardment continued at all costs," he said.

"Yes, sir."

Now something else was moving above the horizon.

At first it was just a slow, knotted contrail, an approaching track of vapor spewing from something unseen, but which eclipsed the lowest stars. Then it grew higher and became vaguely defined: a vast phantasm bearing down like a ghost ship or nightmare locomotive, belching smoke as it came, ever growing, its vertical enormity taking unimaginable form. Pips of flame sparkled within its silhouette like sequins, followed by rippling stutters of thunder. Puffs of smoke proliferated like popcorn and were swept aside by its sundering slow advance. The crowd quailed, screaming, before this unspeakable vision looming up out of the east.

"Holy Toledo," said the general.

The shadow became a man, and this shadow-man took over the sky like a bullying constellation. Because of his size, his movements seemed slow, but he was running—the very image of a generic running man, a spectral Everyman, features obscured. A monstrous caricature of humanity, all the more mind-bending for its mocking absurdity.

As banks of howitzers began to open up on it, General Chesnutt could estimate its range by the sound delay—just under fifty miles. Fifty miles!

Now its rumbling footsteps began to be felt: low, sustained tremors quite different from the thudding artillery barrage. As the quakes intensified, the crowd of protesters erupted into panicked flight, some trampling each other to reach their buses, others collapsing in supplication before the stunned MPs, begging for protection.

Distant batteries of klieg lights came on, their beams probing the monster like pale feelers, spotlighting peepholes of detail: tan fibers like immense burlap, gullied badlands of tarred bristles and oiled leather, a shining eye like a wet planet suspended in space. Forty miles. Tiny slivers of light rose from the ground and puffed ineffectually against the colossus, harmless as sparking flint. Chesnutt shook his head. Thirty miles. He heard the whistle of approaching aircraft, saw more slivers descend, more puny explosions. Twenty miles. He wasn't expecting much—even the BLU-82 deep-penetrators had proved useless. Without nukes they didn't have a prayer. As Major Queen had predicted, they were just pissing it off.

Then at once the giant seemed to be falling. It leaned over in all its vastness, legs buckling, right arm stretching down to stay its collapse…

"Oh my God," Chesnutt gasped. Thin cries of mingled hope and dread could be heard from the bystanders as the mountain rocked.

But the giant did not collapse. Instead its outstretched fingers gouged into the land with the force of an asteroid impact, scooping down five hundred feet deep and excavating twenty thousand tons of rock and soil in a single running handful. The friction and pressure created an enormous pyroclastic explosion that spilled from the closed fist in a billowing incandescent column, raining fire and choking ash on the already flattened countryside.

That goliath fist now rose high into the air, thousands of feet up, a mile and more, until it was above the giant's head. Still running, the behemoth cranked back its arm in grotesque imitation of a baseball player winding up for a pitch—*Oh no*, thought the general—and catapulted all that great load of superheated rock and dirt into the heavens. The tumultuous mass hurtled upward in a tremendous arc, peeling apart, spreading as it unraveled into an apocalyptic blitz of descending meteors and a sky-girdling shroud of dust.

Before the impacts could begin, General Chesnutt took up his microphone and said firmly, quietly, "This is to all field commanders, maximum priority: Begin general retreat. Call off the attack and get under cover. *Now*."

$\geq \neq \leq$

"General?"

"Yes?"

"General, there's a local national out here who claims to recognize the giant." Lieutenant Colonel Kaye's voice echoed in the cave. "She says she works in your office on Camp Henry."

General Chesnutt had been contemplating the serene face of Buddha, cut in stone at the far back of the ancient mountain temple where his staff had taken refuge.

"What?"

"She says her husband met with him, just before he disappeared."

"Who disappeared, the giant?"

"No, her husband. His name is Wang."

General Chesnutt didn't have to think too hard—one of his Korean secretaries at Camp Henry was married to a well-known Mr. Wang. Her name was Ms. Jeong. A very efficient woman, and beautiful; Chesnutt liked her and had done her a few small favors over the years, mostly involving keeping the CID and South Korean authorities off her husband's back. This was not just to be nice. Mr. Wang was a fairly minor-scale black-marketer, a shady, flamboyant character with a thousand schemes who would have been prosecuted long ago if he wasn't such a useful informant. The U.S. military bases were his livelihood, and as long as they let him run his shady businesses unmolested, he gladly tipped them off to anything that threatened good relations, whether it be rings of "slicky boys" or more serious anti-U.S. mischief. The general considered it a valid symbiosis, one of the billion squalid niceties required to maintain troops on foreign soil.

But what was Mr. Wang's wife doing here? Suddenly the general thought he could guess who it was who had spilled the beans about this mobilization, for what it was worth now. He regretfully broke free of the Buddha's stone gaze.

"What exactly does Ms. Jeong claim to know?"

Looking at her notepad, Lieutenant Colonel Kaye replied, "She claims that the giant is one of ours, an American civilian living in Daegu. She says the man's name is Lopes. Manny Lopes."

≥≠≤

"Manny Lopes?" asked the president. "Who's Manny Lopes?"

The CIA Director answered, "Full name: Emmanuel Jacob Lopes, age twenty-six. He's a DoD civilian—a GS-11 assigned to Daegu. Computer tech. He's married, no kids, with a wife back in the States—one Ruth Yi. Manny was last seen on a USO tour in the company of a DoDDS teacher named Karen Park, who works at the American school on Camp George. Apparently they've both gone missing. We're trying to locate her, but it's looking like they may have been in Busan on Saturday."

"Manny, you dog. But he's definitely an American?"

"Yes, and so was his mother, but his father was a naturalized citizen, born Ezekiel Lopes in Belize back when it was British

Honduras. Manny Lopes is of mixed ethnicity, Creole I guess, with freckles and hazel eyes. Get this: his personnel file lists him as five feet, three inches tall, and weighing a hundred and forty pounds."

"Well, what the hell happened to him?"

"We're still working on that."

"But you're convinced it's the same guy?"

"Probably. It's hard to tell from the way he is now—everything's so exaggerated he looks more geographical than human. We ought to have final confirmation as soon as the sun comes up."

"Any more details I should know before my press conference?"

"Just some more background. You're going to love this: In 1972 his father was an unemployed calypso singer shining shoes outside the airport in Belmopan, and one day he just wanders in through the gate and climbs into the landing-gear bay of a Pan Am jet. The plane flies direct to LAX, and out pops this poor guy, half frozen to death. It paid off for him—a lot of people took an interest in his case and helped him get established. One of them even married him: an immigration caseworker named Sondra Horowitz—Manny's mother. Sad coda: Both parents were killed in a car crash when Manny was sixteen."

"So that makes him an orphan again."

"I suppose so. Graduated from Woodrow Wilson High School, got an Associates Degree in computer repair, then dropped out and traveled to Providence, Rhode Island, where he worked a few odd jobs and met Ruth Yi. Attended a DoD job fair in Boston, passed all routine background checks, and was shipped to Korea. Seemingly no association with terrorism or quantum research or any kind of high-level physics...but we're not ruling anything out."

"I should hope not."

"Oh, don't worry, Mr. President. Manny Lopes is about to become the most investigated human being since Lee Harvey Oswald."

"Good morning, Major."

"Good morning, General."

"Mr. Queen, it's a considerable relief to me that you were not among the casualties of our recent action."

"Thank you, sir. It was just dumb luck—we were refueling and taking on munitions in Kunsan. Has there been any word about Colonel Warburton?"

"No, but it will be difficult to identify any of the planes downed by that shitstorm—the entire region is cratered and smothered in dirt. From where I'm standing it looks like the Moon. It's tragic—I've known Bob Warburton since he was a cadet. Back in the old days, he and I used to hit the links at Camp Walker quite a bit. Maybe he's still alive somewhere out there, but I wouldn't hold out much hope."

"No, sir. But there are survivors; you made it. How did you manage, if you don't mind my asking?"

"My senior staff and I were fortunate enough to find refuge in the buried wisdom of the East: speaking of dumb luck, we ducked in the first available hole. It doesn't look like most of the forces under my command fared nearly as well, does it?"

"I'm sorry, sir."

The general brushed it aside, "Yes, of course…but I commend you on your unfortunately astute threat analysis. Considering how closely we'll be working together, Harley, I think it's time we were a bit more collegial. From here on out you're my principal advisor in this crisis, my eye in the sky, and you'll need to trade in that gold leaf for a silver one."

"Thank you, sir. I thought I'd be stuck with that rank forever. Although I would have preferred to be wrong."

"I know. Please call me Buddy, Lieutenant Colonel Queen."

"All right, Buddy. And I go by Lee."

"Lee, that's right. All right, Lee, what's your present status?"

"We're in a holding pattern at ten thousand feet above the target. Dawn is just coming up."

"And how is our big friend? Have you evaluated his condition?"

Queen looked at the computer-enhanced image coming over the TCS. "He's sitting motionless in rice fields east of Gwangju. I'd say he's resting. It does look like the attacks had some effect on him: His face appears to be swollen, and there are numerous observable contusions and burns, even from this distance. Superficial stuff to him, no doubt, but probably at least as painful as bee stings. In my estimation we hurt him. Not seriously, but I think that with a really sustained campaign we might eventually harry him to death."

"But only at incredible cost, judging from last night. You think we have the forces to spend on something like that?"

"No, sir. But that's only considering conventional warfare—I'm a bit more persuaded now about the feasibility of going nuclear… if you're exploring that avenue."

"That avenue is still closed to traffic. We're in a reactive posture for the time being: cleaning up, taking inventory and gathering reinforcements. The emphasis right now is simply on evacuating civilians from projected danger zones. Whatever we decide to do militarily, it's not going to be a repeat of last night. No direct frontal assaults—it's too destructive. What Washington wants is a guaranteed, one-shot giant-killer."

"David and Goliath."

"Exactly. So any specific ideas you may have in that regard…"

"I do have one, sir, actually."

"Really." The general seemed slightly caught short. "I should have known you would. Let's hear it."

"This is my take on something Colonel Warburton proposed a few days ago, before we knew what we were dealing with. He wanted my team to mount a very ambitious reconnaissance expedition to the source of what we thought was a geological disturbance. Now, that was before it got up and started walking around, but I think there is still at least some small likelihood of such a plan succeeding. In fact, it may have great potential benefits far beyond simply stopping the giant in its tracks—"

"I'm intrigued, Colonel, but I'm going to have to interrupt you for a moment. I've just received a communiqué from General Stovington that a very unusual phone call has been intercepted by the Forty-First Signal Battalion and is being routed to me. It's listed as time-critical."

"Of course, General."

Lieutenant Colonel Queen sat waiting in the plane's jump seat, feeling his men's inquisitive looks. "I'm on hold," he explained.

A moment later the general came back on the line. "This should interest you," he said. "It's Karen Park."

"Who's Karen Park?"

"The suspected girlfriend of our giant."

Queen inhaled some spit. "No kidding," he coughed.

"She's requesting that we please not resume our aerial attack, as it caused her great distress throughout the night."

"Join the club. Where is she?"

"She has no idea, but says she is clinging for dear life to the side of some kind of 'moving mountain.' She's on a standard GSM 900/1800 frequency, and AWACS has been able to pinpoint the radio signal—guess where it's originating from?"

"Holy Christ."

"I think perhaps we ought to have a chat with her before her phone battery dies, don't you?"

≥≠≤

There was a crackle as Queen was connected through, then he could hear rasps of static—the sound of someone breathing hard into their phone mouthpiece. It was a woman.

"Hello?" she whimpered. "Oh God, are you still there?"

General Chesnutt said, "Yes, I'm still here, Karen. And I have someone on the line who may be able to help."

"Howdy, Karen," said Queen.

CHAPTER ELEVEN:

ON THE FACE

What was it about this situation that kept reminding Karen of *Reader's Digest*? Her mother had long been a big reader of the magazine, had in fact read it in Korea before ever emigrating to the States, so there were always copies of the *Digest* around the house when Karen was a child. It was considered essential reading for anyone interested in being a right thinking, proper-English-speaking, evangelical, Korean-American citizen of the U.S.A. Karen had read every issue for years, enriching her Word Power until she developed a taste for more ironic, subversive literature.

But all of a sudden she felt like she had become a *Reader's Digest* article herself—transported into one of those true-life survival tales that had been so gripping when she was ten.

Fighting for her own life, Karen now vividly recalled one story in particular: the awful account of a woman whose plane had exploded high over the Amazon, and who somehow survived the fall into the jungle. Alone, she had waited amid gruesome wreckage—bloated bodies still strapped to their seats—before realizing that no rescue was forthcoming. Did she give up and die? No—eating someone's rain-sodden birthday cake, she had set out for help, making a long nightmarish trek through the wilderness, swimming crocodile-infested rivers and picking maggots from her flesh with a stick, before finally escaping to civilization.

Now Karen was that woman.

She had just spent the most terrifying night of her life, lost in a wilderness she didn't understand, with jets screaming by and bombs going off all around, and she had no clue whatsoever how it had all come to be.

The last sane thing she remembered was walking on the beach with Manny. Something weird had happened and he had told her to run, run back to the hotel…and she wavered a second, unsure and angry at his macho trip. What happened next was nonsensical, but she thought she recalled being hit in the face and swept away by something that felt like a wave of ice-cold sand. Somehow she had been carried up the hurtling, scourging face of this wall, higher and faster every second until it threatened to either collapse or pancake her into the upper oceanfront levels of the hotel. But then she crested the wave and was snatched into a powerful updraft, arcing high and free-falling through a blizzard of stinging grit.

Karen landed in a kind of sparse cane field, tumbling through bamboo-like stalks until she came to rest against a dark, scaly tree trunk—one of many. Numb as she was with cold, it was a startlingly warm place—steaming-hot, really—and the damp, waxy ground surged and subsided as if with pent-up volcanic energy

Karen had passed out for some time, in a state of shock. Gradually recovering her senses, loath to move, she reluctantly opened her eyes and took in the grim, unstable landscape. Daylight barely penetrated the heavy fog. Serpentine trees or reeds receded into the mist, sprouting like stiff tentacles from an otherwise barren hill. It looked like the bottom of the sea.

Where the *fuck* could she be? Karen felt squirming movement beneath her, and jumped up to find some kind of gigantic, yellowish crab half-buried at the base of the tree—she had been sitting on it.

"Oh my *God*."

That would have been hideous enough, but its slimy, disgusting burrow was shared by numerous slippery creatures like pale slugs, some of which were sticking to her clothes. In fact they were *very* sticky, clinging to her hands and stinging like jellyfish tentacles as she tried to brush them off. "*Shit, shit*," she cried. Then she remembered the cure for jellyfish stings, and yanked down her pants.

The hot pee seemed to do the trick; they washed right off.

Karen looked around at the creepy desolation, freakish as a Dr. Seuss nightmare, searching the gloom for anything at all to attach hope to. There was nothing—nothing except the fact that she wasn't dead yet. It had been hours, and if she wasn't dead, perhaps death was not so imminent.

Though still shaking with fear, she tried taking a few steps, getting a feel for the rolling of the ground. In time with it, coming from somewhere not far off, was a deep, rhythmic roar like an intermittent waterfall. It was a huge, hair-raising sound— what she imagined a volcanic vent or geyser must sound like. That, along with the heat, the smell, and the dense currents of vapor, convinced her that somehow she had indeed been thrown (by a terrorist bomb, maybe?) into the proximity of an active volcano—there was no other explanation. Unless it was a hot spring, like at Yellowstone. For all she knew, perhaps such a thing existed near the hotel: a natural spa, with stinky therapeutic mud baths and soaking pools and ginseng facials and old Korean ladies handing out clean towels. It was making her cry to think about it. She knew it was ridiculous.

The rushing sound was coming from the other side of the wiry trees, and as she began making her way beneath the bramble-like canopy, the ground began to move, to surge upward beneath her. At once she knew it was going to be worse than the other tremors—this was it, the end of the world: she was about to be buried alive in a volcanic upheaval. Steadying herself against the nearest tree, screaming her lungs out, Karen watched in frantic terror as the entire landscape began to *tip over*.

But there was no landslide, no collapse. The ground just leaned farther and farther over as if on gimbals, threatening to overbalance, to capsize, and then, impossibly…it swayed back a little, steadying at vertical and leaving Karen dangling out over a bottomless, soaring cliff.

Stiff breezes gusted through, winds that carried the thrill of dry winter air and dispersed the fog, revealing tumbling clouds with rifts that opened onto snatches of sunlit blue sky and faraway sea. Karen hugged the now-horizontal tree as hard as she could, straddling its horny overlapping plates and moaning from the back of her throat.

This is a joke okay it has to be a joke please God tell me it's a joke…

Her stomach dropped as the cliff ascended like a balloon, higher and higher into the sky. Her ears popped. Finally it settled into a slow, lurching advance, heaving forward as if teetering toward collapse, then righting itself…again and again and again.

Slowly swaying like that, and by this means somehow gliding through thin air as if afloat on huge, billowing effusions of steam, the cliff seemed to fly miraculously from cloud to cloud, carrying her with it.

This hellish ride continued all day. Between the periodic eruptions of dense vapor, Karen could see out past the copse on which she dangled to the ever-changing, dusty landscape far below—a sheer drop of at least a mile. She felt like a hood ornament on a blimp.

At times the cliff would pause in its grinding advance, or swing right or left, offering panoramic views of the whole horizon. It all made so little sense that for the most part Karen didn't analyze it, couldn't grasp it, vacantly focusing on more immediate concerns such as scraping off the slimy things that wanted to attach themselves to her, or just staying awake.

She grew thirsty and exhausted, and searched for some ledge or crevice that she might scramble to whenever the cliff swayed to its backward extreme. During that few seconds it could be possible to use the trees as handholds to traverse the steep face. But she could see no place to try for, and cursed the hellish futility of her predicament.

At dusk she heard the rumbling of a large propeller plane, and by the light of the setting sun she saw it buzz past less than a mile away, banking out of sight. It had caught her by surprise; Karen desperately prepared to wave her jacket in the air if it came around again.

From somewhere out of view, muffled by the cliff, she could hear the squawking bellow of a loudspeaker. It said: *Attention, please halt. Repeat, please halt. By continuing to walk, you are causing great damage, death, and suffering to the populations below. Stay where you are so we can help you. Do not be afraid. Please stay where you are, or we will be forced to respond with force. We do not want to injure you, but you must halt now. I repeat, we want to help you. Please halt.*

Karen gratefully tried to make sense of this message, which she assumed was intended for her. She was unbelievably eager to follow any instructions, and was more than willing to stay put—what else could she do?—but the threatening tone was puzzling, as well as the business about her causing damage. How was she even walking—she could barely move! Did they think she was driving this thing? But there was no mistaking the final instruction: *If you can hear this message, please acknowledge by nodding your head.*

Karen all but nodded her head off. Nothing happened, and she saw no more sign of the plane.

Night came, bringing cold flurries of snow, but at least her moving perch remained warm—the cliff radiated great heat, and was now covered with a steaming slick of oily, salty-tasting water. This fluid trickled and splattered down through the cane stalks, slowly soaking Karen's clothes. It seemed to have the beneficial effect of washing away the slugs. Through the rank vapor she could see city lights twinkling at the far horizon, and stars above.

Lips cracking, she dreamed of soy milk and coffee and great jugs of warm barley water. She was drifting off, losing her grip, when the shrill scream of a jet engine jerked her awake. It was a fighter plane! Several more jets made close passes, above and below, as if signaling. They were looking for her! Karen tried her best to wave, or shout.

Then there was an explosion. It was far away, thousands of feet below, but she saw the huge fiery plume and heard the delayed *BAM!* The cliff seemed to completely absorb the shock—she felt no effect. *How is this helping?* she wondered dully.

Now more explosions began; above her, below her, to either side. Heavy smoke wafted by, smelling strongly of singed hair. The nearest concussions were deafening—she covered her head with her arms. It was like being inside a tremendous fireworks display. White-hot sparks and bits of shrapnel went whistling past or ricocheted off the trees and cliff face, skittering into the void.

After the first hour, Karen was too worn out to react much— it was all she could do to hang on as the cliff's rocking tempo increased, its vast shuddering vibrations threatening to buck her off. At some point she was smothered in choking dust, and had to suck air through her damp shirt. She lost all track of time.

The final attack was a series of powerful airbursts directly above. The force of them was stunning, wringing the breath from Karen's lungs and scorching her clothes and hair, though thickly caked dust and the impervious forest protected her from the worst of the blast. Smoking bits of metal pelted down, and then a large object—the crab-thing she had seen earlier, or one just like it, toppled heavily down onto her back. It squirmed feebly, dangling by one claw from her jacket.

Now that she could see the thing out of its hole, she realized only the front part of it looked anything like a crab, or perhaps an eight-legged armadillo—the rest looked more like a giant grub. Its leather-plated thorax had split open along the back, and glutinous innards were leaking out.

Without thinking about it, Karen scooped out a handful of the albuminous substance and slurped it from her cupped palm. It was bland and sweetish; no more disgusting than an oyster or a raw egg. She gulped handful after handful, retching but not allowing herself to throw up, and finally dropped the carcass into oblivion.

"Oh my God," she groaned. "Oh my God."

And then her eyes grew wide. *No.* Breathlessly, she reached into the pocket of her coat and her hand closed around the familiar smooth oval. *Oh yes please dear God…* With trembling caution, she drew it out and flipped it open, sobbing to see that the battery was still charged. That her international cell phone still worked.

CHAPTER TWELVE:

HIGH ANXIETY

"**K**aren, this is Lieutenant Colonel Harley Queen, Chief of Operations. Are you all right?"

"*No! I'm not all right! What the fuck's the matter with you? Get me the fuck off this thing!*"

"We're working on that, Karen. Stay calm, it's gonna be okay. Can you tell me what has happened to you?"

"How the fuck should I know? Jesus Christ!"

"Do you mean to tell me you have no idea what has happened to you?"

"I was hoping you could tell me!"

Queen closed his eyes. He had really been expecting a breakthrough—that she could shed some light on it all. The general said nothing, as if equally discouraged.

"*Are you still there?*" Karen quacked hysterically.

Swallowing his intense disappointment, Queen said, "Don't worry, I'm right here. I promise you I'm not going anywhere, Karen, but I'm going to ask you to hang up now."

"*No!* God, no!"

"—just to preserve your phone's power. We're going to need it to find you and get you out of there."

"Wait! Where am I? What am I doing here? *What the fuck is going on?*"

"General?"

"Tell her. Make it quick."

"All right, Karen. Here it is in a nutshell..."

As she listened, dangling in space on what she now realized was a *hair*, the full whimsical horror of the situation percolated through her stretched-thin mind, which strained out the least berserk nuggets of information for her to inspect. *Ain't that a kick in the head*, she thought woozily. There was not much left of her to be shocked.

All right, so it wasn't a flying cliff, it was a giant human being, a mile-high titan, who had sprung up out of some mysterious earthshaking cataclysm and was now laying waste to the Korean countryside. Was that really so much more bizarre?

A lot actually made sense now, if that was possible, but one thing she could not quite digest was that it was *Manny*. Cute little Manny Lopes a globe-striding colossus? She looked down the sloping precipice through its canopy of curling black stalks, and wondered what part of him this had been. Nothing was recognizable. She thought of those *Reader's Digest* articles: I Am Joe's Pancreas, I Am Joe's Liver—*I Am Manny's Cootie*. She pictured him as a grotesque, tormented hulk, cringing in baffled hurt from the cruel slings and arrows of the military. Naturally their first thought would be to kill him. Fragmentary impressions of King Kong and Fay Wray whirled amid kaleidoscopic snapshots of her and Manny's brief affair

Sudden grief and pity overwhelmed her; even though she was remorseful about committing adultery, Karen still felt maternally protective of Manny. He was such a gentle little man—a gentleman. So different from most of the men she had dated in her life, especially the military ones. Was it such a crime, two lonely people far from home, giving solace to one another? Was this the price of their one night of passion? If so, it was too high a price. Way too high.

Whatever that Air Force guy was telling her about being rescued, Karen knew that she and Manny were both well and truly fucked.

"Do you really think there's a prayer of getting her off?" asked Dennison.

Queen was donning the harness rig that would allow him to spool down from the Osprey like a spider. After speaking to Karen, he had decided to handle this task himself—she was on the ragged edge of sanity, frozen in place, and might need a familiar voice to coax her off. Besides, he was the only one of his men who still didn't have a scratch. Shouldering the rescue sling, he said, "I don't know, but the fact that she's lasted this long means that it's at least possible to survive in close. Maybe we can get in there long enough for a quick snatch-and-grab. I just need a precise bead on her position—we can't be hovering around there for any length of time. We're tracing her signal via data link with the E-3; as long as the big guy stays put for a few more minutes, we'll be able to get a visual fix and go after her."

"Got her," said Deitz from up front.

"No shit." Queen rushed forward.

The aircraft's pivoting external camera was fixed on a point above the giant's left eyebrow. On the cockpit monitor it looked like a stand of dark trees. The telephoto lens zoomed in on an anomalous black speck until it came into focus as a tiny human figure in boots and a fur-trimmed leather coat, straddling the base of a colossal hair like a stranded flood victim.

"You magnificent bastard," said Queen, "you found her. Check her out."

"Looks like a nit," Deitz said.

"How close do you think we can get?"

"I don't know. That brow is a sumbitch—it's so steep we're gonna damn near have to shave the thing in order to reach her, and our asses are gonna be hanging in the breeze right above that bloodshot mother of an eyeball the whole time. I don't know about you, but I'm not too gung-ho about that staring contest— one wrong movement, one hiccup, one sneeze, and we're toast. We can't count on him sitting still long enough for us to dangle a line and retrieve her. Personally, I think it's asking a lot. And even if he does sit dead still, there's the wind shears and all…it's gonna be hairy, chief. Literally."

Captain Deitz had a tendency to gripe, but Queen knew from experience that he executed every mission with the same ice-cold determination, no matter how hot a place was. If he thought it was bad, it was *bad*—stupid bad—but this time Queen had no choice but to override the laconic, Teutonic wisdom of his second-in-command, probably sacrificing all their lives for a fool's errand. That was the job. Queen knew Deitz had made his peace with death long ago; they all had. Now they had to look it in the eye.

"Like it or not, we have to rescue her," Queen said. "She's our only connection to whatever caused this thing. And we have to do it quick and dirty, pedal to the metal, since like you say he might get up and start moving again at any time. So get on the stick, Slick. *Macht schnell!* Get me down there."

"*Dammit.* No can do, chief. Sorry."

"What? Why not?"

"Take a look."

Out the port side windows, far across the valley, the giant was climbing to his feet.

≥≠≤

"So you can't get at her?" asked the general.

Queen explained, "Well, we don't dare approach while he's in motion—it's suicide. But I'm not sure we have to. Now that he's not as agitated, he's covering less ground, traveling a lot more slowly and impacting a fairly uninhabited region—it's all open country. Maybe he's dying. If we don't disturb him, he may settle down for another nap and we can try for her. At present we have nine flights in rotation for the attempt: three on station and six others on standby—it's just a matter of time."

"How much longer do you expect her to hold out up there?"

"She's lasted this long; hopefully she can last another day. I'm sorry, general, but we all have to wait for the next window of opportunity."

"Whenever that is. No. I'm afraid the problem has become much more urgent since the last time I spoke to you, Lee. As of now, we have to start taking unacceptable risks."

Queen couldn't read the wooden tone of the general's voice. *What do you think we've been doing?* He couldn't see how things could get much more urgent. "Sir?" he said.

Stiltedly, as if reading from a telegram, the general said, "Forty-six minutes ago, at oh nine thirty-seven Japan time, a series of massive tsunamis struck the southern Japanese coastal city of Fukuoka, wiping out the entire port and waterfront."

"Son of a bitch," Queen said. He was dismayed at this new crisis, but even more frustrated with the general for bringing it to his attention—what the hell could he do about it? His hands were full here.

But the CINC was not finished. Slowly, with over-precise enunciation, he said, "The waves preceded the eastward approach of a second giant, wading in from the Korea Strait. A woman, by all accounts. She made landfall just over a half an hour ago, and now all communications in the prefecture have been lost. Half of Kyushu is dark."

Lieutenant Colonel Queen struggled to comprehend this information; it required another complete mental overhaul, something he didn't feel altogether fit to handle. One of his wife's favorite expressions chirped vividly in his head: *Holy guacamole!*

She had gotten Harley Jr. saying it.

Come on, he thought. *Stay focused. One thing at a time.* All he could bring himself to say was, "All right..."

"Get busy, Lee," said the general. "What we need more than anything are answers. Do whatever you have to, but get me some, ASAP. Meanwhile, I'll be breaking the bad news to the Joint Chiefs."

≥≠≤

Tetsui Honda sat in a spare armchair at the Sasebo Senior Hospital, patting his Elvis-style pompadour and contemplating the comic travails of Scrooge McDuck.

He had changed all the linens in his ward, emptied the bedpans, and was seeing how long he could extend a ten-minute break before he had to start mopping the floor. With all the commotion, he didn't think the floor supervisor would catch him—half the staff had left early, and the rest were glued to the TVs.

Down the corridor he could hear the Sisters of Charity— Australian nuns from the nearby Catholic mission, who made regular rounds of all the old-age homes—singing American show-tunes with some of the indigents. This time it was *Oklahoma.* They were led in song, as usual, by the old Korean dame, that Hollywood nut, Shirley Lee. Or as she preferred to be called, Shirley *Yusa*—Madame Shirley.

Not everybody liked working around the Koreans. A lot of the Japanese staff and other patients thought of them as foreigners, outsiders, freeloading on the national health-care system, even though most had been in the country for at least fifty years and were totally assimilated. Some had even been born in Japan.

Tetsui didn't mind them, and thought it was sad how much dingier their ward was than the rest of the hospital. There were supposed to be rules against this kind of thing, but nobody ever did anything about it. It was like the separate Korean line at passport control: understaffed, overcrowded, and unnecessarily demeaning.

Often having felt discriminated against by mainstream Japanese culture for his personal predilections, Tetsui commiserated with the Koreans, and could even understand why a few of them became so embittered by the myriad subtle and not-so-subtle forms of prejudice that they turned to crime or pro-North Korean radicalism. Sometimes Tetsui wished he had a gay homeland to turn to.

Suddenly the singing stopped. It was so oddly abrupt, the voices just wilting to silence, that Tetsui got up and wandered over. The TV had been turned up, and he could hear Shirley's squawking voice babbling, "*Omona*! That's my granddaughter! That's Dorothy!"

Tetsui came around the partition to find everyone blocking the television. From what he could tell, it was still showing the same thing it had for days: endless news reports of the destruction in South Korea, the Brown Colossus, the earthquakes and tsunamis, and the resultant refugee crisis. Tetsui didn't see any reason to panic. Japan was an island—why should the giant come here? He wished someone would just turn it off. It was the same thing over and over again: a lot of talking heads pontificating about possible causes, and broad estimates of the numbers of dead, missing, and homeless. After the first day, Tetsui had stopped watching—it all made him want to block his ears and start screaming. What good did it do to obsessively dwell on it? What could anyone do?

But now something else was going on.

At first it looked like more canned tsunami footage: grainy aerial images of huge combers battering urban Fukuoka, cars being washed down the street, the harbor thick with floating wreckage and capsized or swamped ships. Then he could see that across the bottom of the screen was a banner reading: LIVE REPORT. Yes, another tsunami must have struck.

Shouting against the helicopter's engine whine, the reporter was saying, "...so far, all we know is that it is not the same giant as the one attacking Korea! Repeat, it is *not* the same giant. It appears to be a woman—it is definitely a woman—and she is now well inland and moving eastward! We will try to stay with her so that we can keep bringing you this story as long as we can!"

There was very disturbing, shaky video of something huge and dark moving against a white overcast sky, with the low horizon dipping in and out of view. It all had the raw quality of candid tornado footage. There were several changes of focus, the cameraman zooming in on plumes of smoke and flying debris, then the jumping image resolved into a long-shot that encompassed the whole gargantuan figure straddling the countryside.

Everyone's blood froze in unison—a collective gasp of breath stole the air from the room.

It was certainly a woman. A woman the size of a living typhoon, striding on legs like twin tornadoes, taking whole ranges of greenly forested hills at a stride. Though the image was dark and hazy with distance, it was possible to make out her leather jacket and mini-skirt, her sneakers and striped leggings. Finally her *face*— her brutal face could be seen, resembling a squinting gargoyle hewn from a mountaintop. The people in the room moaned and gibbered with dread at the sight—all except one.

"That's my granddaughter!" Madame Shirley repeated. "That's her, I tell you!"

One of the nuns said impatiently, with an edge of hysteria, "Shhh. No it isn't, Yusa."

"It sure as hell is! I know my own granddaughter! Can't you see she's Korean?"

Tetsui had to admit she did look sort of Korean.

≥≠≤

Everyone in the hospital knew the tragic story of Shirley's granddaughter. There were two subjects that the old lady never tired of talking about. The first was the Golden Age of Hollywood, of which she had first-hand knowledge, having not only been there at the final leg of those glory days, but even worked as an extra and advisor on many of the '40s and '50s B wartime pictures—interchangeably playing Japanese, Chinese and Korean pretty girls. Americans didn't know the difference.

The second subject was less frivolous: It concerned her family's disappearance, years before, into the cruel fastness of North Korea.

Shirley Yusa—Madame Shirley—would never forgive herself for letting her daughter be tricked into following her stupid husband—Shirley's idiot son-in-law—back there during the repatriation movement of the 1960's, when thousands of expatriate Koreans were lured home with promises that they would be able to travel freely and stay in touch with family members in Japan. It was all lies—few who went over were ever heard from again, except through unofficial third parties such as the International Red Cross or the diplomatic offices of neutral countries. And anyone discovered utilizing these channels was liable to be censored in the most unpleasant ways.

But Shirley's daughter was persistent, and over the years vigorously pursued every illicit means of keeping in contact with her mother, even going so far as to obtain a black-market camera and film—film which she could not develop herself, or ever see, but which she could occasionally smuggle out in the bags of sympathetic Swedish or Cuban diplomats. It was by this means that Shirley learned of the birth of her granddaughter, Dorothy Lee, and was able to trace the hollow-eyed little girl's growth. She also learned just how desperately her daughter was struggling to keep their spirits alive in that blighted place. They coped by living on memories and dreams; and the fabled paradise they clung to the most was not their own, but Shirley's.

Thus, for the first eight years of her life, little Dorothy was raised on a secret diet of silver-screen glamour and Tinseltown legend—all the magic of Grandma's Hollywood. Named after Judy Garland's character in *The Wizard of Oz*, Dorothy was taught by her mother that North Korea was as provincial as Kansas, and just as colorless, but that someday she would fly away to a land where skies were blue and, "the dreams that you dare to dream really do come true."

Though trapped in a bleak, famine-plagued land, Dorothy's mother was determined to provide a Technicolor inner life for her child, and it was this forbidden fantasy of beauty and possibility— reinforced by family ties more solid than any rainbow—that sustained mother and daughter through suffocating years of psychological pressure and harshly enforced public conformity. Dorothy even learned to sing and to tap dance, ostensibly participating in rallies for the glory of the Great Father or the Glorious Motherland, but privately in homage to her invisible fairy-queen of a grandmother, who watched from across the sea.

Dorothy's most prized possession was a carefully preserved postcard showing Grauman's Chinese Theater on Hollywood Boulevard, which she and her mother handled as if it was a religious relic. That postcard was a window of light and hope, proof of a corporeal Oz far beyond the reach of the State Security Department. Sent by Dorothy's grandmother to her grandfather in Japan many years before, with an American airmail stamp, the card read:

Dear Kyong-won—I am finally here! It is more beautiful than I ever thought possible. Mrs. Sakamura is very nice, and tomorrow we have an appointment with Mr. Howard at Universal. Everyone in America is very helpful. They say I will be hired more easily if I use an American first name, and the one I thought of was Shirley, since my sister and I saw all those Shirley Temple movies before the war. I will write again soon. Wish me luck!—Shirley Lee (Lee Dae-jong).

Then the inevitable happened: Madame Shirley learned third-hand from a friend at the Japanese State Department that her daughter and son-in-law had been arrested, her granddaughter taken into state custody.

Shirley spent years appealing to any authority she could, but was unable to learn the fate of her granddaughter. Years went by, then decades. The old lady's health deteriorated, but she continued babbling to anyone who would listen about her family trapped in North Korea.

With the help of the nuns, Shirley started tape-recording long, rambling epistles to her granddaughter in the hopes that some day, perhaps even long after Shirley herself was dead, these hundreds of hours of recordings might eventually reach the girl; so that she would know that through all the years, and whatever she had been through, Dorothy had never been forgotten.

And then, one day in 2008, Shirley had an unusual group of visitors at the hospital: a party of brisk, serious men representing Interpol, the U.S. State Department, and Japan's Ministry of Internal Security, who wanted her to look at a photograph and tell them if she had any knowledge of the recent whereabouts of the person pictured. Shirley put on her reading glasses and studied the photo.

It was a cropped blow-up of a face in a crowd—a stiltedly ghoulish woman framed by banal, anonymous people. Yet her very ugliness was a clear echo of the pugnacious cutie she had been. Shirley recognized her immediately.

Hands trembling to hold the photo, she had croaked, "*Dorothy.*"

The men explained that Shirley Yusa's beloved granddaughter was accused of being a North Korean spy, wanted for a number of high-profile political assassinations in Japan and elsewhere.

It had been the last straw—the old lady went batty, reverting almost totally to her nostalgic world of Hollywood showstoppers.

Until now.

Shirley Yusa pointed to the TV and repeated, "That's Dorothy! That's her!"

Tetsui Honda shook his head in pity. Everyone was ignoring the poor old woman, caught up in their own private horror of the moment, praying or crying to themselves. Shirley's senile outburst was just the final bizarre touch to the whole nightmare.

We're all going crazy, Tetsui thought. *Or maybe we're already crazy.*

But then he noticed that one particular clique of hospice residents was paying serious attention to Shirley, fervently nodding and whispering together.

It was the radical *Choch'ongryn*; the old-school Pyongyang supporters. Not all members of *Choch'ongryn*—the major organization of the *chaeilkyop'o*, of Koreans living in Japan— supported North Korea, but these grumpy old gentlemen certainly did, and made no apologies for it. Tetsui thought they were nutty, but he had to admire their wildly ambitious notions of overthrowing the governments of South Korea, Japan, and America.

Despite their penury and declining years, they remained politically active, agitating for reunification and fancying themselves power brokers of international consequence. As such, they were shunned by most of the other elderly Koreans, and spent all their time in each other's company, grumbling and firing letters to the editor about the latest capitalist outrages. Tetsui thought of them as the Beagle Boys.

Out of the corner of his eye, Tetsui noticed as their leader, a tall, stooped old character named Mr. Oh, furtively separated himself from the others and shuffled into the hall. He went to the pay phone near the deserted nurse's station and made a call, cupping his hand around the receiver and glancing every which way, as if fearful of being overheard. Tetsui could only catch a few words: *"Of course I'm sure it's her! I trained her, didn't I? Just get me out of here and I'll show you!"*

This kind of thing was not unusual for the Beagle Boys, who were very paranoid about their geriatric plots and schemes, and normally Tetsui would have smiled.

But as he watched Shirley Yusa squawking, and the surreal horrors unfolding on TV, anything seemed possible.

Maybe the crackpots were inheriting the Earth.

CHAPTER THIRTEEN:

TALKING TURKEY

Two men talked privately, half a world apart, one in a plane and one in a car, both astonished that the fate of mankind could be decided by their phone call.

The one over Korea said, "Mr. Secretary, the situation is spinning out of control. We now have threats on two fronts, and if the one on the Peninsula is not resolved soon, there is every likelihood that the increasing force imbalance will trigger an opportunistic invasion by North Korea into the South. Since we are accused of having caused this crisis, and seem to be unable to stop it, the North Koreans can claim altruistic motives for any action they take, and if we fight them we look like we're putting political dogma above human life—it's their golden opportunity. And don't think the Chinese aren't watching. If they think the North can get away with it, they might just jump on the bandwagon, claiming security. Who could blame them? It's our mess; it's their backyard. Unless we take decisive control at once, the whole Pacific theater will be extraordinarily vulnerable, and after that, who knows? Most of our alliances are still shaky after Iraq; there could be a worldwide domino effect. We have to act."

"By 'act,' you mean go nuclear."

"That's right, sir. I have reliable sources in the field telling me that nukes are possibly the only thing that can bring these giants down. Right now we have a valid rationale for using them, and a clear shot, but once hostile nations become involved it'll be a free-for-all that's almost guaranteed to escalate into war."

"War. I see." The Secretary of Defense, General Mike Cutler, pondered this from the back seat of his limo. In moments he would be at the White House, briefing the president. "The problem I'm having, Buddy, is one of scale. There are issues on the table that are too big to comprehend. We've all been conditioned since the 'duck and cover' drills of our childhood to think that nuclear war is the ultimate level of violence, and it's very hard for me to judge it the lesser of two evils…and yet, that is what I am forced to do."

"I realize that, and if there was any other—"

"Please don't interrupt. It is equally hard for me to accept that my country—our country, Stan, which we have dedicated our lives to serve—could have given birth to something so…so beyond comprehension, and nurtured it, and set it loose. And that I may now be the one to preside over the final, incredible catastrophe. That, or nuclear war. That's the choice you offer me, Stan. That is what you're asking me to present to the president."

"I don't quite understand, sir. What's the choice again?"

Secretary Cutler suddenly seemed confused, preoccupied. Caught up in a momentary reverie, his words spilled out like a confession: "Zounds, Stan. You ever read Shakespeare? *Zounds.* This is humiliating. This is humiliation on a historic scale— national humiliation. It pains me to say this, and you have to keep this in the strictest confidence, but North Korea is right. They know. The bastards have us dead to rights, and by heck if they aren't going to town with it. Man, they are *flying.*"

"Know what? It's not even clear what they're accusing us of."

"All they have to know is that we did it. Boy oh boy, I wouldn't have believed it. You want to know something? I still don't." He took a deep breath. "For once, what Pyongyang alleges is true: Several weeks ago, a highly placed quantum physicist with the Brookhaven National Laboratory apparently stole unstable experimental materials that were supposed to have been destroyed. The man—a Professor Wilfred Isaacson—was unstable as well, as you can imagine. Exactly what he did with these materials is unknown, but we do know that he was in Busan at the time of the disaster there, having apparently missed his scheduled flight out. We also know that two other crucial people were in Busan at the time, checked into the very same hotel as Dr. Isaacson, very near ground zero: Manny Lopes and Karen Park."

"Oh my God."

"Yup. Yup. I told you. And I'm willing to bet our new giant is in the mix somehow, too. Anyway, whatever happened between those four, I'm being advised that, quote, 'The quantum dynamics of the event suggest that any interaction with it on a nuclear level would be, at worst, potentially devastating on a cosmic scale, and, at best, unpredictable,' unquote. Can you believe that? You still think we should go for it?"

General Stan "Buddy" Chesnutt remained silent for some time, furiously considering. As he saw it, there were three possibilities. On the one hand you had global conflict—essentially World War Three—in which every long-standing grudge would flare up like a box of matches and human civilization itself would be the tinder, burning down until there was nothing left but two giants and a handful of shivering peasants trying not to get stepped on like cockroaches.

On the other hand, if the giants could be knocked down quickly enough, the surprise success could be claimed as a victory for the U.S. and the world; the political fallout (though probably not the other kind) might be surprisingly light, tempered by relief and the ample demonstration of American willpower.

Then there was the third hand…a freakish and false appendage, most likely imaginary. In any case, the general did not care to consign the fate of the world to it—it would be like quitting without a fight. How could he live with himself in the sordid aftermath of war, knowing there had been a better option left untried? Besides, what was to keep other countries from using atom bombs against the giants? If that meant the end of all things, such an end was probably inevitable—all the more important to gamble big now, when it counted. Peace or oblivion: in the context of this waking nightmare, even the latter sounded curiously restful. No, it definitely had to be nukes: nukes now, or nothing. Let the chips fall where they may.

"I do, sir," Chesnutt said finally, voice hoarse with emotion.

Secretary Cutler breathed out, "All right, Buddy, all right—we'll do it, then. You know, part of me is glad."

General Chesnutt's brain was spinning; he felt dizzy, nauseous. He had expected some discussion, an interval of debate, a larger consensus—he didn't expect to be totally responsible for this. "Glad, sir?"

"Well, I've been seeking guidance about this since last night—praying to the Big Guy—and it seems to me that everything happens for a reason, wouldn't you agree? I mean, if you forget all the geopolitical bullshit and just focus on surrendering yourself to the Lord's will, you can't really go wrong. I guess what I'm trying to say, Bud, is that I believe we have been put in this time and place because we have His work to do, and however hard it is, we should go forth with the confidence of the righteous."

Another voice was coming through Chesnutt's earpiece, vying for his attention. Miserably, he said, "Excuse me, sir, I have Colonel Harley Queen on another channel. His flight group is shadowing the first giant. He says he has something urgent for me—this may be important."

"Let's hear it. Put him through."

"Yes, sir. Lee? Lee, you're on with the Secretary of Defense, General Cutler."

"Good morning, Harley," said Secretary Cutler grandly. He felt tired and threadbare as a hobo king.

"Good morning, sir."

"Harley, General Chesnutt and I have been discussing the unreasonable limitations imposed upon you and all our other brave troops on the front lines of this thing, and I may have some good news for you."

Harley Queen's voice was sharp with concern: "Is it about exercising the nuclear option?"

Slightly irked, Secretary Cutler said, "As a matter of fact, it is. I was just about to deliver my recommendation to the president."

"Don't! Jesus Christ, don't do it, not yet!"

"And why not?"

"Sorry, sir—I may have a better idea."

CHAPTER FOURTEEN:

SCHWARTZWALD

Queen wondered if he was truly the best man for the job, or just a death-chasing freak, a lemming. This thought occasionally troubled him, that he should be blindly entrusted with the lives of men equal or superior to himself, men whose souls were open books, men who risked their lives only out of necessity, not desire, and to whom shame was anathema. Men who assumed Duty and God were the same thing.

Once again he was leading these men—his *Boanerges,* his Sons of Thunder—into an insane, probably suicidal endeavor. Why did they keep letting him do it? Didn't they know how bogus his authority was, how arbitrary? The funny thing was, he knew they did, and yet they would automatically die for him…as so many had already. Their lives accrued like ruinous interest on a debt—someday soon it would all come due, payable in his own blood. Colonel Queen was satisfied with that arrangement.

In the meantime he depended on this strange devotion, and

could only pretend to be worthy of it. Certainly this mission would put it to the test yet again…maybe for the last time. But he thought that every time.

Spread-eagled, their webbed suits taut with wind, the ten still-ambulatory men of Habu Flight soared in a loose V-formation, diving through the air not so much like lemmings but like flying squirrels, plunging earthward under a Cheshire-cat grin of a moon toward the smoking jungles of a high, dark tower. A pinnacle that swayed above the mountainous Korean landscape, lurching forward in hundred-knot, half-mile-long surges; a vast battering-ram upon which Queen and his people would splatter like bugs on a windshield unless their timing was ridiculously perfect.

The mellow burr of Queen's voice came over all their headsets like a deejay on a midnight jazz station, belying the mortal intensity of the moment: "…eight thousand feet…delta formation…seven thousand feet…trim rate of descent to ninety fps…maximize foils…approach vector two-seven-two…six thousand feet…go to linear glidepath…stay tight…final approach solution at seven, six, five, four, three, two, one, *mark*…all right, ten seconds to LZ…synchronize and rig to deploy…stay with me…"

Following Queen's prompts (from information he was receiving over his helmet display via radar data link with a circling AWACS), the team aligned themselves to match as nearly as possible the speed and direction of their target—or rather where they anticipated their target would be once they reached the projected midair rendezvous. They could only hope it wouldn't change its mind.

Had they been Navy pilots, accustomed to landing planes by seat-of-the-pants extrapolation on the pitching decks of storm-tossed ships, they might have appreciated the similarities—though unlike carrier jockeys, they had no jet-powered cocoon, no deck controllers, no big rubber band to catch them, nothing but silly webbed suits and their own flimsy bodies. They would only have one crack at landing; there would be no chance to abort. It was success or death.

Strung out single file to maximize lift, they now descended on the nearest thing to a landing strip that they were likely to find on that vast, black-tousled crown (and in all honesty it was a pretty fair approximation of a runway): the razored part in Manny's hair. Six hundred feet long, bright white in their night-vision goggles, it stood out from the surrounding darkness like a moonbeam-lit country road, a luminous scar through deep backwoods.

The fliers were helped by the very thing that prohibited the near approach of powered aircraft: the turbulent, steamy updraft. As they veered in close, it buoyed them up hard, tossing them around some, but pillowing their descent to such a degree that the men felt like they could hang there all day, plying this humid trampoline like condors riding desert thermals. They luxuriated in the head-clearing interlude of precious time, feathering and making last-second adjustments in speed to create the illusion that the violently hurtling island below was a stable patch of ground on which a reasonable person would choose to set foot.

Then time was up. The last few hundred feet went by fast, the naked glowing avenue rushing up to greet them. At the last possible second, less than fifty feet off the deck, all ten men fired rocket-propelled drag chutes barely large enough to arrest their descent. This was the most crucial moment of all: the touchdown had to be feather-light so as not to give them away, yet too light and they might never land at all, but be ripped into the giant's brutal wake.

Chutes deployed, the men were instantly yanked up short, settling like dandelion seeds (and just about that size, relative to the behemoth below), their feet touching bottom as gently as stepping off a down escalator. This microsecond of false leisure was barely long enough to release their chutes and hit the deck—an instant's hesitation would have meant being dragged backwards by the howling winds and flung over the brink. The ten liberated parachutes ballooned wildly up and away like plastic supermarket bags, vanishing into the night.

"All right, we are on the ground, on station," announced Queen, laying flat as possible. They had splashed down in a shallow wash of hot greasy fluid, giant's sweat, and he didn't want to get any in his respirator. The bottom was silty over a bedrock-like substrate—presumably the scalp. Queen's stomach dropped with each surge of the giant's head, though he wasn't usually much prone to motion-sickness—all of a sudden he had great admiration for Karen Park. "Go for cover, by twos. Go, go, go!"

Whipped by hurricane-force winds, the men squirmed like frantic salamanders across the hot spring-fed streambed and into the dense bordering hairs; a black forest over fifty feet high, with horny trunks a foot in diameter. They were like sequoias compared to the sparse arm hairs the men had encountered previously. What appeared to be banks of dirty snow were actually outcroppings of thickened dead skin—dandruff.

As soon as the men were in the shelter of that fathomless jungle, the wind dropped off to nothing. All that was left was the sound: an unseen banshee chorus. The heat was stifling, but the men's night-camouflage body suits had temperature regulators; plastic capillaries began circulating coolant around groin and armpit.

"This is un-fucking-believable," said Dennison, staring in wonder at the alien wilderness as he unzipped and stowed his nylon glide foils. "Check this shit out."

"Wanna make dandruff angels?" said Deitz.

"Quiet." Queen had been doing an equipment check when suddenly he froze, listening. Out of nowhere came a tremendous creaking and crashing, as of a hundred trees being felled at once. The ground shook. The uproar was moving toward them, and through the canopy they could make out a thing like a vast boulder grinding and mashing down the forest.

"Scatter!" he shouted, breaking left and running as fast as he could between the twisting black columns.

The very air seemed to compress and crackle with static electricity as the vast object bulldozed through, crushing down great swaths of trees that miraculously sprang up in its wake, only to be slammed down again on the return pass. Back and forth, back and forth. Searching. Scratching.

Queen heard a brief, hopeless scream from one of his men nearby, abruptly cut short, but there was nothing he could do, trapped in the path of that demonic pestle himself. It was a *finger*, or rather a finger*tip*, big as a whale and gaining on him like a freight train, its broad striated underside flattening giant hair follicles with enough force to cause shockwaves and searing gusts of heat friction, and its blunt, ivory-colored fingernail plowing up thick epidermal crusts like a backhoe ripping concrete. As keratinous timber began slamming down around him, Queen dove for the base of the nearest trunk and huddled there.

This was the end; it had to be. He winced as a log-like follicle nearly squashed him, inches away, and waited to be smeared out of existence by that hellacious digit. Here it came now, plunging down on him. *Shit, shit, shit...*

Then it passed, the enormous hairs springing back up with uncanny resilience, catapulting greasy detritus every which way. Queen was alive, unharmed, and realized that he had been spared by the narrowest of margins, sheltered between the bent trunks of two of those flexible but ultimately crushproof hairs.

Relative peace returned to the forest. Afraid of triggering another attack, Queen hardly dared move. "Radio check," he said softly. "Report in, but stay where you are. What's your status?" He swept his infrared flashlight around 360 degrees, but couldn't see any of his men in the green glare off the trunks. Speaking calmly, he repeated, "Report in, squad. Where are you?" The place looked utterly deserted.

"I'm here, chief," whispered Carl Dennison, tapping him on the shoulder.

Queen almost jumped out of his skin. "Jesus! What the fuck?"

"Sorry, boss, something's wrong with my radio."

"That's okay. I'm just glad as hell to see you."

"Same here. Where is everybody?"

"I don't know; we've lost line-of-sight, and I think my com is funking out, too. Maybe the static discharge shorted it out. We're gonna have to backtrack and find everybody."

"While I was running, I thought I heard Roy buy it."

"Me too, but I'm hoping he was the only one."

"Did you see that fucking finger?"

"Don't talk about it."

"I know, but do you think it's safe for us to move around?"

"No. Now go. *Lightly*."

"Just call me twinkletoes," Dennison said shakily.

As the two men cautiously retraced their steps, creeping along on cat feet, Queen asked, "How the hell could that woman survive here for so long? It's fucking hell."

"I don't know. She hasn't budged and given herself away."

"It's not just that. How could she survive the bacteria and everything else? She's got nothing!"

"I haven't seen too many bacteria, have you? I don't think there's much in the way of flora around here, either. It's pretty antiseptic."

"Are you kidding me?" Queen looked around at the rank swamp surrounding them. "It's a fucking jungle!"

"Not really—I think what we're seeing is pretty ordinary stuff: sweat, sebum, shed epithelium. Only the quantities are extraordinary. It's the sweat that may be helping her the most—it contains a natural disinfectant called lysozyme."

"That's revolting."

"Don't knock it. It's protecting us, too."

One by one, most of the men found each other. There were two casualties: Staff Sergeant Steve Hannigan, the big NASCAR buff, was missing, presumed dead, but they found Lt. Porfirio "Roy"

Roybal—the little that was left of him. His body looked like roadkill that had been all but disposed of by busy traffic, rendered not only anonymous but indefinable by species. Hamburger. Roy had liked to say he was from the *real* Las Vegas: Las Vegas, New Mexico.

They left him there and spread out so as to not draw further attention, fanning toward Manny's forehead. It was not a tremendous hike; the top of that scalp, enormous as it was, measured less than twenty acres. What made it slow going was the slippery uneven footing and their cautious pace—no one wanted to bring the wrath of the Finger down upon them again.

Nearing the grove's edge, they began to feel a cool breeze. Tall hairs rustled as powerful gusts washed through, and there was a sense that beyond the farthest trunks lay open country—a bare, windy plateau. It got colder and still windier, the chill slightly ameliorated by huge billows of steam that rolled in like surf.

"Coming to the anterior hairline," said Dennison.

Then they were there, bracing themselves against the furious tempest as they took in the view, like tourists overlooking Niagara Falls. In front of them, the shiny moonlit dome of Manny's forehead extended outward, sloping gradually downhill until it vanished from sight somewhere below. It was not absolutely smooth, but resembled a pitted mudflat prickled with sparse reeds. Slime was being blown off it into their faces. Beyond was the panorama of the night landscape: the Earth from six-thousand feet up, black with a few distant twinkles of light. It was a breathtaking sight, and dizzying; the dark horizon swayed like the sea, re-apprising them of their unstable platform.

"Now for the tricky part," shouted Dennison.

They were prepared for this—as prepared as any human being could be. As elite AFSOC operators, most of them had started out by distinguishing themselves first as Navy SEALS, Army Rangers, and the Marine Force Recon, or combinations of these. In Queen's flight only Deitz and Wayne Aponte, piloting the

CV-22, were lifelong Air Force men. AFSOC constituted the Air Force's sole forward ground-combat capability, and its people prided themselves on their ability to conquer any terrain. They were modern Ninjas.

Yet they weren't prepared for this.

They began by shedding their heavy equipment, which was stowed in various packs and pockets all over their bodies. Most of it was batteries, computers, and audio components; there were no weapons, and very little food or water. After thus lightening up, they fastened lines to several hairs, hoping to distribute the weight so they could rappel down the face without alerting their host. Acrobats though they were, none of them had ever attempted to rappel down a cliff in a 100-mile-an-hour gale—a cliff that was moving. A cliff that was a slimy, slippery oil slick.

They said nothing, worked without meeting each other's eyes, knowing it would be tempting the obvious. Once again, Queen went first, crawling into the wind. He could feel his body wanting to peel off the ground and fly away, but the oozing pores and ridges offered unexpectedly good purchase; before he knew it he was twenty yards from the sheltering hairline, inching ever more steeply toward the abyss. Lieutenant Dave Mahfouz was following, then Dennison and the rest.

Queen carefully oriented himself feet-first and began to descend. Suddenly it was easy going—the wind supported him, and every time the giant surged forward the g-forces mashed Queen into the wall. He found that handholds were superfluous; he could move around freely, like a human fly. If he didn't have to keep wiping greasy spray off his goggles he would have felt exhilarated.

The cliff was now vertical; he was halfway there. He could see below him the dark copses of the eyebrows, jutting out into space, and below that the tip of the nose. He could not yet make out the woman, Karen—the object of all this. He hoped she was still there.

Then the giant turned its head.

Queen was caught off guard—he felt g-forces pulling him left and tried to find a secure handhold. It didn't seem like a big deal. Then suddenly the wall lurched sideways and he lost his grip, flailing in space. At the last second he tried to snag a passing reed, but the mounting centrifugal force prized it from his fingers. All at once he was helplessly flying outward at the end of his line, dangling from the end of a whip. *"Holy sheeeee—"*

Above him he could see Dave also clinging for dear life as the rope swung out perpendicular to the forehead, so that for a moment it seemed to be a wind-tossed tightrope leading back to the hairline. For a brief instant, looking down, Queen could see Manny's whole face in the moonlight, nearly a thousand feet high, stern and rough-hewn as an overgrown Easter Island deity. Then he was falling, plummeting back down to that unforgiving brow. *This is gonna hurt*, he thought, bracing as best he could for the impact.

Something dark and unimaginably huge veered in from above: Manny's right hand. It came with a sonic boom and crashed glancingly along the dome of the forehead, causing thunderous shockwaves and raining down dermal debris as it cut Queen off from the others. The leading edge of its thumbnail snared their line like a 747 intercepting a kite-string.

Thus, just as Queen was about to slam headlong into the cliff, he abruptly found himself jerked short and yanked upward again as if at the end of a bungee cord, feet touching the speeding wall so that he could actually *run* upward, vertically, like Batman scaling a tall building. He could no longer see anyone else; it was him alone charging that humongous hand. Momentum dying, he scrambled for a foothold, any purchase, beseeching, *Come on now, come on…*

The line parted.

Queen slid, tobogganing facedown amid a mudslide of oily debris. His respirator and goggles were ripped from his head as he struck a gauntlet of whip-like canes—actually the finest fuzz on the human body. The tough stalks slowed his fall, as did the fierce updraft; also the angle of the slope was becoming slightly less steep.

Still clawing for handholds, he skittered to a stop in a slough of litter that had collected on a kind of ledge. It was the puckered, charred rim of a crater about twenty feet across; a grisly sump overflowing with lava-like congealing blood. Steam-heat wafted from the hole as if from a volcanic vent. Thirty-foot-tall eyebrow hairs leaned splintered and smoldering away from the breech, and sticky blood cells had been blown everywhere by the wind, resembling gelatinous red condoms.

"Holy shit," Queen groaned in pain.

From somewhere just below him, a cracked and weary voice cried, "Hello? *Hello?*"

He couldn't believe it. Summoning his strength, he called down, "I'm here, Karen."

≥≠≤

"Oh my God, thank God," she sobbed. "Please get me out of here. I want to go down now. Please take me down."

"We're working on that, ma'am, trust me. But you're gonna have to hold on a little longer, okay? Just a little longer—you're doin' great, honey. Just stay where—"

"Stay my butt! I'm not your honey, asshole! Fuck you! I don't need you to tell me how great I'm doing, I just need you to get me the fuck out of here!" Her voice quavered to pieces. "Get your ass down here now! *Now!* Oh God please *help me…*"

I'm not Rambo, for God's sake, Queen thought. He removed a small laser beacon from his pocket and activated it. "Be right with you," he said, wincing in pain as he moved. "Don't you worry."

He gingerly made his way around the giant's wound and fastened a safety-cable to the nearest hair. Now he could see Karen Park hanging just below amid the stalks, her back to him. Though badly bruised and starting to stiffen, possibly with a sprained rib, Queen easily rappelled down to her. "I'm coming down now, okay?" he forewarned, so as not to surprise her. "Just above you, don't move…"

"I don't think I can move," she whimpered. "I lost all circulation in my legs; I can't feel my toes."

"That's okay, you don't have to do a thing. Just hold still while I get this harness around you." Kneeling between her legs on the base of the follicle, he removed the extra harness vest he was wearing and put it on her, snugging all the straps. She shrieked at every bob of her perch. She was filthy; encrusted with ash and dust like the victims of Pompeii.

"All right, you're all set. Ready to take a little trip?"

"Yes—God, yes."

"Hold on while I flag us a cab."

He could already see the plane coming.

≥≠≤

Queen and Deitz had discussed the unheard-of aerial maneuver, but both of them knew it ultimately had to be Deitz's show; he was the pilot.

Mike Deitz had flown in all kinds of adverse conditions, often at night and occasionally under enemy fire, and he was an old hand at mid-air refueling. He couldn't honestly say he had ever been scared in the air. But he had never imagined he would have to match speed with an unpredictable, hostile six-thousand-foot juggernaut, ride its furious pressure-front like a porpoise surfing the bow wave of a supertanker, and hold position there long enough to retrieve personnel from an obstructed vertical incline.

It was truly ridiculous, and if the colonel had not already demonstrated the impossible by attaining the site on foot, Deitz would never attempt it. He had certainly not expected to; he had never expected to see Queen or the others ever again, figuring the plan for a turkey from the get-go. Acquiring their laser signal had been the surprise of his life, and not a pleasant one. Deitz didn't care if he died because of somebody else's fuck-up—every career soldier expected that. He just didn't want to be the one responsible—now it would be *his* fault if they all bought it! He was pissed.

Leading the giant by about a mile, Deitz dropped down to the altitude of its crest and reduced velocity to below stall speed. The Osprey's onboard computers automatically compensated by swiveling the engine nacelles to their vertical mode, transforming the aircraft into a functional helicopter.

Deitz and Aponte watched with something like religious awe as the giant loomed up behind. At about an eighth of a mile, they could feel the aircraft pitch forward, as if given a shove, and then suddenly drop. His control surfaces all but useless, Deitz compensated by throttling up and simultaneously executing a hard yaw, threading the pressure envelope at an oblique angle that allowed the wind shear to harmlessly roll over them and carry them along like a kayak in tumbling rapids, finding equilibrium by facing upstream into a chute. That was exactly what it was, Deitz thought: now he was in the chute, suspended in a bubble of force and completely at its mercy.

The airframe was vibrating badly—the Osprey throbbed with a deep sound like the guttural chants of a thousand monks—but as long as his ship didn't come apart on him, Deitz began to think they might actually have a chance.

The stick jerked in his hand like a gaffed marlin. He knew it was important to remain centered before the giant; drift too much in any direction and they would fall into the sideslip—it would suck them in like a garbage disposal and spit nuts and bolts out the back end. Likewise, even though it was night, he still had to be conscious of the giant's line of sight, dropping in close and from a high enough angle that the brow would shield them.

The giant was now so large on the cockpit monitors that it was no longer recognizable as anything remotely human; they could have been hovering above a desolate mountain peak. Every couple of minutes, towering eruptions of vapor buffeted the aircraft. Directly below, just a hundred feet away now, Deitz could see the downhill slope of the forehead, pocked with ordnance strikes, and the thatches of brush that were the eyebrows.

Yes—there they were. In the radioactive green light of his night vision scope, Deitz could clearly make out the two tiny figures perched on a limb in the left eyebrow, just where he expected them to be. One was standing and waving an infrared strobe— that was Queen, all right.

Yeah, yeah, I see you, he thought. *Don't get your panties in a bunch.*

They were walking on clouds, dancing on air. As they were hoisted out of danger, soaring free at the end of a steel cable, Queen clutched Karen Park to him as if she was his partner at a tango marathon, dead on her feet but still in the game. He felt a flooding pity and tenderness, affection borne of respect for her toughness, mixed up with wonder at what he and his team had accomplished so far. Now he just had to pull off the rest.

Leaving the pair dangling, the straining Osprey lifted them up and over the hump of the forehead, back to the hairline where Dennison and the team were waiting with the stowed equipment. There, as gently as possible, it set them down again. Queen unclipped the cable and waved Deitz off. He watched with sick resignation as the craft banked away, seemed to be doing all right, then suddenly spun and came apart, plunging out of sight.

You magnificent bastard, Queen thought, heartsick. *You beat me to it.*

In the punishing gale, it took Karen a few minutes to realize she was still on Manny's head; that the aircraft was gone.

"Wait," she cried, as Queen hustled her under the cover of the trees. "Wait—what's going on? Why are we still here?"

"Sorry, Karen, but we can't leave just yet."

"Oh yes we fucking can! *I* can! I fucking well can, and I will!" She suddenly became a flailing dervish of pain, scratching, punching, biting. Dirty fighting. She screamed, "Get me the fuck out of here, you jarhead son-of-a-bitch!"

He was shocked by the unexpected force of her assault—she almost cold-cocked him before he managed to pin her arms and lug her to safety. He could taste blood. Queen wouldn't have liked to know what she could do if she wasn't debilitated by exposure and thirst. For the first time in days, he had to laugh.

"Karen—Karen, calm down. Calm down—*ungh*! It's because I need your help—I need your help with Manny, you understand? He knows you! Listen! I need you to talk to Manny! That's why we're here!"

"*Fuck you! Fuck you!*"

"I know, and I'm sorry! It sucks, but you're the only one who can help him. You're friends, aren't you? He might listen to you!"

"I'm his lover, not his wife! And how the *fuck* can he listen to me? I'm a fucking flea!"

"I know that. I know that. Stop. But we have special synthesizing equipment—Carl, tell her."

Carl Dennison said, "That's right, Karen. We can modulate and amplify your voice so that it comes out at a very low frequency that Manny may be able to interpret."

"See? You can talk to him. You can *save* him, Karen, and thousands of others."

"You're out of your fucking minds!"

Queen let go of her, stood in front of her and laid out his cards: "Look, it's either that or we all die here. It could happen any second—we've already lost four men getting to you. There are no more planes coming. We're all depending on you."

"Why me? Why don't you get his wife to do it? This is her job, not mine!"

"Because she's back in the States and you're here. And because she told us they just broke up—she asked for a divorce. We thought talking to her might upset him."

Divorce? Well that explained a lot. *Jesus.* "You know, I was about to break it off with him, too, before all this happened."

"Does he know that?"

Karen looked around at the men like a cornered savage, then shook her head no. Her hair was molded into wild fins of crusted dirt, and tears had cut channels through the filth caking her face. Suddenly the strength seemed to go out of her and she sat down. Dennison handed her a bottle of water, and she eagerly drained it in one long swallow. Wiping her mouth, she said, "Got any Motrin?"

Queen said, "You're pretty bad-ass, you know that, Karen?"

"Don't patronize me, okay? I'm not in the mood. How do I talk to Manny?"

"Just as soon as you're ready to take a little hike."

"A hike! Where the fuck are we going now?"

Queen hesitated, but Dennison chimed in, "We have to get down to his eardrum."

CHAPTER FIFTEEN:

LIVING LARGE

Manny was tired and thirsty and scared. Sweat stung all the places where tiny bombs had gone off—every inch of exposed skin, it seemed. For a while there he had felt like he was being attacked by angry hornets, and really began to panic: *Leave me alone! What did I ever do to you?* But then he had thrown a few handfuls of dirt in the air, and it seemed to discourage them. At any rate, the harassment had stopped...for now.

Manny wished there was some way to let them know he meant no harm. He didn't think telling them did any good, and when he tried shouting it only seemed to cause more destruction—he had actually seen squadrons of strange gnats flare up like struck matches in the path of his raised voice. The only way he could think of to demonstrate goodwill was to watch his step, tread lightly; and this he was being extra careful to do, staying far away from any sign of civilization. It wasn't easy.

The situation was especially frustrating because at the same time he felt like the only answers he was liable to get would come from these tiny creatures, these super-bright bugs. In any case they were his only company, and they had obviously been here longer than he had. Maybe they knew what was going on—he remembered *Gulliver's Travels* and wondered if it might be possible to make contact with them somehow. Be Gulliver among the Lilliputians.

Right after the initial shock, Manny had been hit with an epiphany: *This is it*, he thought. *I'm famous.* All his life he had felt that something special was in store for him—that he had an important destiny—but he had always dismissed it as idle dreaming. Now, for the first time since his father had smuggled himself to America, the name of Lopes would be a hot commodity. Discovering an intelligent insect civilization—Bug World!— that had to be newsworthy, whatever else it was. Guaranteed fame. Once he was out of here, Manny could start by holding a press conference, then get a Hollywood agent to auction off his exclusive account, then expand it into a magazine story, then get a book deal and a producer credit on the movie—all greased with free media coverage. He would be set for life; he would be huge.

If he ever got out of here. In the meantime he needed to understand the situation, to calmly and methodically analyze what he was seeing.

In this way Manny held terror at bay while night closed in, jumping on every crumb of ultra-miniaturized technology like a fevered prospector shouting eureka over flakes of gold dust. Everything he found was in ruins—he could not so much as approach without destroying stuff—but he did at least recognize the fractured remains of highways and towns, of tiny vehicles scattered about like dead ants. Actual cars and trucks! *They're copying us*, he thought. *Mimicking our technology on a microscopic scale—incredible!*

He desperately wanted a look at one of the tiny inhabitants, and spent some time sifting dust in the hope of seeing one of these mysterious mites. Were they humanoid? Perhaps aliens from another planet? But the light was bad, and without a magnifying glass he didn't think he could find one. In any case it was more than likely that any such delicate, tiny creatures were being pulverized beyond recognition before he could get a close look. Ugh—that was a horrible thought.

At one point he found a miniature railroad switching-yard, which by the robust nature of its metal constituents was at least somewhat intact. The industrial tank cars looked like strings of candy, or like the small ceramic resistors on a circuit-board. They fell apart at once when Manny tried to handle them, but before they puffed into flame and smoke he was able to decipher lettering on their sides, like micro-printing on drug capsules: SANG-HWA. It was in Hangul!

Damn!

Manny didn't know what to make of this unnerving proof that he was still in Korea...or some miniaturized facsimile of Korea... or some schizoid hallucination of Korea.

And then *they* had attacked.

It was much like the time Manny walked into a patch of stinging nettles: As if out of nowhere, searing pain raked his bare flesh. But this agony was rendered visible by crackling sparks, as of a thousand static-electric shocks. Earth and sky were suddenly alive with the flashes of fireflies, and from them came darting spider threads, pale blue streamers of smoke that zipped in and bit deep, with a sharp *pop!* Too fast to dodge. He recoiled, covering his face with his hands. It had seemed to go on forever.

What *were* they—really? Where was this? Was he a giant, or had they shrunk—or was this some alternate reality where nothing made sense? For a while Manny wondered if it was a reality *show*—one of those hidden-camera things, setting him up to look stupid. But he quickly realized it could be nothing like that. This wasn't "real" enough—he would have instantly recognized that reality and jumped for joy; here the very laws of time and space were all screwed up. No, this was a genuine phenomenon, the most extraordinary thing he—and probably anyone else—had ever seen.

Unless he was simply raving nuts. Or could he be dreaming, deep in a coma? Or had a stroke? An aneurysm? Hit by lightning? Manny was afraid to trust his own senses or his capacity for reason. His thoughts kept going around in circles with the shambling gait of a mad cow: fame and fortune or despair and death? Overstressed, his mind was starting to crash like a virus-infected computer, swamped in endless permutations of a single plea: *What does it mean? What the hell does it all mean?*

Finally he just had to stop, sit down, and zone out for awhile. Throw up. Meditate. Maybe even go to sleep. But something was gnawing at him, interfering with his rest, and at last it forced him back to his feet.

On top of everything else, he had to take a leak.

For many hours (he wasn't sure how much time had passed) this had seemed the least of his problems, but now it was finally rising to the forefront—if Manny didn't relieve himself soon, his bladder was going to explode.

But where? That hasty sun was already rising again, pointing him out for the whole tiny world to see. His surroundings seemed fairly uninhabited, sere and rugged, with only a few brown agricultural plots mowed amid the sparse green nap of pine forests. The blue sky was empty. But Manny thought he could feel millions of little eyes on him. He had always been a bit piss-shy—he could never go if someone was nearby, and often froze up before he could finish at public urinals. This, however, took stage-fright to a whole new level. Not only was he self-conscious, but he was afraid that he might rile his audience, causing them to renew their attacks at the moment when he was most…exposed.

So Manny wandered around in growing desperation as he searched for some semblance of privacy, until at last he could hold it no more. Turning his back on the lowlands, he entered a range of brushy gray mountains with patches of snow on their steep upper flanks. The tallest summit rose just over his head. Finding a shadowed ravine, he faced the back and unzipped his pants. His penis, larger than a Saturn V moon rocket, was erect, not from arousal but from the need to go, and Manny went—just barely in time.

The powerful stream shot out not as a clear yellow arc but a foaming white one; a million-gallon-a-minute jet such as would be produced by a colossal water-cannon or the opening of a dam's floodgate. It plunged down from a height of over two thousand feet, losing part of its volume as vapor before thundering upon the mountainside as a steaming, saline bludgeon—a punishing deluge that gouged out boulders and trees and turned the ravine into a cataract of tumbling brown slag. Hundreds of refugees were caught in the vile flash-flood that swept up everything in its path and finally emptied its cargo of salt and ammonia-laced debris miles downstream, into a reservoir.

Manny was aware of none of this. He gave in to blessed relief; the steaming, muddy trickle was only something to avoid stepping in. And in any case, what could he do about it? *When you gotta go, you gotta go*, he thought defensively, zipping up.

"Manny, can you hear me?"

The voice—*Karen's* voice—spoke as if from inside his head. The clarity and nearness of it caused him to jump with fright. Had he not just relieved himself, he would have peed his pants.

Staring around, heart hammering painfully, he thought, *No! There's no one there! It's your imagination!* He tried to hold himself together, but at the base of his fear was the terrifying knowledge that hearing voices was final proof that he was crazy, and getting worse.

"Manny—it's me, Karen Park. Can you hear me? Answer by saying yes or no."

"Oh God," Manny moaned, breaking into tears. "Please God, no. Not this."

"Don't be afraid—it's really me."

"Stop it! God!" Manny clamped his hands over his ears. "Just stop it, stop it!"

There was an uproar of some kind in his head. "*Not so loud!* Manny! Don't do that! We're inside your ear—the pressure's killing us! Listen to me!" The voice was clear as ever—he couldn't shut it out.

"Karen?" he ventured hesitantly, hating to say it aloud.

"Yes! Yes! It's me! Oh my God! Manny! I can hear you! I can hear you!"

Manny's reserve collapsed. "Oh God—Karen? Is it really you? Where are you?"

"In your ear, dummy! It's disgusting! I'm here with a bunch of soldiers. They have some kind of audio thingy so I can talk to you! This is incredible! Incredible!"

"Karen, I don't understand what's happening. I'm afraid I'm losing my mind."

"Welcome to my world, buddy-boy."

CHAPTER SIXTEEN:

STEERING COMMITTEE

"**a**nd so, gentlemen, this leaves us with a range of interesting options. I invite your thoughts on the matter."

The men in the room were stunned; they had had no idea such an ambitious covert operation had been authorized, much less successfully executed. In one stroke, it wiped out all their hectic war-planning of the past few days. Most were deeply resentful of the president for stealing the show out from under them: billions of dollars worth of emergency defense appropriations up in smoke!

The Chairman of the Joint Chiefs of Staff, Robert Moss, cleared his throat and leaned forward. "Mr. President, I'd like to be the first to congratulate you and General Chesnutt on a...remarkable accomplishment."

Several other men at the table, members of the President's party, immediately contributed their lukewarm applause as well. The rest made no pretence of approving anything the president did, and were already maneuvering for political advantage. The

Chairman of the House Armed Services Committee, Steven Cathcart, said, "Now wait a minute. Mr. President, in a matter of this importance, don't you think we should have been given the opportunity to at least discuss this plan of yours before it was put into effect?"

"Thank you, Steve. I wish I could say it was my plan, but I can't take much of the credit—it's really Colonel Queen's doing. He's been in the thick of it from the beginning. General Chesnutt is recommending him for the Congressional Medal of Honor."

"Hear hear," said Defense Secretary Cutler. As a retired general, a war hero, and an appointee of the previous administration, his support of the president cowed the complainers into grudging silence.

The president stepped into the breach: "In answer to your concerns, gentlemen, there was simply no time to debate the issue in advance. However, we now have certain choices to make, and it is absolutely crucial that we take full advantage of this little windfall as soon as possible, since we don't have any idea about its shelf life. Your thoughts, please."

Chairman Moss was first to speak. "Well, I suppose it depends on how accommodating our giant is. What can we get him to do?"

The president deferred to the defense secretary, who replied, "From what Chesnutt says, just about anything his girlfriend tells him to. He's psychologically vulnerable from the isolation, and she's his only lifeline."

"And we're hers."

"Exactly."

The men in the room began murmuring intently. Secretary of Defense Cutler cut them off: "Gentlemen, this gives us some heavy leverage in the region," he said. "Essentially we can do anything we want and blame it on a rogue behemoth. The only downside is we have to play dumb—we can't give any advance notice of the giant's movements, even to our own people, or the jig is up. Other than that, it's a total freebie."

This idea hushed the room like a ghost at a séance, frightening and yet grotesquely fascinating.

Secretary Cutler said, "I think the first thing we ought to do before commencing these proceedings is give a little prayer of thanks for the grave burden and responsibility we have been entrusted with by the Almighty."

There was solemn agreement, and the men all bowed their heads as Secretary Cutler intoned, "We thank you, O Lord, for this power we have been given, and which we wield in Your service, to smite down the forces of evil in the world. Amen."

Frustrated by the delay, the president said, "All right, gentlemen. Have at it."

Every man ransacked his most fanciful wish list, for once able to ignore the bureaucratic devil of prudence.

Chairman Cathcart said, "Excuse me, Mr. President, but we're talking hypothetical pure strategy right now, without political constraint?"

With a shrewd look, the president said, "That's right, Steve. You first."

"Okay." The man took a deep breath. "Since Pyongyang is working so hard to pin the blame on us, my suggestion would be a North Korea's Greatest Hits collection that includes strategic sites in Ich'on, Hwangju, Chunghwa, Pyongyang—"

"Okay, I get it—"

"—Chungsan, Sunch'on, Kaech'on—"

"Stop already."

"Followed by a world tour, with selected stops in China, Russia, the Middle East and Africa. Just for starters, mind you, assuming he lasts that long. I'm sure we can all think of an intractable problem or two that would benefit from the Baby Huey treatment."

There was guarded assent around the table.

The president said, "And what about Giant B? The woman?"

"Naturally we should follow the precedent so successfully set by General Chesnutt and Colonel Queen, and have a team infiltrate her at once. I assume that's why you've been holding off military action, isn't it? Two giants for the price of one?" This drew a chuckle from the room.

"That may not be so easy," the president said. "She's just been ID'd as a North Korean sleeper."

"What?" The bottom seemed to fall out of the War Room.

Consulting a sheet of paper, the CIA Director said, "Her name is Lee Yoon-sook, alias Dorothy Lee, alias Chara Yusa, alias Mudong—she's part of a cell that was operating out of Busan. So far that's all we know. But we think there's a good chance she may have her own defensive tactical team, because three separate attempts to board her have failed."

Chairman Cathcart exploded, "So the North Koreans *were* involved! After all their crying, they've been playing us for suckers! Well, I think that removes any doubts about where we ought to apply force. I say we ride roughshod over the border and give the Great Leader a taste of his own medicine."

"Not so fast," said the president. "I don't think you understand, Steve. This woman—a known enemy agent—is in Japan, heading for Tokyo. What do you propose we do about it?"

"We've got forces prepared to engage her at any time. What the hell have we been waiting for? Give the word."

"Conventional forces—that's bullshit. You saw what happened last time. And this is Japan, the most densely packed country on Earth. It'll be a wholesale massacre."

"So I assume you're not proposing nukes, then."

"No. I'm proposing that before we do anything else, we go with the recommendation just advanced to me by our point man in the field, Colonel Queen."

"And what was that?"

"That we go one-on-one."

CHAPTER SEVENTEEN:

HEAD AND SHOULDERS

With Manny under control, Queen and his men did what they were trained to do: set up a forward airfield. Soon there was a row of infrared landing-lights and a flashing beacon atop Manny's head, and a helicopter caravan began depositing supplies, people, and equipment around the clock.

A hidden tent-city sprang up amid the follicles, replete with decontamination showers, generators, science lab, canteen, and Patriot Missile batteries—an encampment soon dubbed "Hair Force One." Everything was surrounded with spindly wire enclosures called Faraday cages, which shielded instruments and men alike from the rampant electromagnetic bursts. Crude fortifications were built, using greasy chunks of dead skin cells in place of sandbags.

A series of lines and rope ladders carried commerce from the scalp to the smaller installation tucked within Manny's right ear, as well as to observation posts on both his shoulders. None of this was visible from the ground, and the skies were kept clear for fifty miles around by a cordon of constantly patrolling fighter aircraft.

"Okay, Karen, here's the situation as I see it," Queen said.

They were standing, fastened to a tether, on the reed-choked hummock of Manny's *antitragus*—a cartilaginous scenic overlook at the breezy entrance to Manny's outer ear canal. Above them was the soaring rim of the auricle, and to the rear yawned the hangar-sized cavern that was the ear canal proper. Below hung the bristled, bulging earlobe, sixty feet long, and then a five-hundred-foot drop to Manny's right shoulder. The late-afternoon sun was in their faces—it was a hell of a view.

After her initial contact with Manny, Karen had been sedated and slept for twenty-four hours, rehydrating via intravenous drip. While she was out, Dennison examined her from head to toe and freeze-treated with liquid nitrogen all the strange critters that had taken up lodging in the folds of her body.

Upon awakening, she had inhaled four MREs and been shown to a modular shower station, where she was thoroughly steam-cleaned with several cycles of hot water and disinfectant. At first it was heaven. Then Karen saw some of the stuff that was coming off her and suffered a momentary melt-down...but Dennison gave her something, and afterwards she felt a bit better. Not altogether well, but better.

"Am I going to die?" she had asked groggily.

"Die? I don't think so," Dennison said. "Why?"

"I, uh...*ate* something before. Something alive."

Dennison paused from disinfecting and patching her sores. "What was it?"

"I don't know. A big bug. I was so *thirsty*."

"What kind of bug? You mean like these things we're pulling off you?"

"Sort of, but much bigger." She spread her arms to illustrate. "It was when I was trapped out on the eyebrow. I was out of my mind with thirst."

"Did it look like this?" Dennison clicked his ballpoint and

crudely sketched an ugly, grub-like thing with eight stubby legs.

"Oh my God, that's it." She cupped her hand over her mouth, nodding. "That's so nasty. What is it?"

"Nothing to be afraid of. That's just our little buddy *demodex folliculorum*—he's a benign parasite that likes to hang out in oily places on the face, such as around eyelashes, blackheads, any oily follicle. There are probably hundreds living on you right now— well, no, we've just been decontaminated—but there normally would be. It's no big deal; they just eat sebum."

"Gross."

"Kind of, but it probably can't do you any harm to eat one."

"A giant, mutant louse?"

"For one thing, it's not a louse. For another, it's a mite. But before you freak out, realize that on the molecular level it's just another form of protein—the chemistry is basically the same as your average sushi. It only starts getting weird at the quantum level. Think of it like lobster. They're actually distant cousins."

"Oh, thanks, Dr. Science—I really needed to hear that."

But talking to Dennison had made her feel better. So much better, in fact, that she was now remembering what in the depths of her previous misery and exhaustion she had forgotten: the utter, screaming insanity and raw terror of what Colonel Harley Queen so blithely referred to as "the situation." Also, she hated heights.

"Okay," she said, gripping Queen's arm. "Shoot."

"Well, I'm sure you'll agree that we need Manny in good spirits. That means that I need you to reassure him, comfort him. You can imagine what he's going through; just try to soothe his anxieties so that he knows he's not alone, that we're all doing everything we can to help him."

"*Can* you help him?"

"I don't know. That's not up to me. I know there are a lot of people working on it as we speak. At the moment, you're the one who can help him the most, Karen, just by keeping him talking. It's important that you don't let your own fears creep into the conversation—that won't do Manny any good. Keep things light and upbeat. If he starts sounding depressed, steer things in a more positive direction."

"You want me to lie to him."

"It's not about lying. It's about keeping your boyfriend on an even keel so that he can function. One panic attack and it's all over. It's for his protection as well as everyone else's."

"Is that why you bombed us to kingdom come? For his protection?"

"I'm sorry about that. We just needed to stop him—he was heading for a major population center and a nuclear power plant. We tried to communicate with him first, but it was ineffective."

Karen remembered the talking plane—*oh my God*. "Is *that* what that was?"

"We used loudspeakers, but we didn't realize that we needed to broadcast at a much lower frequency in order for him to understand."

"You mean because of the size of his ears?"

"That's part of it, but it has more to do with the size of his brain. The increased distance his nerve impulses have to travel means he perceives everything much slower—even the passage of time. To him, ordinary speech is probably indecipherable twittering, like the sound you hear when you fast-forward a tape, or it may even be too high-pitched for him to hear at all. That's why there's the long processing-delay when you talk to him, because your voice has to be stretched out, and his has to be condensed. And his days must feel considerably shorter than ours. That's fortunate, because it gives us a little breathing room—on his timescale he won't be in dire need of food or water for some time yet."

"He said he was thirsty."

"Thirsty, yes; he wants a drink, but that doesn't mean the same thing as being dangerously dehydrated, as you were when we found you. Don't worry, we'll find him some water. That's the easy part."

"I don't think I want to know the hard part."

"You already do: keeping him happy."

"You know, I'm engaged to be married."

"We thought you might be concerned about that. Here." Dennison handed her a sealed security envelope. "This arrived by fax this morning."

Karen couldn't help giggling at the absurdity. "For me?"

Dennison wasn't smiling. "Yes."

She tore it open. It was a handwritten note from her fiancé, Yukio. It read:

Dearest Karen,

I know what is happening to you, and what you must do. Sometimes we must put our own feelings aside for the greater good—that is the definition of a hero. Nothing you have done or will ever do can change my feelings for you. Have courage, my darling, my wife, and know that I am with you in spirit, and eagerly await your triumphant return.

Eternally, Yukio

≥≠≤

Manny was beginning to feel like the moose in the Dr. Seuss story, or like a debutante practicing her posture. He could barely move without having to forewarn the ever-increasing population on his head and shoulders. Worse, they *itched*.

"How long is it going to be like this?" he asked Karen.

"I don't know, honey. Not much longer. You're being very brave."

"I wish I could see you."

"Me too, baby. I'm right here."

"I feel like I've lost my mind."

"Me too. But we haven't—it's the situation that's crazy."

"I just don't understand how this could *happen*."

"I know. It's weird, all that quantum crap. You'd have to be

Einstein to make sense of it."

"But why me? Why us? What did we ever do?"

"Nothing. It was just pure chance, honey. We were in the wrong place at the wrong time. Look at the bright side: at least we're alive, and together."

"I'm alive for now, but what am I supposed to do for food? Fine, I can drink water from lakes and reservoirs, but how am I going to keep from starving to death?"

"That's the first thing on the agenda. They're pointing you to some industrial food-storage facilities so you can at least have a nibble. Enough to tide you over until they can come up with a solution."

"Are they getting anywhere with that? Can you at least give me some idea of how it's going?"

"I guess it's all highly technical, but everybody seems pretty optimistic. The way they explained it to me is that your body—your 'quantum matrix'—is kind of a balloon blown up with Dark Matter, and they just have to figure out how to let the air out. It shouldn't be any harder than it was to get it in there. I definitely don't think you should worry."

"Oh, you don't? Oh goody—I feel so much better now."

"You know what I mean. Just take it one day at a time."

"I'm trying to, but my days are a lot shorter than yours."

"Yes, which means things are happening twice as fast as you think. Be patient. It'll all turn out okay."

"Easy for you to say."

"Hey, you don't think it's been difficult for me, too? I could've died up there. And it's no picnic living in your head, lemme tell ya. Have you ever looked inside somebody's ear? It's gross!"

"I'm sorry, Karen. I didn't mean to complain—I don't know what I would do without you."

"That's okay, it's a weird situation for everybody. Hey! We're going to get through this!"

"I know, I know. I love you."

It was the first time Manny had said those words to her, and Karen felt a deep chill. "I love you, too," she said queasily. "All right, here comes the latest course-correction: Turn left ninety degrees and continue in that direction for about twenty minutes. You should cross a major highway—that's the Jungbu Expressway. Try not to step on it."

"That's a big ten-four, good buddy. Just tell me one thing: Where are we going?"

"I told you, to some kind of food-storage facility on the southern coast."

"What kind of food?"

"They're telling me it's a holding depot for surplus bulk trade goods—it's so the government can manipulate market prices on imports like high-fructose corn syrup and wheat gluten."

"And that's what I'm supposed to eat?"

"Unless you'd rather wait for a McDonald's."

"No thanks—I already ate three of those."

"Did you ask for them Super-Sized?"

"You know, that's kind of insensitive."

"I'm sorry, honey. You know I didn't mean anything. I'm just trying to cheer you up."

"I was kidding. Besides, Super-Sizing is no longer offered at McDonald's. Or Mickey D's, as they prefer to be called."

"You big dummy."

Feeding Manny directions, Karen felt as if she was in the cockpit of a weird, padded spaceship. There was not a lot of room. Wearing comically large sound-canceling headphones, she was seated inside an igloo of anti-acoustic foam batting, between a cool air blower and banks of TV monitors. The shelter was secured inside Manny's cavernous ear canal by tent pegs that had been driven into resinous brown outcroppings of earwax. Fluorescent lights made the tent glow.

Queen, Dennison, and a very terrified Samsung sound engineer manned laptops that processed Karen's voice and transmitted it via a set of highly amplified, 5000-watt subwoofers to Manny's eardrum, which filled the rear of the dark cave like a forty-foot-high gong. There was a constant loud throbbing from Manny's pulse in there, making it a difficult place to work at the best of times, but when Manny spoke, using even his softest voice, this organ and the cavernous canal leading to it quivered and thrummed with a pounding reverberation so intense that it could cause spontaneous vomiting and internal bleeding to any unprotected bystander. These bass vibrations were in turn picked up, recorded, and digitally condensed so as to render them sensible to ordinary ears.

Karen was abiding the long processing interval between her speech and Manny's reply, watching the external video feed. She was eating a Lotte chocolate bar. The main TV picture was a forward view of the bobbing landscape, with smaller side and rear views inset like thumbnails. Superimposed on the bottom right of the screen was a digital compass and GPS coordinates.

"Karen," said Queen.

"Yeah?"

"Let me tell you what we need to do."

"Okay."

"This may be a little hard for you to deal with—I want you to understand that there is just no other option. If there was another option, we would do it."

"I'm listening."

"Karen, you told me before that you have no idea how Manny got this way."

"That's right."

"That you and he were just on a USO tour, you took a romantic walk on the beach, and bam!—everything went nuts. Is that right?"

"I didn't say it was romantic. I was there to end the affair."

"Okay, but that's all it was? You and Manny were together the whole time? He didn't meet with anyone, or disappear for any length of time? Nothing strange happened?"

"No. The only weird thing was at the end, on the beach. That scream…and the whatever-it-was. The Event, I guess."

"And you've never heard the name Wilfred Isaacson? *Doctor* Wilfred Isaacson?"

"Nope. Sorry."

"That's too bad, Karen, because it would really help if you knew something. Something we could use against *her*. As it is, we have no choice but to send Manny."

"Send him where?" she asked suspiciously. "Against who?"

"Does the name Lee Yoon-sook mean anything to you?"

"No."

"Dorothy Lee?"

"Nope."

"Let me tell you a little bit about her. She's North Korean, born in a little town called Chinsong, on the Chasong River, not far from the Chinese border. She was orphaned at age eight when both her parents were arrested by the North Korean secret police—her father and mother had been North Korean expatriates living in Japan, and had accepted a government offer to return to North Korea. The terms of the repatriation were supposed to include regular contact with the wife's family, but this was never allowed, and the two got into trouble for complaining too loudly.

"Lee was sent to an orphanage, and then to the Mangyngdae Revolutionary Institute, where she was indoctrinated into the philosophy and methods of the State Security Department. As a young woman, she became a member of the Korean Worker's Party—the North Korean elite. In 2003 she entered Japan on a diplomatic passport and promptly disappeared. Then the assassinations began—eleven in Japan, nine in South Korea, all targeting opponents of the regime, all unsolved. Yoon-sook was not suspected at first…until she was spotted in the background of separate press photographs taken at different times, of two different victims."

Queen paused, then said, "She is now twenty-eight years old, and is considered very dangerous. She was considered very dangerous even before she became a mile-high giantess, and right now she's ravaging southern Japan on her way to Tokyo. The only thing that might be able to stop her is your boyfriend, Manny."

Karen's face twitched, her mind stuttering over this indigestible kernel of information. "She's what? He *what?*"

Queen said, "She won't respond to low-frequency hails, and a few minutes ago she obliterated the infiltration team we tried to drop on her. Opened her mouth and inhaled them. She's wiping out military and strategic sites as she goes—the country's whole infrastructure is breaking down, blacking out prefecture by prefecture. In a matter of days Japan will be back in the Stone Age, defenseless."

Karen was still trying to catch up. "You're telling me there's *another* giant?"

"Yes."

"Not just Manny?"

"No."

"And you want him to *stop* her?"

"Yes."

"Stop her how? By killing her?"

"It depends. We're hoping it won't come to that."

"Stop blowing smoke up my ass. What if *she* kills *him?*"

"She won't, not if we can help it—Manny has some training in Tae Kwan Do, and he's going to have the combined strength of our Armed Forces up his sleeve."

"So to speak."

"So to speak."

"And you expect me to tell him all this?"

"That's what I'm asking you. Do you think you can persuade him?"

"Why don't you just order him to? Isn't he still on the payroll?"

"We could try that as a last resort, yes…but we have no leverage if he refuses. Karen, this is very, very important." He reached out and touched her shoulder. "Can you do it?"

Karen retreated a step, warding him off with an upraised hand, her face scrunched up as if whiffing acrid fumes of horseshit. She didn't know what to believe. Then she let out a long, shuddering breath and stared at Queen searchingly, shaking her head.

"We're all fucked, aren't we?" she said helplessly. "Yeah, I'll try."

Manny took it well—better than Karen expected.

"What else can I do?" he replied. "Sure, I'll give it a shot."

"They don't expect you to kill her," she said, flustered by his easy acquiescence.

Karen had assumed he would refuse out of hand, and who could blame him? It was stupid! She was upset that he wasn't giving it the proper weight, and here she had promised not to do anything to dissuade him—why did she let Queen put her up to this? Too late, she realized that Manny was probably doing it for her, the idiot. Just as Queen had been counting on.

"You don't have to prove anything; don't try to be a hero," she said. "Just get her to stop any way you can. But you have to be on guard in case she attacks you, and the military will be there to back you up."

Manny asked, "She speaks English, right?"

"They think so. If not, we'll translate for you."

"Okay. Well, point me in the right direction, and let's see what happens."

"Are you sure about this?" Karen ignored Queen's warning look and said, "You don't have to do this."

"No, it's okay. I'll do it."

"Really? You're *sure*?"

"Sure I'm sure. It's not like I have anything else to do."

What Karen couldn't have known was the thrill of relief Manny felt, discovering that he was not alone. There was another! He was so excited his eyes were watering up, causing great splattering explosions of glutinous saltwater every time he blinked.

In spite of Karen's cautions, Manny couldn't imagine having to fight or kill this other person—this spy woman. He *remembered* her, the murderess who shot that other man on the beach, and then almost shot *him*: that whipcord strength, that *voice*, that harsh piranha face behind the gun. She was the most striking and dangerous-looking creature he had ever seen. Manny didn't doubt that she was a killer—she was scary enough—yet somehow he wasn't afraid of her. In fact, the very thought of meeting her made his blood pound in his head and his ears hot, as if he were a teenager anticipating his first date.

What Manny knew that Karen didn't—that no one else could— was that all ideologies faded to insignificance when you thought you were the last person on Earth. When it was brought home how totally indifferent the universe was to you and the rest of mankind, and how thin the veneer of civilization—a glorified, electrified colony of ants. Ants! They should kill each other for that? Common sense told him that his female counterpart would be so overjoyed to have any company at all in this desolate predicament that the two of them should instantly fall weeping into each other's arms. They *needed* each other, as much as any two people ever had since Adam and Eve.

The fact that she might have killed untold thousands, millions, or destroyed vast tracts of civilization did not mean the same thing to Manny that it did to Karen. It was a totally abstract concept. Not that he didn't care, but he knew first-hand how difficult it was *not* to cause wanton destruction, whether you meant to or not.

They weren't telling him, yet Manny knew for a fact that he himself was leaving an enormous trail of ruin everywhere he went. He was a walking apocalypse, a living weapon of mass-destruction! When he so much as drank from a lake, he fouled it and flooded the whole countryside. It was not something he let himself dwell on; there was simply nothing he could do about it. Was it evil to want to live?

Manny could tell by the sun that he was being guided east again, back toward the sea. That made sense, if he was going to Japan.

"Hey," he said. "Am I going to have to swim?"

It took Karen longer than normal to get back to him. "No," she said. "You can wade all the way to Honshu on the Continental Shelf. The whole Korea Strait is less than a hundred feet deep—you'll barely get your feet wet. It should only take you a couple of hours to cross, and you'll be at Mount Fuji by tomorrow."

"Cool. I've always wanted to see that."

"But first we want you to stop off for a snack at the Goseong Shipping Terminal—it should be coming up soon. Follow the signal planes, and try to walk as softly as you can."

"*Tiptoe…through the tulips…*" Manny sang softly.

"Okay, Tiny Tim. That's enough singing. You're throwing all the instruments out of whack."

"Imagine if I had a ukulele."

"Talk about a weapon of mass-destruction."

Manny had been noticing that the landscape was covered with a thin mantle of smog, and that the green and brown of agriculture was being taken over by urban patches of gray. It had an oddly familiar look to him—the minute traceries of silicon chips and motherboards. Karen helped guide him between the densest concentrations, but he could still see buildings toppling outward like dominoes with every step, and fire blooming in every footprint. *God!* It was so frustrating—so fucking delicate. But at least he had the comfort of knowing that his path had been cleared, the populations evacuated.

Now he could see the ocean, that great leaden puddle. Several airplanes trailing streamers of smoke crossed in front of him, and he followed the twisting ribbons. They ended at an industrial complex on the waterfront, a tank farm that was probably huge by human standards, but to Manny resembled nothing so much as a scrawny patch of toadstools.

"Is that it?" he asked.

"That's it."

As carefully as he could—not just to avoid wrecking the place, but also to avoid dislodging his passengers—Manny crept up and reached his thousand-foot arm for the nearest thimble-sized white cylinder...

Shit! He barely so much as touched it, and the thing toppled flat, spilling its meager contents. Manny dipped a pinky into the spreading wet spot and tasted it: sweet. The next one he tried gently tipping onto the ends of his fingers, so that when it inevitably collapsed, it would at least spill into his hand. This was only slightly more effective; most of the thin nectar ran through his fingers before he could get it to his mouth.

"This isn't working," he said.

"Try the warehouses."

Manny tiptoed to a row of buildings resembling cigar boxes, and delicately tapped one. It peeled open in a dust blossom. Manny licked his finger and dipped it into the cloud; it came out coated white, trailing smoke. He sucked it, tasting something weirdly salty and sweet at the same time. "What is that?" he asked.

"Monosodium glutamate."

"Huh. You know, I'm not really that starving. Can we just get started? I feel like I'm wasting valuable time here."

"Manny, you need your strength."

"Strength? I'm full up on strength, sweetie, and I don't need any size, either. I'm fine, let's just go."

"Are you really sure?"

"Yes, I'm sure."

"Well...all right. If you're sure..."

"I'm sure! I'm sure! Do you want me to just go into the water here, or is there someplace else you had in mind?"

Manny didn't like the idea of just stepping into the sea amid this delicate profusion of dockside industry, with its fuzz of finely-spun wires and spindly cranes, but he had to go to the bathroom.

He wasn't even in the harbor yet, and it was already awash with the ripples he was causing—tiny vessels were battering against the wharves, crumpling like tinfoil and swamping with frothy boils.

These ships were rather disturbing for Manny to see. They were so beautiful in their perfect detail, small as rows of shoes, and yet some of them were huge things—not just abstract geometrical shapes like buildings, but familiar objects of wonder, rusty steel behemoths which Manny had once stared up at in awe, now reduced to tissue-flimsy toys. Because of their size, he could get a pretty good look at them even from a distance; they were a vivid yardstick of what was human scale…and what was Manny scale. They made it all too real for him. He fidgeted, wanting to get out of there.

"Hold on, honey," said Karen. "Hold right there."

"I'm holding."

"Manny?"

"Yes?"

"Um, there's been a change of plans. Hold on."

"I'm right here." He fidgeted, feeling his bowels rumble.

"Okay. Here's what's happening: It looks like the other giant has stopped short of Tokyo and headed west, into the Pacific."

"Good. What happens now?"

"I'm waiting for them to tell me. It's kind of a weird situation. They're saying she's been just lying in the middle of Suruga Bay on her back, not moving."

Manny felt a deep pang of loneliness. "Is she dead?"

There was a long pause, then Karen said, "They think she may be taking on passengers."

"*What?*"

"Japan's defense ministry is reporting sonar signals in the vicinity of her head. There are no ships authorized to be in there. They think it's a diesel-electric submarine, possibly containing enemy agents."

"You're kidding me."

"I know, it's insane. Oop—new report coming in. She's on the move again, heading out to sea."

"Enemy agents from where?"

"They're not sure. But obviously somebody with an agenda, and a navy, and who can communicate with her. That suggests China or North Korea."

"Oh—great."

"I know, honey, I don't like it, either. This is becoming a fucking arms race."

"With real arms. But it sounds like we're jumping to conclusions. If she's been stopped from attacking Tokyo, that's a good thing, right? Maybe the sub is one of ours."

Karen's voice was grim: "She's heading due west, Manny. Towards America."

CHAPTER EIGHTEEN:

END-RUN

"They want to know how good a swimmer you are."

"I'm not sure I can swim the whole Pacific Ocean, if that's what they want to know. How far would it be for me?"

"About ten miles. Not our miles, yours. But the hardest part would be the beginning—once you were past the Japan Trench, there would be a lot of places shallow enough for you to touch bottom. We'd guide you so you could rest along the way." Karen sounded very doubtful. "I'm not trying to sell you on it. Personally, I think it's nuts. For one thing, she has too big a head-start—you'll never catch up with her."

"I think you're probably right. I'm not that much of a swimmer anyway." Manny pictured himself out there, far out of the sight of land, with his feet hanging down in black abyssal depths. One thing he had learned from walking the landscape: this planet was still plenty big enough to make him feel small. "I'm not going to do anyone any good if I drown out there," he said. "What's the alternative?"

"Go overland. North along the Continental Shelf to the Kamchatka Peninsula, and then west following the Aleutian Islands to Alaska. It's more roundabout, the equivalent of a fifteen-mile hike, but you'll make much better speed than she will. The Pacific Fleet will do everything it can to soften her up, and you can intercept her when she comes ashore."

"Boy, you guys have got it all worked out, don't you?"

"Hey, I just read what they give me."

"I'm not sure if I like the idea of the Navy attacking her while she's helpless out there. Especially after she spared Tokyo. How do they know she intends to harm anyone? There's no such thing as a gentle giant when you're this size; it's totally impossible. Maybe *that's* why she went into the sea, did you ever think of that? To avoid hurting people. And now you're going to drop a bunch of bombs on her head."

"Manny! *I'm* not dropping any bombs! I'm just trying to cooperate so that we can get out of this fucking nightmare in one piece."

"I'm sorry, sweetie. I know. It's just that...you can't imagine how empty and alien the world feels from where I'm standing. It's like being marooned, condemned to die, all alone. It's not conducive to hate. All that petty political crap seems light-years away. This woman is probably very afraid, feels very cut off, and would respond best to simple kindness, a human voice. Look how well it's working with me."

"You're different. Besides, they tried that, and they're going to keep trying. But don't forget she's a trained killer, brainwashed to hate America, and possibly being manipulated by state-sponsored terrorists. Once she gets ashore in the States, it'll be too late to get on her good side."

"Not true—I think that's when she'll be the most receptive: when she's cold and tired and waterlogged. She'll be dragging herself ashore, and I'll be standing there to offer her the hand of friendship...or to stop her. Get her before she can catch her breath. But wouldn't it be better to at least try to win her over to our side? Think about it: a friendly face where she least expects to find one. A fellow human being after everything she's been through—you have no idea how much that would mean. Just let me try. For all you know, she's trying to defect."

"Manny, you know it's not my decision. I'm just the mouthpiece here. All I can tell you—all they're telling *me*—is that they're taking everything under consideration."

"How about if I tell them I refuse to go on this walkathon unless they promise?"

"Then you leave them no choice but to go after her with everything they've got."

"Shit. I'm going. You know I'm going. Just tell them to take it easy on her, will you? Leave me something to work with, for Christ's sake."

"I'll tell them. And Manny?"

"Huh?"

"We're in this together, honey."

"I know."

Taking off the headset, Karen said, "I think he's interested in her."

"Does that make you jealous?" asked Queen.

"No, just worried."

"Worried because you think it might make him vulnerable?"

"Yes, and because of what you might do to prevent that possibility. Manny isn't stupid, you know. He knows she's dangerous; he'll take every precaution."

Saying the word *precaution* made Karen think about how she hadn't used any birth control with Manny, and how worried she was about what Yukio would do if she gave birth to a little brown baby. *Stupid!* It was her own fault for getting drunk.

"I feel like fucking Fay Wray," she said uneasily.

Queen nodded slowly, scrutinizing her. "''Twas Beauty killed the Beast."

Karen was caught short. "Don't tell me that."

"I wonder if you're really on board with this mission, Karen."

"What is *that* supposed to mean? Why? Because I think he deserves to know what's going on? Because I don't want to bullshit him?"

"That's part of it. I didn't lose half my men and risk my ass rescuing you so that you could undermine our efforts just because you feel *guilty*, not with billions of lives at stake. Karen, Manny is not the Manny you loved anymore—you know that and I know that. Your job is to *pretend* that he is, nothing more. He has a much more important role to play, and so do you. All of us are on borrowed time here; we can't be thinking of ourselves. Too many lives have been lost already. Feelings aren't any part of the equation."

"Oh my God—this is unreal."

"I know that's hard, and I'm sorry. Look, I have a family, too—this isn't any easier for me. Anyway, your personal feelings for Manny are not really what's worrying me. I'm still concerned that both of you are manipulating things to promote a hidden agenda."

"What fucking agenda?"

"Before we can go any farther, Karen, I need an act of faith from you and Manny. A show of loyalty, something to demonstrate once and for all that neither of you is in the pocket of Pyongyang. That it is not simply your intention to join forces with a known terrorist in order to attack America."

Karen listened to this, agape. Cheeks flushing with anger, she said, "That is the single stupidest thing I've ever heard."

"Then you must've heard some whoppers, because it sounds pretty plausible to me. Look at it from my point of view: You were all in the same place at the same time, you and Manny are a couple of armchair liberals with arguably radical politics who have come to work for the military, you've taken Korean language lessons, and have consorted with suspicious local elements—"

"What 'local elements'?"

"Your landlord, Mr. Wang, for one. Also some Peace Corps people and a local chiropractor."

"Are you serious? That was a fondue party!"

Queen read on, "You travel frequently, keep to yourselves, and have no close friends in either the military or DoDDS community. It all adds up. How can you prove it isn't so?"

"Oh my God. I *can't* prove it, okay? You know that! So where does that leave us? You want a loyalty oath?"

"No, you *can* prove it, Karen. You and Manny can prove it."

"How?"

"The first leg of Manny's course will take him north. Now, he can skirt North Korea entirely by traveling through Japan and along the Kurils to Kamchatka…"

"Yes…?"

"…or he can break through the Demilitarized Zone and wipe out the offensive forces that are gathering there. Our intelligence tells us they are only a matter of hours from a full-scale invasion of the South, under the pretext of destroying Manny. With our remaining forces divided, Manny is the only thing that can hold them back, short of a nuclear bomb. If you can get him to agree to this, it will be the ultimate proof that both of you are as innocent as you claim."

"Oh my God."

"It's a big decision. You should ask him."

"Fine. And what if he doesn't want to? What happens then?"

"He has the right to say no. We can't make him do anything. But it will change your level of involvement—yours and Manny's. He will have to move offshore to Cheju-do and sit out the fighting, or be considered a clear and present danger. Needless to say, America will be out of bounds to him. Meanwhile, our remaining forces will be divided between the other giant and the North Korean invasion forces. We will likely lose South Korea and Japan, but not before nuclear war breaks out. China will probably get involved, and all the superpowers will go head-to-head. Do I have to tell you what that means?"

"Shit," Karen said under her breath, clutching her head in her arms. "Shit, shit, shit…"

≥≠≤

"Everything secured?"

Queen had gone over Manny's whole head, a lightning inspection that revealed a few minor deficiencies, but on the whole confirmed for him that the men knew what they were in for. As if anyone could know such a thing.

"Everything's been battened down as tight as possible," Dennison said. "Unless the stresses are much more extreme than anticipated, they should hold fast. We know it's survivable—Karen has already been through it."

"She wasn't nuked," said Queen wryly.

"No. That's the wild card. Let's hope they don't play it."

"Not unless they want to nuke themselves in the process."

"I know, but still…" Carl Dennison shrugged warily. "Anyway. At your order."

"Don't rush me. I'm working up to it." Queen paused, took several deep breaths, became still, then said, "All right, execute Touchdown."

"Order received and acknowledged. Executing Touchdown." Dennison activated the audio equipment and signaled across the soundproof barrier to Karen.

"Oh crap," she said. Trembling, she picked up the microphone. "Manny? It's time." Her voice was recorded and synthesized and rolled out like hot asphalt. The deep thrumming of the subwoofers filled the ear canal, reverberating against the eardrum. What had taken her less than three seconds to say was spread over half a minute.

Then came Manny's reply, many times louder. It was like a

prolonged earthquake, teeth-rattling, and when it was finished the voice playback was laughably anticlimactic, as usual: "I know," he said. "Full speed ahead."

And at that, Manny began to run.

He had already spent most of the night walking north, being briefed; now it was dawn. They had charted a course that took him far east of Seoul and through the most mountainous and thereby least populated border region, hoping that the four-thousand foot Mount Baegamsan, which straddled the DMZ, would shield Manny's approach until the very last moment.

Manny felt as though he was running along a powdery creek bottom, each footstep kicking up a glowing jet of dust, each plume making way for the next. Mountainsides crumbled as he passed. The ground was springy and very suitable for jogging, its peat-like surface flinging debris like a flapped rug, to bury ponds and thinly trickling rivers. The shockwave of Manny's passing scoured the land down to bedrock. His ears were hot from air friction.

It felt good to run—to just give in to the momentum and not look back. Not think. Running, he couldn't make out any trace of human presence, or of anything extraordinary. It was easy to imagine that this was no more than a patch of undeveloped property, a vacant lot back home, and that at any moment he might hear a bird or a car engine. He desperately missed the ambient sounds of life. All he could hear was the *chuff-chuff* of his footsteps, the pounding of blood in his head. He was dry-mouthed and nervous.

"Approaching the DMZ," said Karen's grainy voice. "Cover up, hon."

Manny carefully raised the collar of his coat up around his ears, hunching over and shielding his face like someone trying to duck photographers. He was moving at a brisk five hundred miles an hour, the speed of a commercial jet (though at his scale, he still appeared to be running in slo-mo)—for Manny, a healthy trot.

North Korean guard posts along the foothills of Mt. Baegamsan saw him a long way off. They had been watching the southern fence line very carefully for hours, ever since it appeared that Southern border patrols were not following standard routines. Around midnight there had been unusual vehicle activity, and then there had been no movement at all. For hours not a single sentry had been seen. The watch captain had awakened the guard commander, who had frowningly surveyed the desolate frontier through night-vision telescopes. Something was wrong: The South had been beefing up security for days, why would they suddenly pull out? Was fighting the giant *angma* draining their forces to that degree already? Not just the extra troops, either— the posts appeared to be abandoned. He had never witnessed such a thing. An alert was issued all down the line.

Now, the commander felt the ground shake, saw the trees wobble, and heard the echo of landslides—then saw the unimaginable as it loomed higher than the snow-streaked mountain in the bright morning sky. He knew exactly what was going on. But it was too late.

Manny never even saw the southern border of the Demilitarized Zone as he approached it. From the height of his eyes, it showed only as a narrow, shaved-looking strip; the fence itself was invisible. At ground level, multiple layers of twenty-foot-tall, razor-ribbon-topped chain link, enclosing fantastic barbed-wire briars—electrified and rigged with motion-sensing fragmentation mines—blew away before Manny's toes like wisps of cobweb. As he crossed the overgrown woodlands of the DMZ, he couldn't even feel the thousands more mines popping off under the thick soles of his feet. Then he was through the opposite fortifications and into North Korea.

On the other side of the mountain, Karen instructed him to cut left. As he did this, he encountered his first resistance: a squadron of hastily scrambled North Korean MiG fighters firing air-to-air missiles. At the same time, homegrown Scuds zeroed in from ground batteries to the north. Some of the missiles crumpled against Manny's shockwave and were deflected, careening out of control into the hills. Most detonated against the massive, trunk-like wool fibers of his coat, leaving marks like cigarette burns. Manny didn't notice them.

"Okay, you're coming up on the Iron Triangle," said Karen. "Run faster."

The Iron Triangle region had been the staging point for heavy Communist troop mobilizations during the Korean War, and was once again the biggest concentration of North Korean forces—a vast base of operations fronting the central DMZ. Now Manny could see patches of antlike activity: seething masses of tiny bugs that were entire tank divisions and supply convoys. Harder to see were the scattering hordes of soldiers—hundreds of thousands of men flowing like wispy shadows over the land. But they saw him.

Suddenly the air was full of smoke strands, weaving across Manny's path like spider silk, terminating in thousands of tiny black puffs. They crackled and stung. He kept running, closing the coat tighter around his face, but it was impossible to keep them all out. Flinching at each snap, he kicked up as much dirt as possible, and scattered big handfuls of soil in all directions. He was getting tired.

The intensity of the attacks seemed to be lessening. He slowed down to catch his breath, clearing his path with a few more showers of dirt, then flapped his coat around over his head at supersonic speeds to clear the sky. Planes and missiles hit this expanding wave of turbulence as if striking a brick wall. Manny winced, tasting blood from a split lip. Looking back, he was startled to see that the landscape was blanketed in thick, rolling dust, spreading outward from his wake like brown magma. There were flashes and spots of glowing orange within it. Fire. Death and destruction. The thought made him a little sick.

"How much farther?" he asked. "I'm beat."

"Lee says that's far enough in this direction. We're approaching the Han River, which could be dangerous to Seoul if you mess with it. You've done enough here. Turn back northeast and we'll make for Vladivostok."

"Not another city."

"No, we'll go around it and wade the Sea of Japan to Hokkaido and then the Kurils."

"Who's Lee?"

"He's in charge of everybody here, on you. Colonel Harley Queen."

"Lee is his nickname?"

"Short for Harley."

"I get it. Is he there now?"

"Yes."

"Can I talk to him?"

"He says it would take time to set up—I guess the computer system is calibrated to my voice. He says congratulations."

"For what?"

"For successfully completing phase one of this expedition. You're a hero."

"Huh, Okay. Well, tell Colonel Queen that I want him to make sure he lets you get enough rest. You shouldn't have to be on the horn with me twenty-four hours a day. We have a long trip ahead."

"That's so sweet. Thank you, honey, but you shouldn't worry about me. I'm okay."

"I worry about you."

"I worry about you, too, snuggums."

"Moogly-poo."

"Sweetie-banoonie."

"I love you."

"I love you, too."

≥≠≤

The War Room was deadly solemn. Things were happening so fast—vast losses, vast gains. Every minute a new report of incalculable destruction and death.

"That's it," said the Chairman of the Joint Chiefs. "We've just confirmed that North Korea has lost most of its invasion force— its whole southern front is completely wiped out, and the border is impassible virtually from coast to coast. Ten armored divisions, sixteen infantry brigades, fifty miles of minefields, all gone in one fell swoop. We've leveled the playing field, Mr. President. There is officially no longer any threat of a conventional attack from the DPRK."

"Holy God," the president said, obviously shaken. "All right. What about an unconventional one?"

"We don't think so. There's a rumor that the Great Leader was in Ch'onam reviewing the troops when the shit hit the fan. They're still too busy looking for him. And Manny is already far offshore, in international waters."

"What about China, or Russia?"

"Nothing so far. Vladivostok just took a big hit to its Navy base and waterfront from Manny-spawned tsunamis, but so far the Russians are treating it like a natural disaster. The Chinese, too. I think they're looking at North Korea and counting themselves lucky that the threat is moving towards Japan. They may be waiting to see what we're going to do."

The Secretary of Defense said, "Oh, I'm sure we'll think of something."

The other generals chuckled grimly.

The Chairman of the Joint Chiefs said, "Frankly, Mike, there's a lot more we can do on this side of the pond. Are you sure we should be bringing him to our backyard?"

Secretary Cutler snapped, "He's proven his reliability, Bob."

"And also his extreme menace."

The president interjected, "That's why we need him. Gentlemen, considering what's just become of the Seventh Fleet, I don't think we have any choice, do you? Do any of you?"

CHAPTER NINETEEN:

THE MILE-HIGH CLUB

Harley Queen and Karen Park were alone in Manny's ear, finally taking a respite from the monotony of adjusting his course. Until now it had been impossible to point him in a direction and leave him to it; unless there were clear landmarks to follow, he tended to drift. Without constant tweaking, he'd have wound up in Siberia. But now the Continental Shelf was a broad, shallow track that Manny could wade along by feel, allowing them to rest for a while.

Karen really felt like she was in a strange airship of some kind, a tottering zeppelin with feet. The video feeds from all directions showed land as a distant smudge on the northern horizon, with puffy clouds casting their shadows upon the sea. The size of their wake was truly astounding, and there were reports of undersea earthquakes with every plunging step.

Manny was plodding along knee-deep, following a series of comparatively shallow undersea ridges that connected Asia with the United States. They were as clear as a dotted line on a map. Without much navigational help, he had been able to trace these shallows northward around the Kamchatka Peninsula, and then west across the Aleutians. Deep trenches on either side made it very hard for him to lose the trail, even in low visibility or at night—it was like being on autopilot.

In a matter of hours they would make landfall in Alaska, and begin the race down the West Coast.

To help keep Manny going in the intervals when Karen needed rest, Psy-Ops had recommended playing upbeat music over the tympanic sound system, just so he didn't fall into a funk. They wanted to discourage him from thinking too much. To this end they chose neutral selections from the Top-40 canon, with a few gung-ho country songs thrown into the mix. Karen's suggestions, based on Manny's eclectic tastes—from Elvis Presley to Elvis Costello—were declined as being "too conducive to idiosyncratic modes of thought" and "not pro-cooperative."

"What do you think?" Karen had asked him as the music cut in.

"Wow! That's amazing!" Manny replied.

"Really?"

"Yeah! Thanks, sweetie!"

In fact, when Manny first heard the music, he was so surprised and gratified that he accepted it without really caring what kind of music it was, and afterwards he was too embarrassed to complain, not wanting to hurt Karen's feelings. They weren't playing it that loudly, anyway—he supposed he could live with it…for now.

Inside Manny's ear, at human scale, the tunes were not recognizable as music at all, but as a constant, bass din, just another layer of sound added to the ambient throb of Manny's internal processes. Nestled in their anechoic igloo and wearing sound-canceling headphones, Karen and Queen could only feel the deep, rhythmic vibrations, a constant, full-body vibro-massage which had the unexpected side-effect of first pleasantly loosening their pent-up muscular tension, and then giving them a ticklish sensual awareness.

Karen was trying to nap, to forget about the untold thousands being killed by tsunamis in their wake, but the electric pulsations were beginning to make her antsy—she felt like she was hyped up on caffeine, like she could scream. Fiddling with the microphone, she looked over at Queen, and he too was frowning, arms and legs crossed as he tried to concentrate on the monitors. Although they were alone, the big tent seemed very close. Sensing her looking, he glanced up and their eyes met.

"You should be trying to sleep," he said.

"I am," she said. "But I think I'm too wired."

"Do you need a sedative? I'll buzz Dennison."

"No, it's not that. How long do you think Manny can go like this? He hasn't had any sleep for a week."

"You know how it works—that's probably about a day to him. Less."

"I know, but…"

"You're worried about him."

"Of course I am. Even though I know it's over between us, I still have feelings for him."

"Sure, I understand. That's all right."

"What about you? Your wife must be worried to death about you." Karen had noticed the gold band on his finger.

"Probably. It goes with the job. I don't handle the whole husband thing too well—it's actually easier for both of us when I'm on assignment."

"That's kind of sad."

Queen shrugged. "Not really. It's just something we've had to overcome. You either make do, or you don't. In a way we're lucky, because if I was home all the time we'd be miserable. I know that."

Karen couldn't help smiling, "That's a pretty cynical view of marriage."

"Just realistic."

She was having trouble concentrating; her nipples were so hard, they were chafing against the fatigue blouse she had been given. "Do you have any children?" she asked.

"Two. Two boys."

"That probably makes a difference, too. I don't know if I could break up if I had kids."

"Do you want kids?"

"Someday…"

"It's not as easy as you hope."

"I bet."

"Nothing ever works out quite the way you figure it should. You think you're doing everything right, and then something comes along and blows it all to pieces."

"Tell me about it."

"I'm not talking about all *this*." He impatiently gestured around, encompassing the Manny situation. "I don't give a damn what happens to me. But I expected my *kids* to have a chance. If they don't have a future, what difference does it make if I save the rest of the world?"

Karen was reluctant to speak, to interrupt Queen's abrupt inward change. Softly, she said, "They will. That's what we're doing this for."

Queen didn't acknowledge her, caught up in dark thoughts of his own. Suddenly he blurted, "My older son—Harley Jr.—had asthma. He had to carry around an inhaler all the time. That's one of the reasons I got myself transferred to Okinawa from Incirlik, because the air was cleaner. The thing that sticks in me is that for the longest time I felt let down, like it wasn't fair that everyone else's kids were crazy athletes, involved with soccer, football, basketball, and my son was the weakling who couldn't play touch football on the lawn. I was ashamed of him…and he knew it."

"Hey, life is a process, you know? You're probably a better father for it. It's a learning experience—that's the whole point. Nobody's born wise."

"That's just it—Harley was. That kid was noble; he had a big heart. Last summer he got into the habit of walking me to work, and every day we would pass this rain puddle full of tadpoles—

thousands of them. Well, over time the puddle starts drying up, the tadpoles getting more and more crowded together. It was kind of this grim race for time: Could the tadpoles become frogs before their water evaporated? As the days went on, it was obvious they weren't going to make it—they were packed solid in there. I thought it was kind of interesting, a little life lesson to show him that things don't always happen the way they do on TV. But Harley wasn't content with that. He decided to intervene. The next time we went there, he had a big plastic bucket. I thought it was to collect the tadpoles, but that wasn't his idea at all— he didn't want to totally disrupt the scheme of things. He just wanted to tweak it a little. What he did was, he took his bucket up to a school drinking fountain nearby and used it to refill the puddle. It must have taken him ten trips, wheezing like hell, but he filled that thing."

"Did they make it?"

"The tadpoles? Oh yeah. That was all they needed. Over the next week or so they developed little legs and everything. By the time the puddle dried up again, every single one was gone."

"That's great. Great kid."

"Tell you the truth, I've just been realizing that the idea behind this mission came from that. That I shouldn't expect the worst of people. My son educated me. I would've never thought of it otherwise, that's for damn sure."

"Well, that's kind of my philosophy of life: It's all a game of musical chairs."

Queen looked at Karen as if he had forgotten she was there. "How so?"

"I think the Universe recycles itself over and over again, and we all get a turn in each other's shoes."

"You mean reincarnation."

"I guess, but not from one lifetime to the next, like Buddhism. My theory is that it's from one Big Bang to the next. Each Big Bang reshuffles the deck."

"That's a hell of a long turnover time."

"Not really. Death is a time machine—it's instantaneous. And this is in the context of infinity—of infinite Big Bangs. They're God's heartbeats."

"Karen, my mind's been blown enough this week, if you don't mind."

"I'm sorry."

"You know, you just reminded me of something else. On our walks, Harley and I also used to go by this big pachinko parlor all the time—it was just outside one of the camp gates. There were always a few steel pachinko balls in the parking lot that people had lost or thrown away. Harley used to collect 'em and put them in a Grolsch Beer bottle—you know those German bottles with the little ceramic stopper? After a while the bottle got full, and when I asked him what he was planning to do with all those pachinko balls, he told me he just liked having them; that each one was like a wish…a chance to do it over." Queen cleared his throat. "I thought that was kind of cool."

"There's still time to do it over, Lee. You'll make it up to him."

Queen shook his head. "No."

"Yes, we'll get out of this. Why not?"

He looked at her as if across a gulf of inexpressible sadness. "Because Kadena isn't there anymore, Karen," he said. "It's gone, swept away. They're all gone."

All at once, Karen felt like she couldn't breathe, like she was going to explode unless she did something. Shakily, she said, "Lee, I don't…"

Eyes welling up, he looked at her and nodded, letting out a deep, long-held breath.

"I'm sorry, I'm so sorry. Please come here," she gasped, begged, arching her back as if in pain.

He went over. She clutched his leg, and he pulled her shirt over her head, revealing her flushed breasts. Karen's long unwashed hair fell over her face as she fumbled his pants open and released his swollen penis. He grunted as she thrust her mouth over it, sucking hard as a feeding calf, and making hungry whimpering sounds as she plunged. Then suddenly she broke free and fell back against the foam mat, squirming wildly out of her pants.

"Help me!" she screamed, weeping.

Queen yanked the pants off and Karen spread her legs wide, using her fingers to open herself to her widest. He fell upon her, driving deep into the well of her heat, and their bodies and mouths collided ravenously, violently. Their earphones clunked like butting rams' horns. As he pumped against her, she gripped him so hard it hurt his injured ribs, shrieking, "*Um! Um! Yes! Oh yes!*" until with a hammering final paroxysm he came.

They stayed in that tight clutch for a number of minutes, frozen, as he slackened inside her, then little by little began to harden again, swiveling his groin against her and gradually starting to thrust. More controlled this time, he moved his hands over her as they slithered together, bodies lubricated with sweat and grease. Their tongues played, exploring each other's mouths, and when he pinched her nipples she squealed, shuddering.

She tried to turn him over, to mount him, but Queen would not budge. When she tried to force it, he slammed her on her back and pinned her, grinning as he pistoned. Annoyed for an instant, Karen surrendered to the building, unfamiliar pleasure— something new, welling up from deep inside.

"Ohhh, don't stop, don't stop…" she whimpered.

All at once, she was spasming, exploding, perhaps dying, while strangled sounds she had never made in her life came uncontrolled from her throat. As Queen continued moving, she shrieked in ever-higher agonies of joy, until at last it began to be just agony, and she gasped, "Stop…okay…stop…stop…stop…" and he cycled down like an expiring wind-up toy.

With her first available breath, Karen asked, "Did you come?"

"Of course," he sighed. "Did you?"

She wept, "Oh my God. Oh my God."

What neither of them thought of, in the midst of overwhelming grief and passion, was that because the music was playing and the tympanic equalizer was active, all that was required for Manny to hear them was that the microphone be turned on. This happened inadvertently when the mike cord got tangled up in their thrashing feet.

Manny heard everything.

CHAPTER TWENTY:

ZULU BEACH

"Fuck you doin', Skin?"

"Check it out. Wait! Wait! Check it out." Skin was dabbing dots and slashes of yellow zinc oxide down his nose and across his cheeks—flesh that was almost blue-black.

"Skin think he a Indian." Doc Noyz made another grab for the tube.

"Check it out."

"Gimme that shit."

"Fuck you."

It was a cold, gray day on the beach, the ocean flecked with whitecaps. Between sets of breakers, Skin could hear laughter by the water: Crips surfing. Grit swirled across the beach parking lot where he and the other Bloods huddled in the lee of the van, looking like gangly frogs in their donated wetsuits. Mr. Mosely, the fat white man whom the boys called Bozo, slumped in the driver's seat with a newspaper over his face.

Booster craned his neck to see, groaning, "This shit is fucked up. This is boring."

"Maybe Bozo be letting us go for refreshments," Doc Noyz said. "Bozo! What time is it?"

There was no reply. They pounded the gray Chevy van, yelling, "Bozo! Yo, Bozo!"

"Hey! Cut the crap out there!"

"What time is it?"

"It's time for you homeboys to get off your asses and hit the waves."

"When we leaving?"

"Don't screw around."

"We want to take a drive."

"No way."

"Oh, man. Just for a hour. Get us some Cokes." They all laughed, wheedling: "Yeah, Bozo; yeah, dawg; just a hour, pleeeeze?"

"I'll tell you what I *will* do: If you punks don't cut the shit and get your sorry butts out on the waves in about five seconds, I'm gonna take you back to Juvie and you can spend the rest of your weekend staring at the four walls."

"Shit, man, that ain't cool."

"Yeah, man, why you have to be like that?"

"I thought you were cool, man, but you've changed. You've really changed."

Mr. Mosely rolled up the window again, muttering, "Unbelievable."

Skin found another tube of zinc in the beach gear and began adding rows of blue dots to the yellow designs on his face, accentuating the puckered scar tissue of his LBC neck brand. He wished he had a mirror.

"That look pretty, Skin. Get you some lipstick now."

"Fuck you, punk."

"Lookin' all Zulu Beach and shit."

"*Shut* up. Fuck you know about it?"

"Motherfucker think he gone swim back to Africa."

Skin's fist, hard as polished mahogany, caught Booster in the mouth. Droplets of blood made pellets in the sand as the bigger boy tripped over the Styrofoam cooler and went sprawling, grit clinging to his cut lip.

"Mother*fuck*!" Booster scrambled up, wild-eyed, but the other boys instinctively surrounded him, just in case Mr. Mosely was paying attention.

"Be cool, man," they counseled urgently, restraining him. "Sit you ass down before you get us all on report. You best be *knowin'* Skin's crazy." They knew that if Bozo caught anyone fighting there would be no more beach days.

"I'm a bust his *ass*," Booster said, glassy-eyed, trying to get loose. "Bust his motherfuckin' ass…"

"Shit, Skin, what the fuck you think you doin'?" Doc Noyz hissed. "Tryin' to get all our asses back in the joint?"

Skin donned the hood of his wetsuit and said carelessly, "I ain't playin', yo. Fuck y'all." He picked up the longest surfboard, an old, scuffed-up Stanley that he had painted to resemble a Zulu warrior's shield. It was his favorite, the first board he had ever stood up on, and still the only one he could ride the nose on.

"Whoa! Skin think he gone hang ten."

"Shit, man. Don't you never know when to quit?"

"Fuck you *goin'*, Skin?"

"I'm surfing," Skin said over his shoulder.

"He surfin'." They cackled, falling over one another. "Cowabunga!"

Skin walked away, balancing the board on top of his head.

It was a long walk across the beach, a regular Sahara. The sand was freezing. At intervals there were lifeguard stations on stilts, boarded shut for the season, looking dormant. Arriving at the hump of sand overlooking the ocean, Skin could see Jerry plying his big red board in the frothy shallows.

The five Crips looked on from the high-tide line amid beached piles of seaweed and dirty yellow suds. They were too nervous to go in. Skin could see why: Far offshore, huge storm waves—

the biggest he had ever seen, ten feet high at least—leaned up
in foam-webbed jade walls, then slammed down with unnerving
thunderclaps, turning to mountains of brutal, spuming whitewater
that surged high up the beach. It was *rough*.

Over the past few years, most of the gang members in the
program had at least learned to surf, and a few had even become
good enough to be "surf ambassadors" to at-risk youth, setting up
surfing contests between rival gangs. Because of such community
service, some had even had their life-sentences commuted. The
program was called Shoot the Curl (its motto: "If you must shoot
something, Shoot the Curl"). But none of them had surfed in
these kind of conditions.

Skin breathed in the sharp, salty air, and could feel his heartbeat.
He fastened the board's leash to his ankle. Jerry spotted him and
cheerfully waved him down.

The Crips were watching him intently. "You goin' out there?"
asked Das, eyeing Skin's war paint. Das was a skinny kid from
the Mineral Springs Avenue click. When Skin didn't answer, he
whooped, "This sand nigger *crazy*!" The others laughed.

"Yo! Harold!" Jerry called as Skin approached the water's edge.
"Good to see you, dude! I'm glad to see at least one of you guys
has some nerve! Oh man! This is the day we've been *waiting* for!"

Jerry was a former gang member turned championship surfer
and trained lifeguard, who owned a bicycle-and-surf shop called
The Inner Tube in Hermosa Beach. He had been one of the
founding members of Shoot the Curl, and his enthusiasm and
media savvy had generated the program's first government grant.
Five years later he still donated his every weekend, but he liked to
say, "It's pure self-interest: I'm selling the sport. And it's not like I
wouldn't be on the beach every morning anyway."

Now he said, "Hey, you found the sunblock, I see. Awesome.
Ready to rip?"

Jerry was top-heavy with bronze muscles and Samoan good
cheer. What he really loved about the program was the trust: In

the alien surf, boy killers had no choice but to shed their gangsta reserve and trust him. You couldn't bust a cap on a wave; there was no faster way of impressing on guys like these the futility of violence, the joy of nature. And once they had a taste of the sport, there was no turning back.

It had been a tough night for Jerry. First he had heard on the news that a giant was coming, which was shocking enough, but then he had learned that within the next few hours he was going to lose his business, his condo, his program, his beloved beaches, and possibly his life. Not that life would mean much to him if he lost the other things—if he let himself get banished to some overcrowded refugee center in Barstow. And what would become of his boys? Having spent the week at a deserted campground, they had no clue about all this, and he wasn't about to abandon them to the kind of chaos that had happened after Hurricane Katrina. So he decided to ignore the evacuation orders and treat this like any other winter storm. As a surfer, Jerry was used to rejoicing at storm warnings; why should this be any different?

"How come we the only ones surfing?" Skin asked. He was used to seeing dozens of surfers any time the waves were up. It was weird.

"Don't jinx it, man! This is prime."

Skin sloshed into the advancing sheet of foam, feet burning from the cold. A few yards out, sand gave way to sharp shells and gravel. Already the surge threatened to knock him down. He quickened his pace, leaning into the thigh-high tidal current. He could still hear the Crips cackling at him: "Yo, Harold! Harold!"

"Don't pay any attention to them, man," Jerry called over the water. Raising his voice so the others could hear it, he shouted, "They're just too *chicken* to come in themselves—*bwuck bwuck, bwukaaak!*"

Gripping tight to the board, Skin now had to lunge sideways into each broken wave, presenting as little resistance as possible when it body-slammed him. He tasted brine. He would have gotten nowhere, except that between incoming waves the intense riptide wanted to suck him out to sea. The beach began to seem far away.

Suddenly he floundered into a deep trough. A spent wave went over his head and flushed water up his nose, the too-buoyant surfboard trying to spurt free.

"*Whoops!*" Jerry said, quick to catch him under the arm.

Gagging, Skin found the stony bottom and yanked away, embarrassed. He jumped on his board and began paddling out.

"There you go," said Jerry, following. "You got it." Together they ducked under the tumbled remains of a big wave. It was wild, crazy strong. Dragged backwards by the buffeting white flux, Skin felt like a salmon trying to swim upstream. He struggled to the surface, his ears full of sand.

Fuck this bullshit, he thought, but Jerry was still waving him on, suddenly all impatient.

"Come on!" the big man shouted, unusually intense. He kept glancing out to sea as if disturbed by something. "Hurry up!"

Now they swam faster, rushing in the lull between sets so they could get behind the next batch of powerful breakers. They weren't going to make it; it was too far. And something was wrong: Skin's teeth chattered as he watched a great slouching hump of white-webbed green rise in their path. The other waves had been heavy, but this was a monster, a ridge of jade water with dark garlands of kelp, drawing the sea from beneath his board like a river, dragging them into its jaws. The wave blocked the sun, and Skin knew he had never seen such a thing except in surfing magazines. He had learned not to be afraid of waves, but this was ridiculous: Ten feet, shit—it looked more like a hundred. Its sound was that of God taking a breath to blow them out like birthday candles.

Skin was alarmed to see that Jerry was not preparing to duck under as he would normally do, but was paddling furiously to make it over the wave's still-mounting crest. The sight drove Skin to a frenzy of speed, and the two of them skimmed up the soaring face of the waters, hurtling steeply uphill. Skin could feel himself being hoisted high up and carried backwards, the liquid cliff standing his board vertical…and then starting to overbalance, the weight of all that water bending it over like a gigantic fist, to smash him into the sea floor. It was a long way down. Arms pinwheeling, he dangled over that hungry abyss…and barely crested it.

Skin catapulted over the top of the wave, catching some big air and slapping down hard on the far side, as the sea settled back down beneath him with a deflating hiss and the wave's muffled thunder receded toward shore. But it was not over: he could see *another* huge swell coming on, blocking the horizon, and behind that another, and another. He had to keep madly paddling every second, paddling far out to sea, if he was going to get above these things. His arms were aching—what the fuck had Jerry gotten him into? *Gnarly my ass, motherfucker!*

Then Skin noticed that he was alone. He had assumed that Jerry would appear at any moment, but there was no sign of the big man. With growing anxiety, Skin scanned for the familiar sight of that red longboard—nothing. Was it possible that Jerry had caught the wave? He didn't think so: Skin remembered very clearly the last look on Jerry's face, the frantic way he was paddling.

"Jerry!" he shouted. "Jerry!" The man had been the closest thing to a father-figure Skin had ever known. *Don't you be leavin' me alone out here, man*, he thought.

Now he noticed something else: *Where was the beach?* All he could see, many hundreds of yards away, was a swath of muddy-looking gray surge, pouring inland. The whole coastline was swamped; his heart stopped to see the collapsed remains of a lifeguard tower being sucked under the tidal bore. The boys were gone, the van was gone. There was no way he could get ashore through that churning mess—it was a meat grinder. And the sea was pushing him towards it. Seized by the icy tongs of panic, he paddled spastically outward, screaming, "Help! Somebody help!"

Now he was nearing one of the big, anchored buoys that marked the swim line. It rose and plunged deep as the high swells passed over. He made for it and grabbed hold of the ring at its top, holding his breath for long seconds as it dunked him under, down, down. His board got away from him and tugged at the end of its tether, bobbing in the current like an unanswered question. Then Skin and the buoy broke the surface once more. He sputtered, feeling like a worm on a fisherman's bobber.

Clinging there, heart hammering against that painted steel ball, his numb feet brushing against its algae-slimed underside and chain, Skin searched for some way out.

Atop distant bluffs he could see apartment buildings and condos—how long would it take for them to figure out what was going on? From what he could see, the whole coast was awash—it was a real disaster, a tidal wave! Yes! That was it exactly: a tsunami! The Coast Guard would have to be all over it! Motherfuckin' Baywatch!

A shadow covered the cold disk of the sun, a weird blackness like an eclipse. In the sudden gloom, Skin looked anxiously out to sea, hoping for any sign of rescue. But the ocean was getting higher every minute, each swell bigger than the last, and now he could see layer upon layer of gigantic white combers covering the horizon like snowy terraces—waves on a scale he couldn't even comprehend, far away but bearing down fast. Two flexing, vertical shapes—twin waterspouts—twisted upward to the clouds. It was an awesome sight; the sight of his own approaching death. Black outlines of ships stood out like negatives against that white maelstrom, then were swallowed whole.

Released from the bondage of hope, Skin's mind suddenly snapped lucid. He had faced death many times down the barrel of a gun—what was he afraid of? So it was his time. Wasn't like he didn't have it coming. "Bring it on, bitch," he said aloud, shivering. "Let's see what you got."

He let loose the buoy and slid onto his board, paddling hard through whitecapped rollers into the face of that ultimate sundering whiteness, intending as his last act on Earth to surf the biggest wave of all time. *I hope you watchin', Jerry*, he thought. He, Harold Haines Loomis, aka MC Skin, was going to do something no man had ever done.

Then he saw something else, something moving in the sky above the hopscotching funnel clouds. Something not natural. The first thing he thought was of Meemaw telling him Bible stories: *A column of smoke by day, a pillar of fire by night*. Or one of those *Highlights* puzzle-pictures where you have to find the hidden objects: a shoe in the tree, a hen in the clouds.

This was not part of the weather. It blocked the daylight, an inchoate, serpentine mass, hazy with distance and overcast, and insubstantial except where it eclipsed the sun, so big it didn't really register. But it kept getting bigger and bigger and more perverse, resolving into something with a mushroom-cloud for a body, tornadoes for arms, waterspouts for legs—an improbable colossus that transcended the storm.

And now it was nearly overhead and he could almost look up its…skirt.

Skin's mind went blank; his wetsuit flooded with hot urine. *Her skirt.*

It was a She, the thing that was coming—a She beyond all shes. A mega-Her beyond all dreams or imagining. A She-monster wreathed in rainclouds and forking lightning, faster than the waves and yet astronomically slow, her Hi-Top sneakers the size of battleships, her sky-high striped leggings dwarfing Catalina Island, the Pacific Ocean, the L.A. coastline, everything—even the prospect of Skin's own imminent death.

Turning his astonished eyes upward and still upward to space, Skin stared in wonder at this vision of Apocalypse as a fire-breathing dragon-lady, a lollipop-punk Godzilla running in slow-motion astride the waters, her nearer sneaker-shod foot now coming down a mile away, just outside the breakwater.

When it hit, Skin was reminded of old H-bomb films he had seen on TV—Bikini Atoll and shit: A tremendous vertical column of white erupted to the sky, and a shockwave raced outward across the surface of the sea. Skin felt it as faceful of spray and a deep, submarine boom. Then the shoe was already rising again, thrusting upward from under a terrifying dome of water and breaking through to emerge like a birthing volcano out of a second colossal explosion, this one dirty brown with a hundred thousand tons of dredged-up seafloor.

Skin waited in dumbstruck awe for whatever was going to kill him first: The astounding impact wave, hundreds of feet high, that was now sweeping toward him; the airborne eruption of water and debris that was just beginning its fall; or the shoe itself, which looked as big as the Queen Mary as it took over the sky and descended unbelievably upon him. It was only a matter of seconds now.

As it began to get very dark, he turned his board around and paddled hard, exactly as he would to catch a wave, just as the shoe touched down a quarter-mile back. Skin didn't see it, and for an instant he felt nothing except the thrill of acceleration, of catching a ride.

Then his board slammed up into him, drubbing him hard as it accelerated like a rocket ship, a fiberglass magic carpet on a foaming, bludgeoning gusher of whitewater that bounced Skin upward and outward and in every direction for a seltzer-struck eternity, peeling the neoprene hood off his skull like a banana peel as it lofted him end over end, to finally collide with a fast river going the opposite way—*Oof!* His board broke in two, whirling into oblivion.

Stunned, cartwheeling along in the violent current, drowning, Skin felt his limp body strike something solid, then again, and he dully recognized the familiar sensation of bumping along the bottom of the sea after a wipe-out. He was washing ashore.

The strength of the current began to let up, the water rapidly becoming shallower and shallower and all at once whipping away like a blanket, to expose him there heavily grounded, flat and limp as a jellyfish, face-down amid a jumble of mangrove-like roots. He was pinned; his body felt heavy as lead, crushed by gravity. He could barely breathe, but at least the pressure helped force the water out of his lungs. A powerful wind blasted across his back, and he had intense vertigo, as if the ground was moving or spinning beneath him. Moving, definitely.

With effort, he looked up and could see a strange sort of artificial tower sloping above him, one with huge crisscrossed members that had been tied at the top in a colossal bow: a granny-knot. And continuing above that, receding into shadow, an immense swaying trunk a thousand feet high. The treelike "roots" he had washed up on were not natural, but massive interwoven cables that formed a lattice—the whole structure seemed to be made of it, as of some vast fabric.

It was a shoe—a canvas basketball sneaker. He was marooned on a giant's foot.

The sky pitched and rolled, and Skin had glimpses of landscape that swooped in and out of view around the flanks of the roving hill on which he lay. Periodically, everything would shudder heavily to a stop, like a derailing train, and his platform would be overtaken by a second massive object—the other shoe, awesome as a leapfrogging zeppelin—and Skin would have a brief sense of being on comparatively solid ground. Gigantic clouds of dust would billow up on all sides. But then the force of acceleration would press down again, and he would take off.

Skin started to laugh, then cough, hacking out the saltwater in his lungs. *What you complainin' about?* he thought. *Bitch be carryin' you, playa.*

≥≠≤

"Manny, word has just come through: she's there."

"Where?"

"She's just come ashore near Santa Monica. She's in L.A."

"Well, we're almost there, aren't we? Should I start heading west?"

"No, she'll see you coming from a hundred miles away. It's no good now."

"Why not?"

"If she's ready for you, you lose the advantage of surprise. It's better if you catch her by surprise."

"Says who? I'm just going to talk to her."

"That's not what she'll think; we have to assume she'll expect the worst. We don't dare give them any time to prepare a strategy against you. Besides, it's better if you meet in a remote location, to minimize the collateral impact. We can't have you fighting in L.A."

"Well, what did you have in mind, then?"

"Stay in Nevada and come south behind the Sierras. Then you can move around without being observed, and we can pick the best spot to intercept her."

"Cut 'em off at the pass."

"Yep, that's right, podna."

Partner my ass, he thought grimly.

Manny was going along with whatever they wanted him to do—he didn't care. Screw Karen and Queen and all the rest of them. They had each other, and the only thing Manny was interested in at this point was meeting this Yoon-sook, this Dorothy; but since he still depended on them for directions, he wasn't going to argue.

He didn't much like this business of setting up an ambush, but he could see how it might be helpful if handled right; the more surprised she was, the less likely she would be to have some preconceived notion of who he was, and what he stood for. Manny had never liked being pigeonholed: *You're black, so you have to think this way—you're Hispanic, so you have to think that way—you're Jewish, so you have to do this—you're American, so you have to do that.*

Screw all that—finally he was going to be his own man.

Manny was tired and depressed; it had been a long walk. When he had finally crossed the shallow, ice-crusted Bering Sea and come ashore in the white desolation of the Yukon Delta, he wasn't sure if he could keep going. Though he had known full well what to expect, the disappointment of finding America to be just another anonymous wasteland was intense—final confirmation that he was never going home. He was marooned even from himself; there was no Manny Lopes any more.

He knew this because he wasn't jealous of Karen and Queen…or if he was, it was the gloomy, resigned jealousy of the condemned. The ghost. Despite betrayal after betrayal, he wasn't heartbroken or angry or even upset. He was just…separate. Far removed from all sense of purpose or connection. He would have loved to have the noble ideals of Superman or some other fictional superhero, dedicating himself to the good of mankind, but it was impossible for him to harbor any such illusion. Karen's voice was an open circuit to a fading human realm from which Manny was irrevocably divorced. He did mourn it, but it already seemed so far away, so puny. That was the thing—he didn't feel any bigger; it was the rest of mankind that had shrunk to nothingness.

Karen directed him to a nearby glacier-fed lake, where he drank all he wanted and ate his fill of ice—ice by the handful, by the tens of thousands of tons—and after that he felt somewhat better.

Refreshed, he followed thinly peopled inland routes through Alaska and the Yukon Territory, then turned south behind the Coast Range and the Cascades, through British Columbia, eastern Washington State, Oregon, and northern California. It was all the same to him, just a lot of patchy ground crisscrossed with pinstripe roads and mountains resembling mossy termite hills. Everywhere he went, he found the scars of human civilization: industrial pollution, strip-mining, deforestation that looked like mange. To avoid major population centers in central California, Manny had skirted around it through the red badlands of Nevada, through bombing ranges and nuclear test-sites, and was now re-entering eastern California via Death Valley.

The trip had taken longer than expected, mainly because the rugged topography offered some challenges: Mountains that were twice or even three times Manny's height, and which were too steep and crumbly to climb; potentially ticklish active volcanoes and earthquake fault zones; rivers leading to fragile dams and industry; sensitive military sites—he had to avoid them all. The original plan, which called for his traversing the Continental Shelf all the way down the West Coast, had been discarded after undersea disturbances caused by both giants had triggered significant earthquakes and tsunamis all around the Pacific Rim.

But now Manny was on the final leg of the journey, screened between two desert mountain ranges barely higher than his head—the Panamint and the Amargosa—and eager to find this mysterious woman he had chased halfway around the planet. *Lee Yoon-sook*, he wondered, *where are you?*

CHAPTER TWENTY-ONE:

IN 'ER EAR

Lee Yoon-sook sat on the shoulder of Mount Wilson—its crushed observatory level with her head—and glumly watched the sun set in the Pacific. Spread out before her like a Japanese rock garden was the sprawling Los Angeles Basin, with its crystalline outcrop of downtown towers sprouting through a layer of smog.

She could trace the smoke-trail of her footsteps, starting at the seashore and crossing north through such icons of capitalism as Beverly Hills and Hollywood, both reduced now to flaming rubble. She had been too thirsty and tired at first to do more damage than that. But now Yoon-sook had drunk her fill from the San Gabriel Reservoir, and was considering her next action.

"You are the whirlwind," said the constant whisper in her ear. It was a man's voice, soothing and implacable. *"Your breath is the typhoon, your sweat the cleansing rain, and your phlegm the fire from heaven. You render justice with each footstep, spread purity with every glorious bodily humor. You are a scourge greater than Genghis Khan and Attila the Hun combined; you have an army in each hand,*

an arsenal in each leg. You piss destruction and shit death. You are a one-woman superpower, a walking world-war. Nothing can stop you. You are the triumphant will of the Great Father made manifest. You are the collective soul of the people…"

"Shut up," she snapped, barely listening. She felt clear-headed for the first time in days.

The voice kept talking.

Looking around at the grid-like urban expanse, Yoon-sook felt betrayed, resentful, yet strangely devoid of wrath. She was only mad at herself for crying—how many years had it been since she had done *that?*

Dry your eyes, fool, she commanded herself, furiously wiping tears. It was her very lack of emotion that had earned her the code name *Charassi*—Miss Snapping Turtle. That, and her harsh reptilian features. Yet here she was, blubbering away like a child.

That was the problem: she felt like a child again. She had been tricked into remembering what the Socialist Workers Youth League had spent years first prying out of her…and then warping and twisting to their advantage.

All the glorious cinematic dreams her mother had instilled in her, but which she knew only by description; all the lush orchestral music and heavenly songs, wrested from the red velvet-lined jewel case of her deepest psyche and brought to life, spiked with opiates, jacked up to mind-bending intensities of orgasmic Pavlovian bliss and delivered drop by drop back into her parched baby cinder of a soul. Weeks of harsh sensory-deprivation alternating with jolts of pure pleasure—a plush, furry womb containing only herself, an intravenous plastic umbilical, and hour after hour of cathode-ray sunshine from Hollywood's heyday. The reward for a job well done. The incentive to kill.

That was why it had been such a profound shock to hear her long-lost grandmother speaking to her as if from the spirit realm. It was perhaps the only thing that could have snapped Yoon out of the trance in which she had been wandering ever since she first awoke, half-drowned, in a great shallow pond like a reflecting pool, with low banks of mist girding her in.

What had happened to her? All she knew was that she had been fighting for some scientific artifact of great consequence—the thing that at the least would set her free, and might even enable her to challenge the stultifying, amoebic police apparatus that was killing her country, just as it had killed her parents—when she had blacked out for some unknown length of time...only to awaken in this mysterious place.

Darkness falling, she had sloshed aimlessly through the shallows for many hours, as a new day rose and fell with uncanny speed. She thought she was delirious, sick. Finally she saw a phosphorescent crest of lights and made for it. It was the Japanese island of Kyushu.

But not the Kyushu that she knew. Seeing the densely populated landscape of southern Japan from her new perspective gave Yoon-sook her first intimation of what was going on. She did not believe it, or could not, fleeing inward from her own burgeoning awareness like a sleeper clinging to the wishful fabric of a dream.

Then came that voice:

"*Pada konno*, Dorothy. Across the sea. All the answers you seek lie across the sea..."

Before she could react, a second voice broke in:

"*Dorothy, it's me, Shirley—it's your grandmother speaking.*"

" Grandma?"

"*Although I know you can't talk to me, I have found this means of talking to you. It's almost like magic, isn't it, that we can communicate this way.*"

"Yes."

"*If you're listening to this, then I have succeeded at something beyond all my hopes and dreams: to reach across the* uju, *across time and space, and bridge the distance between us.*"

"*Omona!* Grandma—"

"*I know you have probably felt alone for a very long time; you probably still do. But I am here to tell you that you are not alone, and you never were. That's because my thoughts and my love have been with you all your life, no matter where you've been or what you've done. I've been there, by your side.*

"Even now I am with you. No matter where you go, you won't be going alone. You can cross the whole Pacific Ocean, like I did, and you'll always be in range of the sound of my voice. You are a star, never forget that. All these years I stared into the darkness, I never lost sight of you. You glow; you are larger than life, too big for some provincial village. You belong where giants roam, where the red carpet beckons.

"There is a song in English that I know your honored mother taught you, and which I hope you still remember."

And then that piercingly gorgeous melody had begun: the voice of Judy Garland singing *Over the Rainbow*.

Born of a time and place that outlawed any deity but its woolly headed Leader, Yoon-sook had now ironically become a god herself—the real thing, without parades, speeches, or hyperbole.

She was omnipotent.

Yoon had never believed in any higher power. Her constrained existence had not inclined her toward any heavenly plan, not even the one imposed on her country by its leaders. She thought religion was a sop for people too weak to face the harsh realities of life, of which no supposedly loving God could be the author. It was all propaganda, she thought.

But now that Yoon had some insight into being Supreme, she could understand why good gods go bad: gods and demons were the same thing, just as worship and fear coexisted in the human heart. Buddha and Beelzebub were two sides of the same personality; Satan was just Siddhartha with a toothache.

She had seen the ancient temple murals with their baroque scenes of torture and bestial long-tusked demons—how long would it be before she was added to this fright-gallery, her reasonable anger at humanity interpreted as evil incarnate?

Yoon had never thought of herself as evil, because she killed only to relieve pain—blissful nothingness was her gift to the sick, suffering world. As an assassin, she killed with a profound sensation of relief, as if she was hacking through some great stricture of vines surrounding her breast, or to release trapped birds to the sky, or perhaps lancing a huge, horrible boil to drain the poison. Her own black heart the carbuncle.

But murder was addictive, like dope. No matter how many times she did it, she always needed more, and it became easier, more automatic, each time. Why was it different now? Maybe that was it: without the soft, silk cushion of junk it wasn't the same.

Yoon had been led to expect that coming to America would mean something; that it would have some primal, mystical aura that would complete her, fix her in some way...but there was nothing. It was barren as the surface of the Moon—*wolsegye*. Her teachers at the Revolutionary Institute were right: It was all a hoax. Hollywood was nothing! *Hollywood!*

From where she was standing, It was no different than any other part of this dreamlike alien landscape. All the bourgeois symbols of capitalism, all the famous landmarks, were either invisible to the naked eye or puffed into smoke at the slightest touch. It was all just shit.

She had no interest in taking revenge on shit, in defeating and humiliating shit—nor in joining shit. Wiping out the military bases in Japan, and then the U.S. Navy, had given her no more satisfaction than crushing a nest of insects. She would just as readily have stomped on DPRK forces. The futility of what she was doing made her angry.

"Who are you?" she demanded. "You are not my grandmother. Who are you?"

"East," wheedled the other voice, the soothing and strangely familiar male voice. "*Tangtchoguro*—all answers lie to the east.

Go purify the military facilities of Edwards Air Force Base, China Lake, and Fort Irwin. You will then proceed to Las Vegas…"

"I haven't finished here yet."

"Los Angeles has a mongrel population of oppressed blacks and immigrant slave-laborers—they will support the revolution. We dare not waste time; the capitalist warmongers will be planning desperate counterattacks, even upon our beloved Motherland. We must not be distracted from our mission. The victories we achieve along the way will be largely symbolic; our ultimate goal lies to the east."

"How far?"

"No more than a day's walk."

"Why should I go there?"

"For the greater glory of the Motherland."

"Fuck the Motherland."

"Dorothy, don't you understand it's the only way you can go home?"

"Shut up! Don't call me Dorothy. You are not my grandmother."

"But your grandmother is here; we are friends. She only wants what we all want, and that is for you to fulfill your destiny. So that you may earn your reward."

Now that lilting, guileless granny voice could be heard again, speaking as if in the next room: "Dorothy, your *omma* used to love this one. Sing along with me."

And once again came that soaring music, the angelic voice of Judy Garland in *The Wizard of Oz*.

Its effect on Yoon-sook was profound and immediate. Even though some part of her knew she was being manipulated, the power of that song on her was such that it tore down the spindly facade of her skepticism and better judgment, flooding her parched brain with pure, infantile yearning. It pointed the way to ultimate fulfillment. Like a compliant child, she slowly got to her feet, brushing tons of dirt off her sodden reptile skirt.

But the worm of doubt persisted. It was because of the pain, that steadily growing need. Once she had done everything they asked her to do—what then? Could they restore her to her previous size? Could they get her food? She didn't care about any of that. But could they give her what they promised? That was what she clung to, what ultimately drove her. Whether they could or not, the mere promise was enough. It was the only aspect of her previous life that still meant something to her. Meant more than ever, in fact.

Once America was conquered, they promised to turn it and all its chemical-industrial might into one big *yakkuk*, a giant drugstore for Yoon-sook's personal use, to keep her demons at bay until she could be restored to normal size…however long that might take. With the West conquered, they would have unlimited access to all the dope that the planet could produce—supertankers full of grade-A junk, an endless golden fleet, off-loading precious cargo straight into the pipelines of her thirsty veins.

What else did she have to hope for in this miserable life?

"Okay, boss," she said. "Lead the way."

Yoon-sook walked quickly, traveling a hundred and fifty miles an hour. She swept through Soledad Pass and the city of Palmdale, wiping it off the map. A hysterical mob fighting over emergency provisions at the Safeway gradually fell silent at the sound of air-raid sirens and a distant booming.

Boom! Boom! BOOM! *BOOM!*

Then the lights went out, the store windows blew in, and the entire supermarket and its contents were compressed to a thickness of several inches, rammed two hundred feet deep into the earth by the sole of Yoon-sook's left shoe. People who had been glued to the TV all morning ran out of their houses at the first tremor and could only stand in shock before the prospect of sneakered doom descending upon them.

Passing through Saddleback Buttes State Park, Yoon-sook fell under attack by combined squadrons of Air Force, Navy and Marine aircraft, and by Marine artillery out of Twentynine Palms. As "Stormy Weather" played in her head, they showered her with 15,000-pound bunker-busters and depleted-uranium penetrators—everything in the conventional arsenal.

Yoon-sook draped her upper body with her leather coat and screamed as loudly as she could. Her piercing voice was a weapon even at normal frequency and volume; now it was a force beyond reckoning—nothing short of a death-ray. Anything caught in the path of its lethal harmonics was instantly liquefied by sympathetic vibrations, whether animal, vegetable, or mineral. Bridges collapsed, ancient stone buttes shivered to pieces, and aircraft rained from the skies.

The few projectiles that penetrated this sonic field were of little consequence to her. Her epidermis was twenty feet thick, and many times stronger than an equivalent thickness of reinforced concrete, steel, or Kevlar. Beneath it was a thicker layer of impregnable, shock-absorbing subcutaneous fat. She was indifferent to pain, anyway. As she trampled the military installations, her feet automatically traced the dance steps of Gene Kelly in "Singin' in the Rain."

They had already tried all this back in Japan, and more. When she had entered the sea to an Esther Williams fanfare, and been floating very still on the surface of Suruga Bay as instructed, the Americans had used the opportunity to attack.

Guided missiles and shells from eighteen-inch naval cannon had rained down upon her, while beneath the surface a submarine armada had unleashed schools of torpedoes.

At the first wave of lashing impacts, Yoon-sook had dived down deep, to lightless abyssal depths near ten thousand feet, skimming the Japan Trench far below the range of most marine weapons—her body showing up on sonar as an extraordinary phantom shape treading the gulf.

At the bottom of the sea, she felt a peculiar sense of déjà vu:

When she had first come to South Korea from Japan, she stayed in a safe house on Cheju Island, and was strangely affected by the ancient, matriarchal society of women divers she saw there, who harvested octopus, abalone, and other goods from the sea.

Day after day she watched these independent women as they worked at considerable depths with no special equipment, and who were the masters of their world. They looked like extras in a Busby Berkeley production number.

Holed up in her little room overlooking the rocky coast, Yoon experienced a pang of longing like nothing she had ever felt— or perhaps not longing, but regret, as of something golden and irretrievable having passed her by.

On one of her rare outings, she had been taken to a picturesque waterfall, one of the island's scenic attractions, and had been told by her handler, Mr. Oh, that the green pool at the base of the p'okp'o was inhabited by huge eels. He made his hands into toothy jaws to show how formidable these eels were.

A wedding had been going on at the time, using the waterfall as a backdrop. Yoon-sook stared intently at the prosperous wedding party and the bride, silently humming "I'm Nobody's Baby" and feeling more kinship with the eels slithering in the murky green darkness. The groom was her next target, but she would have preferred for it to be the bride; that was one she would have taken care of. Not out of hate, but out of compassion.

She killed out of mercy. This was her programming. Love was a heartbreakingly fragile flower poking its head through a crack in the concrete, doomed to a parched and lonely death. A baby chick that had fallen out of its nest. To Yoon, who loved too much, it was impossible to abandon these to their arbitrary, inevitable fate. She must be the one to put them out of their misery...because she *cared*.

It was intolerable for her to witness the degradation and suffering inflicted upon the innocent, the exploiting of their childish assumptions so that they became slaves of the Great

Machine—that ponderous, invisible, inexorable shucker of souls, which carded and discarded the human spirit like a hellacious cotton-gin, leaving only robots making more robots, perpetuating the Machine to infinity. Better to midwife them through the ugly, bloody truth and help them on their way. To break the cycle.

She had once thought she could spare them, save them, and had only caused greater suffering for herself and everyone else.

After graduation from the Youth League, Yoon-sook had been assigned as her first official project the task of administering security for one of the remote settlements. These were places where undesirables of various types were sent in order to maintain standards of civic quality—not criminals as such, but the deformed, the handicapped, and anyone else whose physical misfortune was a visible affront to the Workers' Paradise.

Yoon-sook had accepted the assignment knowing that it was only a stepping-stone to better things. Without family connections or direct lineage to a hero of the Revolution, the only way to break into the ranks of the Korean Workers Party was by showing total loyalty to Party ideals. Being sent to the boondocks to police a bunch of harmless freaks was a test of her dedication. She just hoped it wouldn't last too long.

Her last day in Pyongyang, she had packed a bag with her few things—a book of the Great Leader's sayings, a handbook of State Security Department regulations, identity papers and travel documents, a baggy dress uniform—and left her dormitory at the SWYL for the last time. She had no friends to say goodbye to—most of the other girls were privileged children of high Party members, and had shunned her from the start. Yoon-sook was not lively and animated, not girlish enough for them. She was not attractive. They called her a lot of things, but the name that stuck was Snapping-Turtle—*Chara*.

Staring out the train window at the broad, pristine avenues of the capitol, Yoon-sook had breathed deep of the rare pleasure of travel. As the urban view gave way to countryside, she opened her little parcel of rice and garlicky *kimchi,* and thought nothing had ever tasted so good.

She got off the train at a rural station in Hamkyonbuk-do Province, near a small town called Kilju. It was the middle of the night, and she was cold and tired from the long train ride. The station was very dark compared with the lights she had become accustomed to in Pyongyang, but she was relieved to find a car waiting for her—an ancient military ambulance that looked like it dated from the Korean War, if not the Japanese Occupation.

"Provisional Officer Lee Yoon-sook?" shouted the driver. He was a sunburned, rustic-looking character with missing teeth and dirty fingernails, but he wore a policeman's cap.

"Yes."

"I am Regional Deputy Director Choi, Ministry of Public Security, Eastern Rural Jurisdiction. You'll be reporting to me. Please get in."

"Thank you, sir."

As she settled onto the hard, rusty springs, he handed her a dirty wool blanket. "It's a long ride to the camp. You probably want to sleep."

"Thank you, sir, I'm all right."

"Suit yourself."

Yoon-sook attempted to stay awake, to maintain a strict and officious demeanor, but the drive seemed to last forever, traversing an endless dirt road through a fathomless black void, and she kept nodding off. The driver, obviously uncomfortable being alone with her, made awkward small-talk.

"We don't get a lot of visitors around here," he said.

"Hm."

"Tell you the truth, I don't get up to the village very often myself, unless there's a problem. The camp pretty much takes care of itself. They don't bother us, we don't bother them. They have their own little council that handles disputes and civil matters. There's really not much need for a full-time security administrator."

What was there to say? Need or no need, she was here. Just to give the man a rest, Yoon-sook feigned sleep, and before she knew it she was asleep, lulled by the jouncing potholes.

She awoke with the morning sun blinding her through the windshield. The car had stopped.

"Hello!" shouted Mr. Choi from outside. "*Ya! Yobo!* I have someone for you all to meet, and I want you to make her feel welcome!"

Shielding her eyes, Yoon looked out at the grassy clearing in which the car had stopped. It was a kind of farmyard shared by several dirt compounds with low stone walls and rough, mud-patched wooden houses. She heard a rooster crowing, and smelled manure.

As her eyes cleared of sleep, she could make out people emerging from the shadows, stepping out from behind walls as if from hiding. At first she thought they were children, and felt a burst of horror when she saw their deeply lined, emaciated faces. Then she realized they were wizened little people—dwarves.

They were dressed like paupers, in the coarsest of peasant clothing, with crude straw hats and woven rush sandals. They looked like a tribe of primitives: Korean pygmies. As they came, they were all bowing and prostrating themselves, eyes on the ground as if in abject submission to some grand and terrible monarch, but it was only Mr. Choi pissing by the side of the car.

Yoon-sook got out and bowed back as much as she thought seemly, while they practically groveled at her feet, murmuring, "Welcome, please. Thank you, thank you. Welcome. Forgive us, please. Thank you, please. Welcome…"

"Thank you," she said. "I am honored—"

"All right, that's enough," said Mr. Choi impatiently.

At the first sign of his displeasure, the lead dwarf gave a command and the others stood straight, chests thrust out and eyes forward, as if at attention. One of them, a stubby-fingered young girl with a pretty face, approached, trembling, holding before her a steaming basin of water and a clean cloth. The deputy director accepted the cloth as his due and vigorously washed his face with it, blowing and sputtering all over the girl.

"Ahhh, that's more like it," he said. "Well, this is the settlement, Miss Lee: Camp Sunshine. Not much to look at, eh? We can't all live in Pyongyang! Your quarters and base of operations are up the hill there, along that path, in the old police barracks. Mr. See here is the council president, and he will assist you in making this place a model community that even the Chief Minister of Public Security would be proud of. Also, I will stay for a few days to ensure that your transition goes smoothly."

It did not go smoothly.

From the first, Yoon-sook had suspicions that Deputy Director Choi was taking advantage of the dwarves, exploiting them in a way that reflected poorly on the Ministry, and these fears were confirmed as the following days wore on.

The villagers were obviously desperately poor and malnourished, yet every time Yoon-sook turned around there was someone offering her a gift of food from their meager stocks. Her office and quarters were provisioned with stores of food, as well as constantly replenished jars of water from the communal pump, and sacks of charcoal for her heat and cooking needs. Not that she had to cook—at every mealtime there was a parade of dwarf-women at her door, proffering delicacies of meat and fish such as she had never been accustomed to in her life. Worse, the deputy director's car became a rolling distillery, jammed with valuable jugs and bottles of bootleg rice wine and *soju* for his trip home.

She would have liked to talk to the dwarves about this, but they wouldn't meet her eyes, much less engage in a frank conversation about illegal activity. Nor would the deputy director himself— after a perfunctory tour of the village, he seemed to lose all interest in her or her mission, and brazenly gave himself over to the business of collecting tribute. This included being visited by the village girls at night. Apparently it was a long-standing tradition.

"This is pure extortion," she told him on the night before he was due to leave. "I must inform you that I intend to file a formal complaint with my section chief at the Ministry."

Choi laughed drunkenly, "You ugly bitch. Don't you know what happens to people who file false complaints?"

"I have documented in detail every instance of corruption."

"*Corruption*. The sound of your voice is like a dying cat. Go away."

As she turned to go, he called after her: "And who do you expect to corroborate this wild accusation? It's my word against yours!"

The man had a point: Yoon-sook knew she could never persuade the locals to testify against him. Nor would the Ministry be inclined to side with her against a senior official. But she could not stand by and let this continue—at the very least she wanted her report on record, so that if and when the truth came out she could not be implicated. She had seen too many instances of guilt by association.

That night, the deputy director came to her door. He had been drinking in the village for several hours, and was red-faced and perspiring heavily. As he came up the hill, several bloodied dwarf-men, including the council president, were pulling at his arms and pleading with him to stop. Though Choi cursed and savagely beat them with a stick, they kept trying. A cadre of dwarf wives preceded them up the path, wailing for Yoon-sook to run and hide.

When Choi threw open her door, she said to him, "This is unprofessional conduct. It will be included in my report."

He beat the dwarves aside and shut himself in with her, pressing his back against the door. "Now I'll give you something to complain about," he said, out of breath. "You know, there are bandits in this region. They sometimes kill people who interfere with their business, and then they vanish into the hills. It's discouraging, but the Ministry understands there's only so much I can do. I'm terribly understaffed." He lunged forward with the heavy stick raised.

Yoon-sook waited until he was just upon her, and then ducked inside his blow and drove her long steel hairpin—her *pinyo*—up under the angle of his jaw and deep into the nerve cluster at the base of his brain. She was well trained in the art of *chaebonghada*. There was not much blood or external sign of violence, but Deputy director Choi fell instantly dead.

"He passed out from the liquor," said Yoon-sook primly, as she opened the door to admit the clamoring dwarves. They checked the body and looked up at her in hushed amazement.

"He's dead," the council president said.

"Bandits," she replied.

There was a week of celebrations in Yoon-sook's honor. Songs were sung, speeches were made. It was a pageant to rival anything in her musty Tinseltown imaginings, and for the first time in her life Yoon-sook felt the almost unbearable sweetness of reality undermining her perpetual death-grip on the past. She was becoming alive.

But it didn't last long.

In the months to follow, some disgruntled official on the other end of Choi's pipeline was annoyed to find the well gone dry.

At the same time Yoon was being initiated as an honored sister into the newly prosperous society of the dwarves, and helping them to permanently secure the fruits of their labor according to strict legal principles, there were whispers in high places. Suspicions were raised, investigations begun.

She awoke one morning to the sound of approaching vehicles. The camp was closed, Yoon-sook arrested. The dwarves—over nine hundred of them—were taken away and never seen again. Nothing could be proved, and it was decided that if Yoon-sook was so talented at murder that she could avoid prosecution, then she should be promoted.

Less than a year after she arrived in Camp Sunshine, Yoon-sook was back in Pyongyang, training for the dreaded Foreign Service.

That bride at the base of the falls made Yoon-sook flash on things she didn't want to remember: of aborted fetuses tossed like dead fish in the bloody gutters of institutional shower rooms, and naked women screaming as their newborn babies were taken from them and killed with a hammer. Other women laughing and joking as they did this, goading Yoon to join along. *Pigs, just pigs*, they had cackled. And eventually she had joined along. In her drugged euphoria she had joined in, laughing and mocking the prisoners along with the camp matrons until the last week of the exercise, when one of the prisoners had been her own mother.

Such thoughts didn't usually last very long—only until her next fix.

But now she was the diver, the eel.

"You are Neptune's Daughter. You are Dangerous When Wet," urged the voice in her ear, and she imagined it was handsome Fernando Lamas speaking, who co-starred with Esther Williams in the film where she swam the English Channel.

Passing directly below the American fleet, Yoon-sook could hear the sound of destroyers anxiously probing for her, pinging her, mapping her, as they set depth-charges for maximum.

It was just like the twittering of little birds—finches, perhaps. Strange finches, increasing, proliferating, to pelt her with droppings.

As she passed far beneath the hulls of the main battle group, holding her breath for the long minutes that were mere seconds to her, Yoon-sook raked her hand across the bottom of the sea, penetrating deep silt and hundreds of feet of underlying bedrock to release a vast, explosive plume of methane from the hydrate slush in which it was trapped.

Over fifty million cubic meters of highly pressurized greenhouse gases rose to the surface, expanding all the way. This extraordinary bloom spawned a series of concussions that preceded it up, enveloping and imploding several nuclear attack submarines and giving some brief interval of warning to the rest of the fleet. But there was nowhere to go; the entire ocean bottom seemed to be rising to swallow them. Alarm klaxons sounded across the waves.

Almost simultaneously, every ship in a twenty-mile radius—essentially the entire Seventh Fleet, minus a few outlying oilers—rose up on a greenish-white dome of gas-propelled seawater, hung by inertia for a moment above the yawning void, and then fell through as the thousand-foot-deep bubble burst. Robbed of buoyancy, the ships simply vanished without a trace. It was as if a trap-door had sprung beneath them.

The erupting gas plume shot high into the atmosphere, spreading and combining with oxygen to create a bomb of megaton proportions. When it detonated a few moments later, the shockwave and fireball cleared the skies of aircraft.

Yoon-sook took her time rising to the surface, ascending through clouds of sinking debris. Catching her breath, she rested then, floating on her back in the sun, cradled by the empty blue Pacific.

≥≠≤

Now she was approaching the Arizona border. The military attacks had stopped, and she warily awaited the next wave. The land was brown, with ranges of bare, conical peaks. One of these, a medium-sized mountain little taller than herself—Funeral Peak—blocked her path, and she made her way around it.

On the far side she was startled to hear a voice speaking English: "Uh, hello?"

Yoon-sook whipped around defensively and found herself face-to-face with a man. A strangely familiar man. A puny, brown-skinned *miguk* with torn clothes and bare feet—the very man she had been about to shoot back in Busan. Before *it* happened.

"Small world," he said, smiling tentatively.

What was *he* doing here? Yoon-sook stood frozen in a combat stance, teeth bared savagely. For once she was at a loss—she did not know what to do.

"Kill him!" the voice screamed in her ear. *"Kill him now!"*

"Sorry to surprise you," said the man, holding up his hands. "I won't hurt you, see? I'm a friend, okay?"

"It's a trick! He is an American puppet! Kill him!"

"Be quiet!" she hissed. "Why is he here? I thought I was the only one!" Her brain was sparking with agitation. "How many more are there?"

"None," said Manny. "It's just you and me. My name is Manny Lopes. What's yours?" He gently tried to approach her, as a rodeo clown might approach a wild-eyed bull.

As he reached for her, Yoon-sook snatched the 9mm pistol from her pocket and aimed it at his head. "Stay back!" she screeched, circling eastward around him.

Manny went rigid, shocked that she still had the gun. It seemed so out of place in this weird, desert netherworld—but then so did the two of them. So much for the colonel's big plan. Typical.

"That's okay, don't kill me," he said, heart in his throat. "No problem, we're cool!"

She kept backing away from him, and then abruptly turned and ran.

Watching her go, Manny felt his nerves jangling like tubular bells. He realized he wasn't scared so much as thrilled, vindicated.

"I think she was just as afraid of me as I was of her," he said with mounting exhilaration. "Did you see that? She didn't want to kill me."

"Don't count on it," said Karen anxiously. "Listen, just stay put for now—that gun changes everything. The science team is evaluating whether it will still fire at this scale."

Ignoring her, Manny breathlessly went in chase.

"Manny, stop. You hear me? Stop!" Karen turned off the mike and shook her head. "He's not listening," she said.

"All right," Queen said. He was not speaking to her, but into a headset. "Yes, sir. We may be able to make that work. The timing's crucial. I understand, sir. Thank you." He turned to Karen and said, "Little change of plans."

≥≠≤

Jogging east, Manny tried to keep out of sight as best he could, following Yoon-sook by her dust cloud. He passed the smoldering embers of Las Vegas, the quickly draining sump of Lake Mead— Hoover Dam was gone. Occasionally he would spot her across the mountain ridges, her face luminous in the moonlight, and pearly billows of dust in her wake. He could see that the military was still harrying her, but it didn't seem to be slowing her down— not yet. Manny knew that eventually she would tire; they both would. He felt like he could sleep for days.

The elevation increased, the Arizona landscape changing from low desert basins to broad, forested plateaus. Snow covered the distant mountains—it looked like an aerial photo on a postcard. And these were real mountains, the beginning of the Rockies. Manny was running uphill, the air getting thin. He was out of breath.

"Manny?" said Karen.

"Yeah?"

"She's entering the Grand Canyon. It could be a trap."

"I'll stay up on the rim and follow her from above. Tell me if she takes a detour and I'll jump across."

"Don't even think about it, Evel Knievel. Not unless you want to cave the whole thing in. Our guys think it's safer just to go in after her—she'll have less chance of spotting you down there."

"Will do."

The rolling earth was covered with tiny green speckles of sage and pine, then it fell sharply away into a broad, eroded gully as deep as Manny was tall, and much wider: a big meandering ditch. This was the Grand Canyon? Manny had never seen it before except in pictures. From his unusual point of view, there was something creepy about it, a great red gash in the planet—the river in the bottom looked like blood. The canyon was deep and dark and murky with the dust of Yoon-Sook's passing.

"Which way did she go?" he asked.

"East, we think. The spotters have lost sight of her, hold on…"

Now Manny could hear something.

Singing. A beautiful, ethereal voice, curling like smoke from deep within the canyon. It was a vaguely familiar tune, and hypnotic: *"Come out, come out, where ever you are…"* Hair standing on end, Manny gingerly started working his way down, following the echoes.

All at once, the ledges crumbled beneath his feet. For all his bulk, he completely vanished from view, sliding in a heap to the canyon floor. A miles-wide explosion of smoke and dust mushroomed from the fissure, and a seismic shockwave rocked the region, registering 9.8 on the Richter scale at Flagstaff (before the machine was destroyed), and over 6.0 as far east as Albuquerque. It was a physical cataclysm almost as great as the eruption of Mt. St. Helens.

≥≠≤

Inside Manny's ear, the effects of the fall were comparatively slight: With Manny's tobogganing body absorbing most of the impact, Karen and Colonel Queen experienced a degree of turbulence not unlike a spacecraft re-entry: intervals of near-weightlessness alternating with vertebrae-wracking jolts.

Equipment broke loose from its earwax moorings and tumbled around, choking dust poured in, but the lovers huddled in their flexible, padded cocoon and rode out the storm in relative ease, listening anxiously to the muffled din. It seemed to go on forever. Queen got respirators on their faces just as they bumped to a stop, the big dome tent sagging sideways.

"What the hell was *that*?" Karen cried. "What happened?" The external monitors showed nothing but static. All the audio equipment was wrecked.

"I don't know. Manny's down." Queen grabbed a flashlight and slid downhill to the door, unzipping the shelter. A solid wall of dust rolled in, along with the booming of Manny's metabolism. "Shit," he shouted, adjusting his headphones. "Stay here until I get back."

"Where are you going?"

"The landline's dead; I have to check up top." He slipped out feet-first—the opening now faced steeply downhill—and started to zip the flap shut behind him.

She blocked it open. "Fuck that! You're not leaving me here!"

"Karen, I can't babysit you and assist casualties at the same time." He shoved her inside.

"I'm coming, whether you like it or not."

Harley stopped and gave her a look of utmost gravity. "Karen, there's something we haven't told you. Men have been disappearing and turning up dead."

"What are you talking about?"

"I mean there's something up on the crown that's tearing my men to pieces and…eating them. It's living in Manny's hair—we don't know what it is. A spider maybe, some kind of predator or parasite. I didn't want to scare you."

"Are you serious?"

"Yes. So please stay here until I get back." Brooking no argument, he went out into the murky void of the ear canal and she angrily re-sealed the quilted Kevlar door.

The tent was full of dust, a dirty fish tank lit by battery-powered emergency lanterns. Karen breathed through her mask and sat for a while, frantically stewing, then half-unzipped the tent flap and peered out. It was pitch black in Manny's ear canal. She could not locate the safety-cable; it seemed to be gone, along with the decontamination chamber and the chemical toilet.

"Hey!" she shouted, voice echoing, but Queen had disappeared. "Asshole," she muttered. "Love 'em and leave 'em."

Karen was afraid for Queen and the other soldiers, but even more concerned about Manny. Had he been shot? Was he dying?

"Hold on, baby," she pleaded to the air, feeling trapped and helpless.

It was a shock for her to realize how scared she was without Manny to talk to. Giant monstrosity or not, he was her only touchstone in this whole twisted nightmare, his goofy, familiar voice the only thing that felt real. Everything else was a bad dream. Even her affair with Queen was part of the madness; how much could she really trust him? *Spider my ass.* Without Manny to share the burden of this situation, it was too big to cope with— didn't fit in her head. She would go crazy sitting here all alone.

"Stay with me, Manny," she muttered. Gritty tears trickled down her face as she opened the shelter and cautiously ventured out. It was hot and booming, but the air had cleared enough that she could see fuzzy brown light at the mouth of the cave. "We're going to make it, just you wait and see."

Scooting along on her butt down the steep tunnel, Karen heard something in the darkness: a slobbering, smacking sound punctuated with distraught whinnies, as of someone weeping and eating at the same time.

"Lee?" she said doubtfully.

Through dissipating dust, and limned by sporadic flashes of blue lightning from outside, she could just make out an oddly distorted human form.

"Hello?" she called.

It was someone—or *something*—squatting against the circle of night at the entrance: a sinister, bushy silhouette that resembled Bigfoot, or at least an impossibly big man. A huge man, in fact, bristling with strange antlers and fronds, and with a disproportionately tiny head that made him look like a cartoon Neanderthal.

Continuing to edge forward as if in a dream, as if she could force this vision to make sense, Karen stopped only when the ogre looked up at her. Lightning pulsed bright and stark. She cried out in horror. What she had thought to be sticks and mop-like dreadlocks were actually ghastly sprouts of fungal matter—sickly colored tendrils entwining a skull all but denuded of flesh, but which seethed with a living beard of giant bacteria.

As Karen drew back in revulsion and disbelief from the sight, the creature rose up before her, sixteen feet tall, with great, club-fingered hands, even more massive clown shoes, and the rags of a tweed suit that tapered in size from the bottom up. Eager eyes and bloody teeth gleamed in a pulsating void of a face.

With a thick, phlegmy voice, the thing slurped, "Hello, Karen. Fancy meeting you here." When she didn't reply, it said in high-pitched tones, "*Dr. Isaacson, I presume.*"

≥≠≤

Wilfred Isaacson had never known what hit him on the beach. He just knew he had been shot, several times, and was on the verge of death. Fleeing that hideous female assassin, he had begged for Yahweh to take him home, and then blacked out. When he awoke, he knew something was wrong.

He was in some kind of waking nightmare: a fetid, steaming black marsh that moved as if sprouting from the back of some vast, unholy beast.

No, this can't be, it can't be, it's impossible, oh Lord, oh dear Lord it's impossible, its IMPOSSIBLE!

Hell. He was in Hell.

Screaming, vomiting in terror and despair, Isaacson had broken down then, sobbing over whatever failure had caused him to be rejected from the gates of Paradise.

"Why, oh Lord?" he had begged from the depths of madness. "Why?"

But even as he moaned and carried on, he knew in his heart of hearts that he was being disingenuous—Yahweh had already warned him loud and clear, years before, when the date of the Apocalypse had come and gone without incident, leaving Isaacson and his fellow Brethren high and dry.

Against the wishes of their families and friends, defying all common sense and social decorum, the members of Isaacson's church had given away all their possessions and divested themselves of every tie to the mortal world in solemn anticipation of the Rapture…and it hadn't come. The minutes ticked off after midnight, and nothing at all had happened.

Oh, the mockery! For some the shame and disillusionment were too much—they lost their faith, drifted off, or even committed suicide—but Isaacson held firm. He reasoned that perhaps there was something he was called upon to do, something he had failed to do. He prayed and meditated upon this long and hard until he finally arrived at the answer. A terrible but inevitable answer, which required of him the ultimate act of faith and sacrifice. And he had done it. He had done it.

But apparently not well enough.

Ah, yes. Yes, yes, yes! Of course! Isaacson was a natural problem-solver, an engineer by training and inclination, and this basic part of his disposition still remained functional amid the ruins of his sanity, like the brick chimney of a burned-down house. Once he was over the initial shock of being damned, it didn't take him long to put his finger on it, to find the serpent that had been hiding in his breast all along, and against which all of his dedication to Yahweh was for naught.

Lust. Lust had damned him, just as he had always feared it would.

It was those *people*. The couple in the next room. Isaacson had tried to ignore their carnal banquet, had covered his head with a pillow and turned the TV way up, had got down on his knees and prayed, had pinched and slapped and burned his throbbing penis with a lighter, but in the end he hadn't been able to resist putting his ear up to the wall and breathlessly listening to every tantalizing moan and thrust.

Oh, Karen, he heard. *Oh, Karen, yes.* Karen this, Karen that.

He wanted her, yes; he wanted Karen so badly, to be the one naked between her generous thighs. He had earlier ridden with both of them in the hotel elevator, and could picture it all so clearly: the big Korean girl and the little brown man. Oh, he had been with them in spirit, and spilled his seed on the barren carpet as they went at it. Only then had he banged on the wall in shame and anger, trying to salvage some belated sense of righteousness. But he had known it was too late—there was no point in pretending otherwise.

Isaacson had always known he was an unregenerate sinner, and that the Lord would neither forget nor ignore the countless "minor" lapses that Isaacson had always been so quick to rationalize away. Was he stupid enough to think he could trick the Almighty? Of course not—it was only himself he had been fooling!

He knew now that was why he had been so ready to martyr himself and deliver mankind over to Judgment: It was because in his hypocritical, conniving heart he thought he was cutting a deal to wipe the slate clean. Well, God had the last laugh. Isaacson had to hand it to him.

Strangely enough, once he adjusted to the idea that he was damned, Isaacson realized he didn't feel so bad. This was not bad at all, not nearly so bad as he had expected. There were no flames, no pitchfork-wielding imps, no lakes of lava. Rather than outright agony, the discomfort was more akin to the most disgusting challenges on *Fear Factor*.

It also called to mind a comedy monologue he once heard that consigned human beings to two varieties: the horrible and the miserable. The horrible consisted of people dying of cancer and other such unfortunates. Everyone else was lucky to be merely miserable. Despite being damned to Hell, Isaacson had to admit he was still squarely in the camp of the miserable. What's more, his *spirit* was lightened—the freight-load of moral terror and guilt was off his shoulders. He could do anything he wanted.

This concept broke on his psychopathic consciousness like warm, golden rays of purest sunshine.

I'm off the hook!

≥≠≤

"What the *hell*?" Karen said.

"*Exactly*," Isaacson slurped, and began capering around like a hulking elf, giggling madly. He crooned, "*Karen, you're mine now, all mine.*" As if revealing a surprise birthday present, he took out his massive, shaggy organ. It pulsated with communal life, a hunk of polyp-encrusted driftwood, dank from the sea. Pus-colored living things sloughed off of it.

Suddenly the ear canal tipped vertical, and Karen found herself in free fall, plunging down a well. Isaacson was hanging in her way, blocking the entrance like a gargoyle, and she fell right into him, her knee smashing his infested prick as though it were a moldy zucchini, both their bodies tumbling into space.

Karen's scream echoed close for a second, then its sound broadened as she emerged in rainy, tropical, outdoor air, her guts clenching up as she dropped to some abrupt and final end on the rocks. After what she had just faced, it didn't seem so bad. She had always wondered what it would be like to skydive without a parachute, to fall from a great height to your death—now she would know. She only hoped it wouldn't hurt too much.

She landed hard in a river of boiling water.

Karen shot down deep, stunned by the painful blow, and then swam madly for the surface. The water—if that's what it was—was not actually boiling, but it was hot, salty, rich with slimy grit, and moving fast. Its powerful current pulled her along like a leaf, and when she broke the steaming surface she could hear its roar.

With her remaining strength, she struggled toward dim shapes of boulders and managed to drag herself half onto land before collapsing.

CHAPTER TWENTY-TWO:

THE ITSY-BITSY SPIDER

Mr. Oh Hyun couldn't believe the luck. No, not luck—this was truly the blessing of heaven upon the Great Leader; a miracle to surpass the glorious albino sea cucumber that had heralded His coming.

From the very start, this mission had exceeded all possible dreams of success. As soon as Mr. Oh had informed his North Korean connections that the woman giant was actually an agent of the Motherland, and that he alone possessed the means of controlling her, Oh had felt the presence of the Great Leader watching approvingly over his shoulder. He felt young again.

Once he got over the initial shock of having to share his mission with a group of Japanese Red Army factionists, Nippon-Islamic *jihadis,* and Aum Shinrikyo cultists—they were the only ones available at short notice to steal and fly the charter plane—Mr. Oh realized what a stroke of good fortune had fallen into his lap. These people might be a catalogue of kooks, but they had no fear, and they shared the same short-term priorities as he and his retired fellows. It was a natural symbiosis!

Of course, under normal circumstances he knew that these fanatics would never have had anything to do with him, being rabid enemies of North Korea's strict anti-religious policies. And he would have never before risked associating with terrorists, what with the Japanese authorities always so ready to detain Koreans on any flimsy pretext. This was a one-time deal. But once was enough to set right a lifetime of iniquities.

Oh had a deep resentment of his adopted country, as did thousands of fellow Koreans, most of whom had lived in Japan all their lives—or had even been born in Japan—yet were never fully accepted by Japanese society, never considered truly Japanese.

No matter how many years in the country—no matter how loyal, how hardworking, how assimilated—anyone of Korean extraction still got shunned on the street, still stood in a separate, longer line at passport control, still got turned down on dates, still got sent to the back, still was refused decent jobs and apartments and credit, still got that *look*.

If the Japanese truly wanted to know why Korean residents felt persecuted, joined loyalist North Korean organizations, turned to crime, or just didn't like them, all they had to do was walk in a Korean's shoes for a week. But they didn't care. That was the problem: it didn't matter to them.

Well, now it matters, Oh thought with bitter satisfaction. *They can't ignore us now.*

He looked around at his fellow team members with a glow of astonishment and pride. They had done the impossible, they had really done it! Their list of accomplishments since breaking out of the senior hospital in Sasebo was staggering.

They had hired and hijacked a charter plane, then immediately contacted Yoon-sook via the short-range radio receiver planted in her skull years before by the State Security Department. A laptop loaded with ordinary audio-editing software served to modulate the signal. Next, they had accessed the autosuggestion mechanism that Oh himself had implanted in her subconscious, using her grandmother's fetish with American musicals as the trigger. Having her actual grandmother handy was just icing on the cake.

Finally, they had transmitted the coordinates that directed Yoon-sook to her critical rendezvous with the North Korean Navy beneath Suruga Bay, where he and his compatriots were able to board her, consolidating their total control.

Oh, and they had destroyed the U.S. Pacific Fleet.

Now they were loose on the American mainland, free to trample as they pleased. The world was theirs!

The only remaining source of concern was Yoon-sook's long-term reliability. Her motivation seemed to have faltered, no doubt due to the pangs of drug withdrawal—not to mention possible side effects of her freakish growth, as well as simple exhaustion. Because of her instability, his superiors had decided that she should not be apprised of the other giant's existence, in fact should be removed from the region entirely and sent to America.

Oh Hyun had not agreed with this directive at first—it made him feel as if his superiors didn't trust him at the helm, and only wanted his female titan far away from the Brown Colossus. As if she might be destroyed by him, or even worse, corrupted. It galled Mr. Oh that after a lifetime of faithful service he would be given so little confidence. Surely he had proven himself the equal of any younger operative—retirement be damned! But Yoon-sook's reaction to the other giant's unexpected appearance in America made it clear that she was indeed psychologically vulnerable.

It was fortunate that she still had her gun, but very troublesome that she ignored his direct order to kill. Foolish woman! With the other giant on their tail, Hyun had thought they would be lucky to reach their primary objective: Washington, D.C. He knew now what he and his crew had earlier only suspected, that the male giant was under the control of imperialist warmongers. That meant there were only two available options.

The most desirable was for Yoon-sook to kill the other giant outright, leaving them holding the sole reins of ultimate power. Of course this would be the best of all possible worlds.

However, if it even slightly appeared that Yoon was not acting in the best interests of the Party, they did have an alternative: Get her close enough to the other giant so that they could destroy them both, preferably in proximity to a strategic American target—the five-megaton nuclear device in their arsenal ought to accomplish that.

But now it appeared that nothing so drastic would be necessary. Mr. Ali, the sentry posted at the rim of Yoon-sook's ear, had just ecstatically reported the unthinkable.

Oh Hyun's elderly lieutenants and the navy personnel in the command center would have scarcely dared believe it except for the closed-circuit video streaming in from the tiny exterior observation post, which clearly showed their adversary half-buried in the dusty, rubble-filled valley of the Grand Canyon.

Looking at the miraculous sight, Oh and his team couldn't help cheering, weeping, pumping their fists with the fierce joy of victory.

The American giant was lying helpless, dead or dying at their feet!

≥≠≤

Manny awoke gagging, as hot, caustic liquid splashed on his face and in his mouth, stinging his eyes and abrasions, turning the dust to mud. It smelled. He tried to turn away, to fend off the noxious stream with an upraised hand, but he found he was pinned, arms crushed down at his sides by the implacable weight of two dirty, wet sneakers. The spattering flow diminished enough for him to see the figure looming above him, pink satin panties at her knees and miniskirt hiked up, bare pudenda thrust forward and dribbling.

"Aaaugh," he groaned, struggling. "Stop!"

She sat down hard on his chest, her knees digging into his shoulders, panties stretched across his throat, and her thumbs gouging his trachea. Her savage, predatory face thrust into his, so close their lips brushed together. She smelled like the beach at low tide.

"*Wonsungi!* Who are you?" she hissed. "What kind of trick is this?"

"I don't know," he choked. "I don't know anything."

"Who did this? Was it you? Your government?"

"Yes. They said it was an accident."

"Accident, okay boss." Her lizard eyes became slits, her pug nose wrinkled contemptuously. "*I pabo nyosok.* I know you are working for them."

"No! I'm alone. We're both alone, can't you see that? It's just you and me now."

"Yes, just you and me." She squeezed tighter. "You think you come to kill me, asshole? I *piss* on you."

"I'm not your enemy. We're—gachhh—both guinea pigs... lab rats..." Manny couldn't breath; his face was turning purple. "They *want* us to kill each other...it saves them the trouble."

She let up, sitting back and staring down at him with the disdain of a mounted barbarian queen, an Amazon. As he gasped for breath, she said, "What do you want from me? Huh? You think we gonna be like Adam and Eve? *Pubu?* You think we gonna have babies and start new life together?"

"No...but we don't have to die alone. We're both going to die anyway; I don't care if you kill me. But then what? Think about it. Do you really want to kill your only real ally in this world? I'm on your side."

Yoon-sook paused, listening to an inner voice, then jerked her head and fell upon Manny. Her lips covered his mouth, and her tongue forced his lips apart, worming deep inside. She sucked the breath out of him, replacing it with her own scorching exhalation, grinding her face into his even as the rolled-down panties at her knees crushed his throat.

Overwhelmed, Manny tried to resist, gulping deep of her suffocating heat, her mouth a humid tunnel with slippery-sweet walls, enfolding him. Swallowing her saliva, he could smell pungent female vapors, and suddenly his every nerve ending flared into urgent flame, more intense than any arousal he had ever felt. His penis, as long and broad as the Hindenburg, pulsed yearningly within his fly, then actually ripped through the bomb-scorched fabric, emerging into the moonlight like a great, tan tower with a gleaming purple dome. He raised his hips to graze her back with this swollen monolith.

She groaned into his mouth, a canny, questioning sound, then edged away, sliding her crotch downward over his torso, pressing his penis backward at an increasingly painful angle until at his utmost discomfort she said, "This is what you want, isn't it? *Songgyo*? Fucking."

Face flushing with shame, Manny nodded.

≥≠≤

Skin was no longer Harold. He was the Anyoto, the Leopard-Man. It was not Skin that killed, it was the Anyoto; it was not Skin that climbed, but the Anyoto. Skin did not have the cunning and the night-vision and the strength to climb a tree with a two-hundred pound antelope—the Anyoto did.

Harold Loomis had not been born an Anyoto. It had been handed down to him.

Harold's street education had in many ways been typical: Born in free-fall from a proliferating, self-perpetuating, multigenerational column of unwed teen mothers and absentee fathers, he was defenseless against the pseudo-anarchic consumer society of gangstas and pimps and preening thugs that were the idols of his peers and elders. It would have been suicide to resist.

Thus he identified with and emulated local gang members from his earliest age, a strutting toddler barely out of diapers amusing the peeps with pudgy-fingered gang signs. True gang affiliation didn't begin until age eight, when he became a runner for the drug dealers who ruled his neighborhood. In this role he learned the business, and after a few years graduated to being a dealer himself.

His mentor in this process was a man named Sampson—a charismatic, intelligent, and much-beloved local philanthropist and civil-rights advocate, who had left the neighborhood to go to college, reputedly became an international businessman, and then returned to the old hometown in triumph and a big black Lexus SUV, spreading his good fortune in the form of generous contributions to the Policemen's Benevolent Fund and folded fifty-dollar bills to starry-eyed boys and girls.

Mr. Sampson never came in contact with the products that his youthful sales force so readily distributed. He was a legitimate businessman, operating out of the back room of a busy laundromat. People brought in their wash, put it through its cycles, and left. It was not unusual for them to forget an item of clothing in the dryer—usually a sock. Frequently this sock contained thick wads of cash.

In the event that there was no sock, certain special boys who had shown particular aptitude were sent out to handle the problem. These boys were given a talking-to:

"Man is a hunter by nature. When you kill, you are fulfilling a destiny as old as life on this planet. Killing is surviving; it's about making the deliberate choice to survive, as opposed to the passive acceptance of fate that is the province of all prey. If you can't kill, you are relinquishing your choice, and it will be made for you.

"In the Ituri Forest regions of West Africa, sometimes a man will fall into a strange trance and leave his hut in the middle of the night. He will run through the night forest like a hunting leopard, and many times he will even use the disguise of a leopard, camouflaging himself with paint and a monkey's tail or a strip of hide as a tail and

*sharp acacia thorns for claws. He might carry a pot of poison to dip
his claws and knife in, for the leopard carries on its claws and teeth
the infectious decayed matter of its kills.*

*"This Leopard-Man, this Anyoto, will stalk and kill anyone
unfortunate enough to cross his path. He will slash their body, drink
their blood, taste their flesh. He will not distinguish between strangers
and close relatives, between friend and foe. He recognizes no society,
no law, no loyalty, no fealty, no fear. He has no kinship with any
tribe, nor with humanity at large. He is the top of the food chain;
the rest are cattle."*

So Skin was inducted into the ancient cult of the Anyoto. By
day he was expected to stay in school and maintain every nuance
of law-abiding respectability. It was not just empty pretense—by
the code of the Anyoto, he had to completely surrender his will
to it, to believe in it and love it, so that at times he himself would
forget he was anything but a civilized, polite boy.

But then, in the middle of the night, the call would come. Skin
would feel an odd numbness creep over him, his limbs moving of
their own accord as if he was a robot. He would watch in sleepy
fascination as his body got dressed and went to the weapons stash,
selecting and checking and loading. And then he would hunt.

Skin was a wreck. It had been at least two days since he had
washed up on the canvas shores of the giant's right shoe, in a
state of shock, and fully expecting any second to be snuffed out
of existence. Then, as the hours went by, he began tentatively
exploring the limits of his pink-laced atoll. It was huge, at least
several football-fields long, sloping down around the front and
sides to terminate at an encircling white palisade. Skin didn't dare
get too close to that rubber cliff for fear of falling off, but he
crawled near enough to see that there was absolutely no chance of
escape that way, any more than it would be possible to step off a
hurtling jumbo jet.

With dreamlike incredulity he rode that endless procession of long, long strides: the unspeakable foot first hoisting him high up into the sky—Skin pinned beneath insane forces of gravity and wind as it soared in a great arc, his stomach fluttering weightlessly at the apex—then plummeting hair-raisingly downward toward palm trees and Spanish-tiled rooftops as the shoe dropped. For a moment, his familiar Los Angeles would seem terrifyingly, tantalizingly close, tempting him to bail out. Then it would hit.

The impact was calamitous, loud and prolonged as a train wreck. The sneaker would come to a brief stop, but there would be no real respite, only a frightening interlude during which enormous walls of fiery volcanic smoke would erupt outward in all directions, completely covering the gardened Southern California vistas— freeway interchanges and high-rises toppling like sandcastles— leaving the shoe in the eye of an infernal brown tempest.

The menacing billows would be just beginning to fold back on themselves, to collapse in upon Skin from every direction, when just like that the heel would bend upward and the whole thing would pivot off the toe, launching once more into the sky. To begin the whole cycle again.

Ducking chunks of flying debris—not just from the ground, but raining down from the giant—Skin knew he couldn't stay where he was; it was death. He had to get higher, to climb. He looked far up the monumental leg, three times as high as even the very tallest building, to where both thighs receded into the misty, shadowed reaches of the giant's skirt, which resembled the sheltering canopy of a vast tree. It seemed much more stable up there than anywhere on the scissoring legs. He could see her mammoth panties.

Skin started to climb. He climbed over twenty-foot hummocks of laces, past pitted and crudely forged metal eyelets thirty feet in diameter, alongside stitches resembling massive twined hawsers, bigger than the cables of a major suspension bridge.

He rested for a time at the summit of the shoe, persuading himself that it would be easy to climb the colossal tower of coarse rope mesh that was the giant's legging, from which treelike stumps of hairs protruded. There was no shortage of handholds, or even niches to duck in for safety, or a rest. Through gaps in the weave, he could make out a rough, waxy substrate that he rightly guessed was the giant's bare ankle. Then he started up.

The itsy-bitsy spider...climbed up the waterspout...

It was a matter of rhythm: right hand, right foot, left hand, left foot. The higher Skin climbed, the less jarring was the ride, and the more confident he became. There was nothing precarious about it; the wind buoyed him against the sheer face, and the fibrous cotton twine offered excellent purchase. He just made damn sure he never looked down.

Think like Spiderman, motherfucker, he thought.

Skin made good time. Less than seven hours after he started, he was under the rocking bell of the skirt, in a cavernous dome of darkness and sweltering, rank heat. It was not the safety he had hoped for, but rather an ominous place, deafening with the industrial-sounding din of friction between giant rubbing materials. The putrescent sea smell reminded him of when they dredged the canals in Venice Beach. Even so, Skin found it a relief after being exposed to the blistering wind for so long. He had no way of knowing that it saved his life to be under cover at that time, shielded from both the military attacks and Yoon-sook's devastating voice.

He felt as if he had been climbing forever, and was becoming seriously dehydrated, but there was a powerful incentive to keep going: In the darkness, he kept feeling things trying to attach themselves to him, like leeches. They burned.

This shit is nasty, he thought in panicky disgust. *I had enough of this Jack in the Beanstalk bullshit! Get my ass outta here!*

Working his way upward along a ledge-like panty seam, he found himself in an increasingly narrow space under the waistline. It was humid and close, pitch-dark, the walls contracting and expanding like a bellows. There seemed to be no way out, and

Skin despaired at the thought of climbing down again.

Just then, there was a change; something unusual happening.

First, the walking of his host seemed to stop, the giant falling still. This in and of itself was not so unusual—there had been many temporary hitches in her progress. But after this intermission everything went crazy.

Violent upheavals shook the narrow chasm in which he perched, the skirt's twenty-foot-thick leather armor buckling like rifts in solid rock, and the heavy mesh of the panties on which he had been climbing suddenly avalanched downward, leaving his feet dangling over an abyss. If not for the narrow crevice in which his upper body was wedged, he would have been dragged down to his death. Everything was in motion.

As he hung on for dear life, Skin looked down and could see something rising from the depths toward him, blocking what little light filtered up. Its sound was that of a giant earthmover plowing asphalt, but it looked alive: mushroom-headed and darkly gleaming. An intense, humid fish-stink wafted up as the thing nosed through the dark, a bulbous, urgently questing grub, hundreds of feet long.

In the commotion, an opening appeared above; just a crimp of fabric as the giant's waist flexed, but to Skin a broad, blinding seam of daylight. He barely scuttled through as an explosive spasm ran the length of the blind monster, and it vomited a tremendous gout of pus-like, ropy venom. The opening clapped shut.

Now Skin was on the giant's clothes, climbing within the deep, shifting folds of her silk top (another lattice of hawser-like strands) and partially sheltered by the thousand-foot-high swinging gates of her open jacket—a world of strange silence and fearful instability on which he didn't want to remain any longer than necessary.

He couldn't see much in any direction, and his muscles were giving out. What was the point of all this? Skin couldn't remember. Weak and shaking, talking to himself, he came to the disturbing realization that at some point under the skirt he had gone completely deaf. There was blood running out of his ears.

Close to quitting or falling unconscious, semi-delirious with weariness and thirst, Skin finally surmounted the foggy ridge of the jacket collar. On that smooth, windless plateau he rested for a long while, basking in hazy sunlight as all around him an astonishing panorama of pink and orange and purple-layered canyon, its escarpments rising higher even than the giant—*Where the fuck am I?*—rose and fell, rose and fell. Above him his host's monumental head could intermittently be seen jutting from reefs of vapor.

Skin would have remained there until he lapsed into unconsciousness and then death, if not for the frost that had accumulated overnight from the giant's breath: a thick, stucco-like rime now melting in the sun. He thirstily lapped at trickles of runoff until his stomach started cramping and his mouth ached with cold.

Muscles spent and twitching, he laid back on the ice, not wanting to move. He never wanted to move again.

But he had come this far; he was going to go all the way.

$$\geq \neq \leq$$

Manny was weeping as he fucked. *Your turn, Karen,* he thought brutally. *Your turn to listen.* He felt ashamed, yet more alive, more like a *man*, than he had since the whole thing had begun.

In some way even the negative emotions that were being dredged up—the heartbreak and anger and shame and fear—fueled Manny's ardor. In spite of himself, he realized he *was* having fun, if fun was the word for this exhibitionistic self-immolation, this erotic catharsis.

It was almost as if by defying all standards of human decency he was testing the limits of this dream world, whether to verify or challenge them, but preferably to bend them till they broke. He was more ashamed and consequently more aroused than he had ever been in his life. Despite having come almost at once against her thigh, he was already at the mercy of forbidden passion again.

Gripping Yoon-sook's hard, sinewy body with all his might, Manny gratefully pounded into her as if in defiance. She was a rock on which he broke like the surf, as cruelly, watchfully stolid as he was abandoned, and her very reserve—that toying, teasing, unbearable holding-back, forcing him to abjectly beg for the slightest reciprocation—was perhaps the sexiest thing of all.

Yet even as he became willing to utterly abase himself, some part of him still feared her, and hated and resented what she had induced him to do. It was ugly, wrong. It went against everything he thought he knew about himself, or would have liked to imagine, so that Manny discovered that he had become a savage, the beast escaped from within. But the savage *was* the giant, predominant, and even these negative emotions were transmuted into that all-consuming hunger, just as Yoon-sook's very fierceness was unspeakably erotic to him, until Manny was on the verge of declaring the deepest love he had ever known.

Finally he could stand it no more. With the force of an exploding wellhead on an oil rig, Manny ejaculated.

"I love you," he groaned in release.

"We call that *chaksarang*," she said, and leveled her gun at him.

Manny froze, still gasping. "You wouldn't kill me."

"Why not? You want me to play *yanggalbo*—the whore; I prefer to play the *yojangbu*. The hero."

"It won't make you a hero to kill me."

"Not just you. You first, then your country."

"It's not my country anymore. I don't have a country, and neither do you. All we have is each other."

"You speak like a traitor," she sneered. "Maybe you hate the *paeginjong* as we do, huh? The Whites? Is that what you are saying? They have oppressed you, used you, and now you want to make *tongmaeng* with me. An alliance to conquer them and make a new world order?"

"Not really. There's no country to rule, can't you see that? Not for us."

"What, then?"

"Be friends. Help each other. What else is there?"

"You are so stupid. You offer me nothing."

"It's all there is. Look around. Did you see anything else out there worth killing for? There's nothing, just us. And I'm starting to think that's all there ever was. Everything else was just make-believe: all the governments and religions and rivalries and languages and sports teams and TV shows and fast-food franchises—it was all just an illusion. Something to block the view. *This* is reality: you and me, here, now. Two people trying to connect. That's all it's ever *been* about."

This sentiment had an odd, familiar sound to Yoon. She had never spoken to an American before, and this was so much like the lyrics of a generic Hollywood love song, or the dialogue from a hundred movies she had seen.

That thing planted deep inside her responded to it; she became confused, defensive, like a sleepwalker torn awake.

Yoon/Dorothy said dreamily, "The problems of two little people don't amount to a hill of beans in this crazy world." Her eyes widened with a look of paranoid dread. "This isn't a movie. Is this a movie?" She stared hard at Manny, then shook her head as if to clear it. "*Anio.*"

Manny realized she was not in her right mind. "Don't be afraid," he said. "It's all right."

"Don't move!" She trained the gun on his forehead.

"I'm not moving!"

"*Opta yosul*—you can't trick me."

"I'm not trying to. I just want to help you."

"I'm sick!" Wild-eyed, she said, "I don't need a friend, I need this!" She showed him her tracked-up arms. "You know *mayak? Ap'yon?*" She winced, doubling over in pain.

Manny didn't dare breathe, but he sensed her cracking up, forgetting to aim the gun. A little more and he could grab it from her! Once he had the gun it would be all over—she was on her last legs, nothing but a ravaged waif now, all the menace gone out of her. Manny felt intense pity for both of them.

"Here, it's okay. Relax." With utmost caution, Manny reached for the gun and gently lifted it out of her shaking hand. She let him.

Her eyes were fixed on something far away, tears streaming down her face. "*Omona*," she whimpered. When she didn't explode, Manny stood up and gently took her by the elbow.

"Come on," he said. "Let's get out of here. Just the two of us." He didn't like being in this canyon, it was claustrophobic, like standing in a grave. She followed meekly as he started to lead her out.

Something caught Manny's eye in the sky above the canyon rim. Glancing upward, he saw words forming out of thin air, out of smoke. Skywriting. The airplanes making the letters were all but invisible, but the words they wrote were large enough:

MANNY—DON'T MOVE

I LOVE YOU—RUTH

Manny froze, confused. *Ruth!* The last person in the world he would have ever expected to hear from right now was his wife. Of all people! His heart slugged in his chest as memories of their life together flooded back. Was she here somewhere? God, he would give anything to go back to her, back to the way things used to be. They didn't know it then, but it was paradise: their beach walks, going to movies and restaurants, even that barfing cat of hers. Manny had never stopped loving her, and never needed her as much as he did right this second.

"Ruth," he whispered, wishing she could hear, "I'm sorry." Then louder, "I'm sorry!"

The letters drifted in space, dispersing on the wind.

Manny was still standing this way, transfixed, when he was

suddenly struck a hard blow from behind. In agony he saw fireworks, long streamers falling from the sky. A snippet of *The Star-Spangled Banner* played absurdly in his head, about the rocket's red glare. Legs crumpling, he could feel a brutal hand in his coat pocket, retrieving the gun. He tried to stop her, but not fast enough. She had it. She had it.

"You think you can trick me?" Yoon-sook pressed the gun into the back of his head. "You wanna trap me and make me your puppet? I am no puppet, understand? Because I know the secret of happiness—the secret of eternal peace. Do you want to know the secret, Manny Lopes?"

Things happened quickly, starting with a bang. Manny thought it was the gun going off. Skull ringing, he twisted around to see Yoon-sook's face seized up in a vulpine grimace of pain. Her head suddenly swelled like a veined balloon, glowing red, with white-hot lava spurting from her ears and nose. Her whole body jerked and her hands clenched, so that she inadvertently squeezed the trigger.

Now the gun *did* go off, shooting Manny in the throat. He slid down the canyon face, blood pulsing through his fingers.

At the same time, there was a rippling series of deep thuds from somewhere above. Great, towering pillars of smoke mushroomed to the sky, ten on each side of the canyon, less than half a mile away, enclosing it within a rapidly expanding shockwave of radioactive dust and flame.

The walls fell.

CHAPTER TWENTY-THREE:

ROCKET MAN

Salim Ali, the Rocket Man from Afghanistan, sat cross-legged on his red prayer rug in the windswept funnel of the female *jinn's* ear. He was wearing bulky winter clothing, a heavy burnoose, and gold-tinted ski goggles. Mounted on a short tripod in front of him, aiming downward rather than toward the heavens, was a powerful celestial telescope connected to a computerized radar targeting system and a high-definition video camera with a live cable feed to the command center deep in the ear canal. Planted all around him was an arsenal of military weapons: ground-to-air missiles, air-to-ground missiles, antiaircraft cannon. All as dear to him as his own sons...and as eager to shed the blood of infidels.

Clicking his prayer beads, the Rocket Man looked up at the face of the Grand Canyon, brilliant-hued in the morning sun, and silently mouthed thanks to Allah for allowing him to live long enough to witness miracles such as these, beautiful and terrible and vast as the events which formed the world. Even if he had to do it in the company of those obnoxious, heathen North Koreans.

Two thousand feet below, sunk in the still-shaded depths of the canyon bottom, was the American giant, its dust-shrouded torso propped on a great mound of rubble. It was helpless, pinned between the legs of the *jinn*, completely at her mercy. At *their* mercy. Even as it struggled, she was having her way with it, tormenting the pitiful titan to its last breath. The kilometer-long pier of her right arm, terminating in that incredible gun, sloped down like a ski-jump toward the enemy's gaping, dusty face. Any moment she would shoot—why didn't she shoot?

"Shoot, shoot," Ali muttered, trembling in frustrated anticipation.

Overwhelmed with dread and wonder as he watched this obscene spectacle, he failed to notice a sleek black form creeping over the brink of the ear, behind and beneath him at the base of the cartilaginous knoll that was his lookout.

Sprawling in the channel of the ear canal, the dark shape rested for a few minutes, chest heaving as it gibbered and wept—a sound the Rocket Man would have heard, had he not been wearing ear protection.

With a start, the gangly figure saw him on his lookout perch and became very still. It cautiously picked itself up and stared in a comical posture of disbelief down the yawning tunnel of the she-giant's ear canal, following with its eyes the electronics cables that snaked from deep inside that living grotto to the missile battery at the entrance. Then it flattened itself against the wall and started climbing again.

It moved slowly but deliberately, scaling the sheer rise by using stiff, reedy ear hairs for handholds. Inch by inch, it crept up and around the sandbagged fortification, topping the hummock and rising to its feet behind the seated lookout.

The Rocket Man sensed something and turned his head, doing a double-take as his mind tried to comprehend this ragged specter that had risen out of nowhere: a wild-eyed, weirdly painted devil wearing the shredded remains of a wetsuit—a voodoo frogman.

Its face and flesh were ravaged and sprouting hideous growths.

Dropping his prayer beads, the Rocket Man grabbed his AK-47 machine-gun. But he was too late—by the time he brought it around, the stranger was upon him, both hands on the barrel and a rock-hard bare foot kicking him in the chest. Losing his grip on the gun, Ali fell backwards, knocking the telescope into the abyss, and was arrested at the edge by the safety cable.

Before he could gain his footing, the wooden stock of his own weapon clouted him in the head, and the Rocket Man sagged against the wire, unconscious.

≥≠≤

Skin was as high as a jet plane.

Even in his thermal wetsuit he was cold, his face wind-burned, his lips chapped and bleeding. Weird roots were growing out of his nose and ears. None of it fazed him—he was the *Anyoto*.

What he did now, he did for that dumb-ass Samoan, Jerry—the only one who ever gave a shit, and who was now drowned and dead for no good reason because of whatever it was these chickenshit motherfuckers thought they were doing up in this giant bitch.

Jerry, man, I know you wouldn't like it, Skin apologized with all sincerity, *but I gotta do what I gotta do, dig? Don't think I be backslidin' or nothing'—I remember everything you ever taught me.* He kissed his two fingertips and showed them to the void. *Peace. I hope we still tight when I see you.*

Facing the dark portal of the ear, Skin tried to make sense of what he could see in there. He wasn't sure what he expected to see, but it certainly wasn't *this*.

Protruding from that well of shadow was a shiny steel boat propeller—a big one. And behind it, filling the cavern, was a matte-black shape like a railroad tank car with fins.

It was a submarine.

Skin knew that much; what he didn't know was that it was a Soviet-era DSRV—a Deep Submergence Rescue Vessel—sold at auction during *glasnost* and re-registered with the North Korean Navy, for which it had served admirably for years as a low-sonar-signature, deep-sea spy vessel. Its name was the *Kobukson*—the Turtle Boat, after the famous armored ships of Admiral Yi Sun-shin. Skin couldn't have known any of this, nor would it have made any difference to him if he had.

He climbed down to the sub, using power cables to clumsily rappel to the bed of the ear canal. Someone had been using the place as a toilet. There was an intense sonic vibration in there, not unlike the bass thud of really monster amps—Skin could feel it in his marrow, but he still couldn't hear a thing. There was also a gruesome object down there, cast aside as if it was a bundle of refuse: a withered corpse, bound and wrapped in clear plastic. It was a dead old lady—Skin thought she looked Chinese. A profusion of disgusting foliage had sprung up around her.

He hurried past the body and under the keel of the submarine. The vessel looked even bigger from below, propped up on struts, with a pillbox-like escape hatch jutting down from its steel belly, and a bundle of wires trailing from the opening.

As skin approached, a man's legs dangled out of the hatch and dropped to the ground. When the man ducked under the flange to come out, Skin bashed him in the head. He was Asian, wearing some kind of foreign military uniform. Another Asian man appeared, and Skin bashed him in the head as well, dragging the body out of the way as the man's fallen radio barked staccato gibberish. Both men were wearing bulky earphones. Skin hunkered underneath the hatch and climbed up the short ladder within.

Passing through a cylindrical antechamber, he heard voices above, and cautiously raised his head above a second opening.

It was like a cramped space station—all pipes and wires and buttons and glowing readouts and video monitors. Seven Asian men were packed together in this cluttered capsule. Four of them were officious-looking sailors in gray uniforms, two were old-timers fiddling with a large reel-to-reel tape player, and one was a bearded civilian.

They rewound and listened to the playback. It was a quavering old lady's voice speaking in what Skin took to be Chinese. She sounded like she was crying, and he correctly assumed that she was the same lady now rotting outside.

The civilian said in English, "If I have to listen to this shit one more time, I am going to lose my mind completely. This is worse than Guantanamo."

"It has gotten us this far. Be thankful."

"It is Allah, the Compassionate and Merciful, that has brought us this far, not this infidel nonsense."

"Well, if I have to listen to your Allah business one more minute, *I'm* going to go mad."

"Watch out, blasphemer, or you will get what is coming to you."

"I thought we agreed, no ideological debates."

"He's the one who keeps bringing it up!"

"Piss off."

"You piss off. What are you going to do about it? Blow yourself up?"

"I just might."

"That's your solution for everything."

As Skin rose from the deck behind them, the men matter-of-factly turned to him as if expecting one of their own, and then went stiff as if they had touched a live wire, their faces frozen in alarm.

Before they could make a peep, Skin cut loose. The AK-47 made a horrendous racket in the tight space, filling the chamber with sparks and spent shells and blue smoke. Shrapnel winged Skin, but he didn't flinch, leaning his whole weight against the gun's leftward pull.

By the time the long banana-clip was empty, it was difficult at a glance to distinguish one body from another, or even how many there had been. Skin noticed that one of the ravaged torsos had a strange device fastened to its waist, a metal box with a blinking red LED and a clock timer. There was also a loud warning alarm, but he couldn't hear it. The timer was counting down like a microwave oven. It was in the single digits, almost done: 4...3...2...

That was the last thing Skin ever saw.

CHAPTER TWENTY-FOUR:

RIO COLORADO

Karen could barely move—she thought she must have internal injuries, probably broken ribs. The hot yellow torrent had drained downstream, leaving her limply clinging to the edge of a tepid, muddy basin. The Colorado River was dammed up with Manny's body and a million tons of rock; upstream from him it was probably filling up to create a reservoir.

"I'm sorry, Manny," she wept. "We blew it, didn't we? I'm so sorry, honey."

Karen had been unconscious until the firing of the gun. That huge detonation—the equivalent of many tons of TNT—had violently jarred her awake, just as it triggered further avalanches up and down the canyon. If not for the shielding of the enormous pistol, which contained and focused the blast, the explosion might have killed her, or anyone within a half-mile radius. As it was, the prodigious forces were largely muffled, spent on accelerating a forty-foot-long, thousand-ton, Teflon-coated steel bullet to near-supersonic speed.

Spawning an intense shockwave, the massive projectile emerged from the gun's muzzle ahead of a blinding jet of superheated plasma, hotter than the surface of the sun. It punched through the air like a space capsule during re-entry, incandescent red at its blunt tip, and covered the two thousand feet to Manny's throat in less than a tenth of a second. It struck with the force of a ferrous meteor, and if it had hit anything else but Manny's impregnable hide, it would have caused immense destruction and gouged out a crater hundreds of feet deep. But Manny absorbed the brunt of the impact.

Deafened by the blast, unable to move, Karen managed to turn her head enough to see a plunging, foaming, lava-like wave descending on her like a spring flood. Blood—a million gallons of blood. Red as tomato soup, it thundered down the riverbed, engulfing everything in its path. In a second it would be upon her. Karen watched with grief and weary, doomed fascination as it came.

"It's okay," she said, bracing herself. "It's okay, it's gonna be okay…"

Karen wasn't afraid until the very last instant, when she could smell it—a brazed metallic stench like a foundry—and feel its hot breeze in her face. Even then it wasn't Manny's blood that scared her, but what she saw washing downstream with the blood.

In the high, tumbling face of that living flood—which Karen could actually see now was a scarlet porridge of red and white corpuscles, greasy yellow plasma, and a quarry's worth of churning, grinding stones—there was also a multitude of long-tailed giant tadpoles, all wriggling and leaping out of the pink spume as if in crazed migration. Sperm. It was almost as if they sensed her, all of them crowding the wave-front in manic anticipation of completing their one objective.

Karen was cut off mid-scream.

CHAPTER TWENTY-FIVE:

MEET ME IN ST. LOUIS

Ruth watched the whole thing on CNN.

It was quite a show: The B-2 bombers launching their supersized bunker-busters from high above the Earth. The nukes homing in, their deep-penetrating warheads boring underground. The Grand Canyon, one of the Wonders of the World, which took millions of years to create, slowly and majestically caving in.

Burying her husband Manny alive.

The president patted her arm. "I'm sorry, Ruth," he said. "It was the only way. A grateful nation thanks you for your sacrifice."

"It's like a movie," she said dully. She had been crying and screaming for a week, now she was all cried out. Cried out and burned out. All she wanted to do was lie down. Sleep. "Manny loved movies."

"He didn't suffer, I promise you. We couldn't do anything for him; he couldn't survive in our world. He wouldn't have lived much longer anyway. You spared his suffering, Ruth." He motioned for the TV to be shut off.

A glint of sudden animation lit Ruth's face, bright and uncanny as the images onscreen.

"Wait," she said.

CHAPTER TWENTY-SIX:

SLOUCHING TO BETHLEHEM

Within that vast, smoldering pit of rubble, something stirred.

Amid the seismic aftershocks, a peculiar vibration. It got stronger. Rocks crackled, then roared. A dome formed, and fissures opened, spewing jets of blue flame. The avalanche debris bulged until it could rise no higher, then exploded. Lightning danced in the roiling smoke.

It emerged.

Birthing itself from a womb of rubble, something rose, tentacle by tentacle, limb by limb, swelling forth from the Earth like an unspeakable flower from an alien bulb. Its monstrous blooming head was the flower bud, with curling tendrils where purple-dyed topknots had been, and four burning eyes bright as the sun.

The thing had a face as weirdly beautiful as it was terrible, its former two heads melted and reshaped into one, its face baked to a crackled finish like an old china doll. Its amphibian naked body was the same, consumed by nuclear fire and remade eerily featureless, half-formed as a fetus. Two fetuses fused into one—

Siamese twins conjoined from head to groin. It had eight limbs: four legs, four arms. Its male and female parts had been scoured smoothly sexless, a paragon of androgyny that was perversely erotic as a Hindu deity made flesh. One arm terminated not in a hand, but in a gun. It was hard to tell where the flesh ended and the metal began.

The thing started walking.

The voices in its binary brain were silent; it was alone. That was all right. It felt oddly well—the pitiful human cravings were gone, love and junk burned up in the furnace of its belly. Its new body was powerful and clean. It could survive in this world now. The angry fleas seemed to have given up their attack, but they would be massing somewhere, poised for a final assault. They were welcome to try – the newborn creature knew that there was nothing to stop it from wiping out all of human civilization if it so chose. In fact, it thought it might just do that.

They had made it a God. Well, let them feel God's wrath.

My world, it thought jealously. *Mine!* A town stood in its path, and the Deity was so disgusted by the infestation of its planet by these revolting creatures, these *insects*, that it had to vomit.

The One God opened its two mouths and fire came out.

A river of nuclear plasma enveloped the remains of Flagstaff, Arizona, and instantly reduced it to ashes. A pine forest burst into flame, and the sweet smell of wood smoke impelled the Deity to reach down and scrape up a handful of several thousand burning trees, inhaling them with the force of a tornado.

Delicious, it thought. How nice that everything on Earth was so edible. Not just the living things, but the inorganic matter as well. In fact, the whole planet was one big tart, its surface as tender as a pie crust and its filling hot and red as baked cherries. Life was good.

Pondering such things, the Deity wandered the Painted Desert and the nations of the Navajo and Hopi, crossing into New Mexico.

It passed just north of I-40, immolating with one breath the ten thousand pickup trucks bogged down around Gallup, and a stopped Amtrak train whose passengers craned their necks to stare in reverent dread at the phantasmagorical figure striding across the bare desert expanses. The thing and the landscape were all of a piece: Faded with distance and the washed-out light of noonday, the colossus appeared as elemental as anything in nature. Even the incongruity of its tentacled head seemed somehow organic to the surreal backdrop, already the scenery of peyote-induced dreams.

The Almighty crossed the Continental Divide where it intersected the Jicarilla Apache Reservation, at the foot of the considerable mountain range it had been approaching all morning. Peaks nearly twice God's height, plush green and glazed like cakes with white icing, marched jaggedly north and south into the distance. The Rockies. Human habitation—the towns of Gallina and Coyote—showed as mangy spots in the pine shag.

The Deity stopped for a drink, destroying the Abiquiu Dam in the process, and continued on through passes in the Sangre de Cristo Range, trying to stay as low as possible in the thin air, which was making it a little woozy, damping its fires.

Then it was leaving the Rockies behind, coming down from the Turkey Mountains into the prairies—a sprawling landscape like a wrinkled brown hide, inset with bodies of water like mirror fragments, scored with geometrical lines of human commerce. The Deity was not very familiar with this region, but it vaguely remembered that there should be no major landmarks (at least none that a being its size would be likely to recognize) until the Mississippi River.

All it could do now to be sure of heading east was to keep the morning sun ahead of it and the afternoon sun behind, events so frequent that it had lost all track of time. Occasionally the Deity detoured to erase a city: Albuquerque, Santa Fe, Taos, towns large and small, it didn't matter.

The Superbeing left New Mexico and crossed the Texas

Panhandle into Oklahoma, passing close to Enid, Ponca City, and Bartlesville, pulverizing a fifty-mile stretch of Interstate 44 where it entered Missouri, and cutting a tornado-like swath of destruction through Joplin and southern Springfield. But before it could reach St. Louis or the rusty creek of the Mississippi, the One God encountered the first thing to stop it in its tracks:

A wall. A solid wall of dust.

It was an extraordinary thing: a dust cloud fully ten thousand feet high and at least a hundred miles long, stretching diagonally across the mossy hinterlands of Mark Twain National Forest from Rolla to Poplar Bluff. An orange-brown curtain hanging suspended in the atmosphere, higher than God's head and impenetrably deep and murky. It was hard to reconcile with the surrounding greenery and cloudless sky.

The Deity was reluctant to venture into the dust without knowing how far it went. Some lingering remnant of animal instinct, which feared being blinded. Then the Enormity had a thought: *What am I afraid of?*

Laughing as it plunged into the cloudbank, God walked boldly forward, knowing there could be no real obstacles, determined not to falter. The bright daylight went hazy yellow, then orange, then opaque brown—solid as a wall. A weirdly familiar odor of engine exhaust permeated the gloom.

Unexpectedly, God stumbled over something: a string of some kind, stretched across the ground at shin-height. A bell tinkled nearby.

"Now!" shouted an American voice.

All of a sudden, three enormous figures—beings God's size—rushed it from the dense murk. The Deity instinctively raised its gun hand, but someone hit it from behind and God sent off a wild shot that sheared the top off Mudlick Mountain before rebounding all the way to Cairo, Illinois.

"Look out, it's got a gun!" another voice cried.

The Almighty tried to shoot again, but its ammunition was all gone. It could regenerate more, but not soon enough. As one of the shadowy attackers closed in, God opened the furnace doors of its mouth and vomited a stream of liquid fire. But something went wrong: The terrible dragon breath fell short, a sudden wind blasting it back into God's face. The Deity inhaled its own fire and dissolved into a fit of coughing.

A sputtering roar filled the air, a mechanical sound, and suddenly God could see what it was: One of the enemy was wearing a leaf-blowing machine on his back. *He* was the one who had raised all this dust, and *he* was the one who now dared challenge the Enormity's fiery dominion. This horse-faced boy! This leaf blower! God laughed, dealing a judo kick that knocked the fool on his back, then pinned him to the ground with all eight limbs. This time the fire would find its mark. Now they would all know God's wrath!

A powerful blow struck God on the back of the head—a cast-iron frying pan.

God blacked out and toppled like a multi-trillion-pound sack of potatoes, causing a powerful earthquake that rattled the Plains states. Volcanoes erupted, dams broke, parts of California slid into the sea. A hundred miles to the northeast, the gleaming Gateway Arch warped and twisted and finally sheared apart, its two halves falling into the slopping-over waters of the Mississippi.

≥≠≤

Karen thought she was dead.

Washed up high and dry, miles downstream, she had survived her fall from Manny's ear, and then the canyon's collapse, only to watch this slithering, scarlet berm of living magma rolling toward her now, rebounding off boulders with sludgy explosions of liquid human tissue, steaming and hissing as it came, and the jostling, phallic heads of a hundred thousand eager sperm leading the charge. All this poured down the river bottom, rushing upon her, and with her last strength she let out a hopeless scream.

She was cut off by a hand reaching down from above to grab her wrist.

"Karen! Help me!"

She looked up in weary amazement to see Harley Queen leaning over a shelf of rock, yanking her upward by the arm. He looked like he too had taken a beating; there was blood streaming from his scalp.

"Come on!" he shouted, struggling to lift her. She was a big girl; he needed her help.

Karen wanted to say *I can't*, but seeing his set face and feeling his furious grip on her wrist shamed her into trying to climb. One of her legs was broken and something else was wrong with her back, sending bolts of agony through her body when she moved.

Crying out from the pain, she found a foothold and boosted herself upward, just as the hot, rampaging current sloshed into her. It knocked her sideways with the force of a moving car, and Queen used the momentum to swing her up and over the ledge.

The two of them lay there, gasping, as the river of Manny's lifeblood tumbled past.

EPILOGUE:

HOME SWEET HOME

The house stands alone on its eroded plateau, incongruous as a ship left high and dry after a storm. A ramshackle Dutch Colonial heap set askew against the violet rim of the sky, all funny angles and its tilted roof glazed with snow, it looks like some godforsaken homestead abandoned to the wilderness. Just a sad little house on the prairie.

Except that Casa Shapiro is as tall as Mount Everest, soaring high above the weird desolation of the Jersey shore. And hardly abandoned: as night approaches, flickering yellow lamplight shines in the kitchen window, attracting swarms of bizarre insects. The gnats hover outside the screen, tuning their sensitive antennae to the frequency of the thunderous noises coming from within. They listen to us.

"Hello? Can you understand me? *Habla Español?*"

"How is she supposed to talk if she's gagged and tied to a chair?"

"Doesn't matter; I don't think she can talk anyway. I also don't think she's a she."

"Well, I'm not going to call her an *it*. Besides, she's more a *she* than a *he*—anybody can see that. And they said she spoke English.

That's what they told me."

"They said a lotta things. Trust me, the Army will tell you anything."

"Shhh. They can hear you out there."

"I don't care. I did my time for Uncle Sam. Phew, that is a puss only a mother could love."

"I don't care. She's *mine*, and I think she's awesome."

"You would, kid. More like Medusa's turnip-headed kid sister, you ask me."

"Bill! Don't be rude! As long as she's under my roof, we treat her like a guest. And for another thing, she's not yours, Joey, for heaven's sake. You act like she's some mail-order bride. She's *all* our responsibility; she's one of us now. She just needs some solid food, maybe a little make-up and some decent clothes, and she'll be fine. I'll take care of that, don't you worry. It'll be good to have someone else helping out around here, so that maybe I can finally—"

"Watch out!"

"What!"

"She moved."

"Oh—you scared me. She's not gonna bite, for heaven's sake."

"It's not a bite I'm worried about. Did you see her breath? Who knows what she's liable to do? She looks dangerous. They said be careful."

"Give her a chance, for Chrissake. Here, give her some *kreplach*."

"Ma, you're gonna make her puke."

"Shut your fresh mouth! She needs something in her system."

"She doesn't know what that is!"

"Well, we don't have no chop suey, so she'll have to get used to it. If she's gonna be living here."

"I'm still not used to it, and it's been twenty years."

"Oh, oh, now he's Mr. Smart Mouth. You better watch your lip, sonny-boy. Instead of wising off, you oughtta be down on your knees thanking me for putting up all this wholesome food during that Bird Flu scare. Didn't I say it was gonna come in handy? Didn't I? We'd be in a pretty pickle without it, waiting for those vegetables to grow. That reminds me, did you put that leaf blower away? I don't want you leaving it outside overnight."

"Yeah, Ma, you asked me that already. Yes, I put it away. What, you think someone's gonna steal it? I don't see us having much use for it in the near future."

"Good, because I'm not letting this place go to pieces. Not when we have company. Don't you dare laugh!"

"*Ow!* I'm not laughin'! Jeez! I'm just not sure this qualifies us as proper *hosts*, kidnapping her and bringing her home all hog-tied, is all."

"Well, that's a fine thing coming from you, Mr. She-Can-Have-My-Room. You're the one who wanted to do it. You and Audie Murphy here."

"Hey, it was that General Queen's idea."

"General, schmeneral. He's not the one who would've had to bury you if you got shot. You're lucky neither of you idiots got yourselves hurt; that would have been a fine thing with no doctor anywhere to—*Oh!* Look, she's eating, she's eating! *There* you go! It's good, isn't it? See? She likes it, smarty-pants."

"Look out! She's gonna puke!"

"Whoops, don't overdo it! That's okay, that's okay, honey—one bite at a time."

"Give her room. She's trying to say something."

Parched lips part, whispering cracked syllables.

"What was that she said?"

"I think she said thank you, Ma."

"You're very welcome," Dottie says grandly. "Welcome to our home. Wait—what did she just call me?"

"It sounded like 'Auntie Em.'"

"Auntie Em?"

"Shhh! Listen!"

"*There's no place like home, there's no place like home, there's no place like home...*"

ACKNOWLEDGMENTS

My sincere thanks to Ross Lockhart, Jeremy Lassen, and the other fine folk at Night Shade Books, who gave me the privilege of joining their incredible family of authors. Thanks also to my agent, Laurie McLean, for bringing this 10-year project to happy fruition. And thanks most of all to you, the Reader, for joining me on this journey.

NIGHT SHADE BOOKS IS AN INDEPENDENT PUBLISHER OF SCIENCE-FICTION, FANTASY AND HORROR

ISBN: 978-1-59780-194-2 . ❨ $14.95 ❨ Look for it in e-book format!

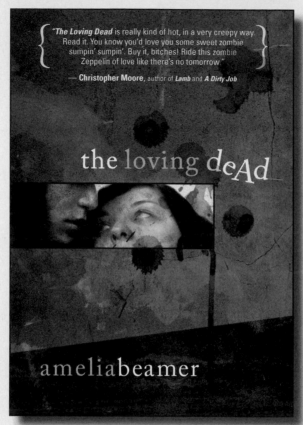

{ *"The Loving Dead* is really kind of hot, in a very creepy way. Read it. You know you'd love you some sweet zombie sumpin' sumpin'. Buy it, bitches! Ride this zombie Zeppelin of love like there's no tomorrow." }

— **Christopher Moore,** author of *Lamb* and *A Dirty Job*

the loving deAd

ameliabeamer

Girls! Zombies! Zeppelins!

If Chuck Palahniuk and Christopher Moore had a zombie love child, it would look like *THE LOVING DEAD*, a darkly comic debut novel by Amelia Beamer.

Kate and Michael, twenty-something housemates working at the same Trader Joe's supermarket, are thoroughly screwed when people start turning into zombies at their house party in the Oakland hills. The zombie plague is a sexually transmitted disease, turning its victims into shambling, horny, voracious killers after an incubation period where they become increasingly promiscuous.

Thrust into extremes by the unfolding tragedy, Kate and Michael are forced to confront the decisions they've made, and their fears of commitment, while trying to stay alive. Kate tries to escape on a Zeppelin ride with her secret sugar daddy—but people keep turning into zombies, forcing her to fight for her life, never mind the avalanche of trouble that develops from a few too many innocent lies. Michael convinces Kate to meet him in the one place in the Bay Area that's likely to be safe and secure from the zombie hordes: Alcatraz. But can they stay human long enough?

NIGHT SHADE BOOKS IS AN INDEPENDENT PUBLISHER OF SCIENCE-FICTION, FANTASY AND HORROR

ISBN: 978-1-59780-290-1 (($14.99 ((Look for it in e-book format!

"Terrifying, darkly hilarious, tougher and meaner and faster than a .45 hole-in-the-head—Roche delivers a fast-paced, gripping thriller where the showdowns make other zombie novelists look like they're playing with dollies."

—Violet Blue, author of *The Smart Girl's Guide to Porn* and many others

THE PANAMA LAUGH

THOMAS S. ROCHE

Ex-mercenary, pirate, and gun-runner Dante Bogart knows he's screwed the pooch after he hands one of his shady employers a biological weapon that made the dead rise from their graves, laugh like hyenas, and feast upon the living. Dante tried to blow the whistle via a tell-all video that went viral—but that was before the black ops boys deep-sixed him at a secret interrogation site on the Panama-Colombia border.

When Dante wakes up in the jungle with the five intervening years missing from his memory, he knows he's got to do something about the laughing sickness that has caused a world-wide slaughter. The resulting journey leads him across the nightmare that was the Panama Canal, around Cape Horn in a hijacked nuclear warship, to San Francisco's Mission District, where a crew of survivalist hackers have holed up in the pseudo-Moorish-castle turned porn-studio known as The Armory.

This mixed band of anti-social rejects has taken Dante's whistle blowing video as an underground gospel, leading the fight against the laughing corpses and the corporate stooges who've tried to profit from the slaughter. Can Dante find redemption and save civilization?

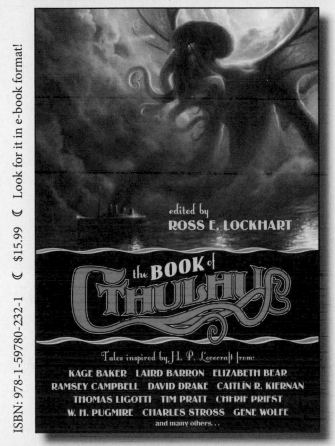

ISBN: 978-1-59780-212-3 ❨ $14.99 ❨ Look for it in e-book format!

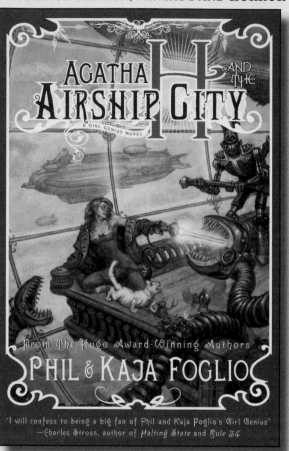

AGATHA **H** AND THE AIRSHIP CITY

A GIRL GENIUS NOVEL

From The Hugo Award-Winning Authors

PHIL & KAJA FOGLIO

"I will confess to being a big fan of Phil and Kaja Foglio's Girl Genius"
—Charles Stross, author of Halting State and Rule 34

Adventure! Romance! Mad Science!

The Industrial Revolution has escalated into all-out warfare. It has been sixteen years since the Heterodyne Boys, benevolent adventurers and inventors, disappeared under mysterious circumstances. Today, Europe is ruled by the Sparks, dynasties of mad scientists ruling over—and terrorizing—the hapless population with their bizarre inventions and unchecked power, while the downtrodden dream of the Hetrodynes' return.

At Transylvania Polygnostic University, a pretty, young student named Agatha Clay seems to have nothing but bad luck. Incapable of building anything that actually works, but dedicated to her studies, Agatha seems destined for a lackluster career as a minor lab assistant. But when the University is overthrown by the ruthless tyrant Baron Klaus Wulfenbach, Agatha finds herself a prisoner aboard his massive airship Castle Wulfenbach—and it begins to look like she might carry a spark of Mad Science after all.

From Phil and Kaja Foglio, creators of the Hugo, Eagle, and Eisner Award-nominated webcomic *Girl Genius*, comes *Agatha H and the Airship City*, a gaslamp fantasy filled to bursting with Adventure! Romance! and Mad Science!

"*Southern Gods* is scary, smart, and effective both as Lovecraftian fiction and as a Southern Regional novel set in 1951."
— DAVID DRAKE, author of *Balefires*

SOUTHERN GODS

JOHN HORNOR JACOBS

ISBN: 978-1-59780-285-7 ☾ $14.99 ☾ Look for it in e-book format!

Recent World War II veteran Bull Ingram is working as muscle when a Memphis DJ hires him to find Ramblin' John Hastur. The mysterious blues man's dark, driving music—broadcast at ever-shifting frequencies by a phantom radio station—is said to make living men insane and dead men rise.

Disturbed and enraged by the bootleg recording the DJ plays for him, Ingram follows Hastur's trail into the strange, uncivilized backwoods of Arkansas, where he hears rumors the musician has sold his soul to the Devil.

But as Ingram closes in on Hastur and those who have crossed his path, he'll learn there are forces much more malevolent than the Devil and reckonings more painful than Hell . . .

In a masterful debut of Lovecraftian horror and Southern gothic menace, John Hornor Jacobs reveals the fragility of free will, the dangerous power of sacrifice, and the insidious strength of blood.

NIGHT SHADE BOOKS IS AN INDEPENDENT PUBLISHER
OF SCIENCE-FICTION, FANTASY AND HORROR

ISBN: 978-1-59780-143-0 ◖ $15.95 ◖ Look for it in e-book format!

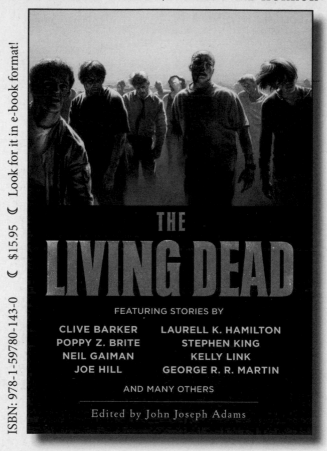

THE
LIVING DEAD

FEATURING STORIES BY

CLIVE BARKER	LAURELL K. HAMILTON
POPPY Z. BRITE	STEPHEN KING
NEIL GAIMAN	KELLY LINK
JOE HILL	GEORGE R. R. MARTIN

AND MANY OTHERS

Edited by John Joseph Adams

"When there's no more room in hell, the dead will walk the earth."
From White Zombie to *Dawn of the Dead*; from *Resident Evil* to *World War Z*, zombies have invaded popular culture, becoming the monsters that best express the fears and anxieties of the modern west. The ultimate consumers, zombies rise from the dead and feed upon the living, their teeming masses ever hungry, ever seeking to devour or convert, like mindless, faceless eating machines. Zombies have been depicted as mind-controlled minions, the shambling infected, the disintegrating dead, the ultimate lumpenproletariat, but in all cases, they reflect us, mere mortals afraid of death in a society on the verge of collapse.

Gathering together the best zombie literature of the last three decades from many of today's most renowned authors of fantasy, speculative fiction, and horror, including Stephen King, Harlan Ellison, Robert Silverberg, George R. R. Martin, Clive Barker, Poppy Z. Brite, Neil Gaiman, Joe Hill, Laurell K. Hamilton, and Joe R. Lansdale, *The Living Dead*, covers the broad spectrum of zombie fiction. The zombies of *The Living Dead* range from Romero-style zombies to reanimated corpses to voodoo zombies and beyond.

Edited by John Joseph Adams (*Wastelands*), *The Living Dead* is 230,000 words of zombie fiction (34 stories!), collecting the best tales from *Book of the Dead*, *Still Dead*, and *Mondo Zombie*, along with the best zombie fiction from other sources.

NIGHT SHADE BOOKS IS AN INDEPENDENT PUBLISHER OF SCIENCE-FICTION, FANTASY AND HORROR

ISBN: 978-1-59780-190-4 ◖ $15.99 ◖ Look for it in e-book format!

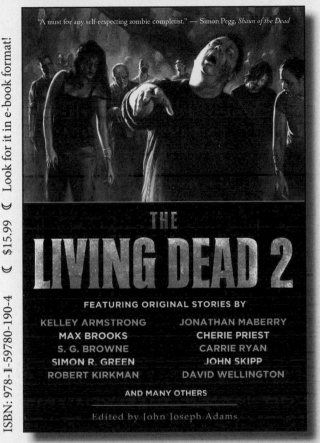

"A must for any self-respecting zombie completist." — Simon Pegg, *Shaun of the Dead*

THE
LIVING DEAD 2

FEATURING ORIGINAL STORIES BY

KELLEY ARMSTRONG   JONATHAN MABERRY
MAX BROOKS   CHERIE PRIEST
S. G. BROWNE   CARRIE RYAN
SIMON R. GREEN   JOHN SKIPP
ROBERT KIRKMAN   DAVID WELLINGTON

AND MANY OTHERS

Edited by John Joseph Adams

Readers eagerly devoured *The Living Dead*. *Publishers Weekly* named it one of the Best Books of the Year, and Barnes & Noble.com called it "The best collection of zombie fiction ever." Now acclaimed editor John Joseph Adams is back for another bite at the apple—the Adam's apple, that is—with 44 more of the best, most chilling, most thrilling zombie stories anywhere, including virtuoso performances by zombie fiction legends Max Brooks (*World War Z*, *The Zombie Survival Guide*), Robert Kirkman (*The Walking Dead*), and David Wellington (*Monster Island*).

From *Left 4 Dead* to *Zombieland* to *Pride and Prejudice and Zombies*, ghoulishness has never been more exciting and relevant. Within these pages samurai warriors face off against the legions of hell, necrotic dinosaurs haunt a mysterious lost world, and eerily clever zombies organize their mindless brethren into a terrifying army. You'll even witness nightmare scenarios in which humanity is utterly wiped away beneath a relentless tide of fetid flesh.

The Living Dead 2 has more of what zombie fans hunger for—more scares, more action, more... brains. Experience the indispensable series that defines the very best in zombie literature.

ABOUT THE AUTHOR

W. G. Marshall was born in Torrance, California. He sold his first short story at age 16, and has since written for newspaper, television, and public radio, as well as starting his own alternative paper, *The Dark Horse*. After working his way across America, he spent a decade freelancing in Asia, Europe, and the Middle East. He currently lives and writes in Providence, Rhode Island.